PRAISE FOR REBE

"Deliciously thrilling—and thrillingly ex....."

—*Kirkus Reviews*

"Hanover's book is dark, ominous, and oppressive from the very beginning, filled with heart-stopping, head-spinning twists, bizarre characters, and a spiraling sense of impending doom. This book is for those who enjoy something very dark and very different."

—*Booklist*

"Sharply written and deftly plotted . . . [and] the best sort of psychological suspense. It hooked me from the first page and kept me guessing until its surprising, satisfying conclusion."

—Cristina Alger, *New York Times* bestselling author of *Girls Like Us*

"A fast-paced thriller about identity and love."

—*Publishers Weekly*

"Fascinating. I was captivated."

—Francine Pascal, bestselling author of the Sweet Valley High and Fearless series

"As immersive and fast paced as it is shrewd, compelling, and heartbreaking."

—Ray Kurzweil, inventor, futurist, and *New York Times* bestselling author

"A page-turner that more than delivers on its premise."

—Allison Raskin, *New York Times* bestselling author of *I Hate Everyone But You*

SEEMs PERFECT

ALSO BY REBECCA HANOVER

The Last Applicant

For Young Adult Readers

The Similars

The Pretenders

SEEMS PERFECT

A NOVEL

Rebecca Hanover

LAKE UNION
PUBLISHING

Published by Lake Union Publishing, Seattle

www.apub.com

Amazon, the Amazon logo, and Lake Union Publishing are trademarks of Amazon.com, Inc., or its affiliates.

ISBN-13: 9781662520501 (hardcover)
ISBN-13: 9781662509308 (paperback)
ISBN-13: 9781662509315 (digital)

Cover design by TheBookDesigners
Cover image: © Mark Fearon / ArcAngel

Printed in the United States of America
First edition

To the squatters who've been living in my house rent-free for over a decade: Leo, Quincy, and Naomi, my OG San Francisco kids. You inspire everything I do.

SEEKING: SF Bay Area Roommate

32yo female questing for a roommate in cute Noe Valley neighborhood! My 900 square foot one-bedroom is an ideal home for two. It has a separate, cozy nook off the living room with a futon, perfect for someone between homes who appreciates city living and all that San Francisco has to offer. Rent is $1200, negotiable depending on move-in timeframe (the sooner the better!). About me: yoga teacher. Plant-based lifestyle (but omnivores are welcome!). I'm a SF native living in this condo for the last sixteen years. Been in my family for even longer. Hardwood floors, lots of light, kitchen renovated in the early aughts. DM me for more details—I'd love to live with you!

Chapter 1

I dread looking under my mattress.

I'm afraid. And it's not that I'm worried about ghosts lurking there. I don't lie awake past the witching hour, frightened of the fairy-tale wolf who ate Grandma, or the witch who bakes children into shortbread. Those stories never scared me as a kid, and I'm not scared of monsters now, though maybe I should be. If monsters were unpaid bills . . . well, then. I should be terrified.

Every time I go to pull out the thick stack of unopened envelopes I've stuffed between the slats—AT&T, the mortgage payment, the water bill, the notice from my orthopedic surgeon informing me that I'm past due on the out-of-pocket payment for my meniscus surgery last July—I can't do it. I freeze, do a 180, tell myself I'll tackle them when I'm feeling braver. Or, maybe, never. Because the cold, hard truth of exactly how much debt I'm in, down to the last ugly cent, would sink me. I know what I've done. I know why I'm here and exactly how I got to this place.

I also know I will dig myself out. It's what I do, what I've always done. I'll do it now.

Somehow.

It's why I placed the Craigslist ad. I know, I know. Craigslist, is this 2001? What can I say? It's the best place to find roommates. Remarkably, it's where people still look for them, even now.

It's where I find *her*. A princess among a sea of frogs. I placed the ad on a Thursday at 8 a.m., then checked obsessively for bites all day. There were none, at first, except for a dude who definitely wasn't interested in being my roommate and was either a troll or a megacreep; his "hey, hot mamma" comment made that pretty clear. By the time Friday rolled around, I began to despair when no one else serious had responded. By that point I'd only received a few more odd responses (*Is there central AC?* No, definitely not. *Would you be fine with three large dogs?* Also, no). None of these were even remotely promising. Not even close to workable. How hard was this going to be? And what if there was no one suitable out there?

It was hard to focus on anything else. I needed this. I needed *someone*. A warm body, at this point. Hoping for a nice person around my age who could actually be more than someone to help pay the rent, and might even end up being my *friend*, seemed like asking for too much. I was desperate. I would take whoever I could get.

On Saturday, Pip's message arrived. She was interested. She needed a place to live starting yesterday. She was a children's tutor. Check, check—this seems too good to be true, but check! Could we talk on the phone? Much easier than text, she asked me, and I almost didn't let myself believe it. Was it going to be this easy? I dared to hope but reminded myself that all the stars were going to have to align. When she called me five minutes later, I nearly did a happy dance. Maybe we could get this sorted quickly. Maybe I'd have help with the rent much sooner than I even thought.

She introduced herself on FaceTime as Penelope Stone but explained she goes exclusively by Pip. Then she said, in her jaunty, affable way, that her given name is "ridiculously unwieldy" and she "never uses it." Speaking to her that first time, I felt an instant connection to her, and to those words. My own name is beyond generic. Emily Hawthorne. There are approximately seventy thousand of us on the internet alone, so no one can ever find me in a search. There's something comforting about being anonymous. But also, something bleak. The mark I have left on the world in my medium-to-short time here has not been recorded. Inviting the question, Have I left one at all?

We spoke that first day for forty-five minutes, and they flew by. I could only feel relief at the sight, on my cracked phone screen, of her friendly face and messy blond topknot, and the ease with which she talked about her life, her goals, her challenges. We seemed like we were connecting—like two people who randomly meet at a party and actually choose to keep talking to each other!—and after I hung up, I searched for a rudimentary lease online, found one that claimed to be the very definition of standard, downloaded it, and immediately sent it her way. She'd returned it to me, countersigned, by the next day.

Is it sort of wild that we haven't met in person and she's moving in today? Sure. But we both felt it, like this was meant to be. And anyway, what other choices did I have? Except for the guy with the three large dogs, about zero.

It's a Saturday morning, and I'm pacing my condo barefoot, walking those creaky wooden floors that Aunt Viv always calls "patinaed," but I suspect would be deemed "worn" by any unbiased appraiser—if I'm being honest with myself. Which I try to be. It's best for one's mental health, isn't it? I'm a yogi, for fuck's sake. I have to strive for Zen, preach positivity. My whole identity revolves around radical self-acceptance. Hard to stick to, given that I haven't had a truly good day in months. Ever since . . . Seth. Our breakup. Which was, categorically, a thousand and one percent my fault. The truth is, I'm starting to think all my gratitude journaling and meditation is a bunch of horseshit, vaguely disguised as wellness. It doesn't help that I'm also starving. Intermittent fasting is not all it's cracked up to be, no matter what Gwyneth Paltrow says. Unlike me, Gwyneth isn't fasting because groceries cost a literal fortune these days. Opening my fridge is almost as painful as confronting the bills under my mattress. Tomatoes cost a whopping two dollars and twenty cents *per*, and at my last trek to Mollie Stone's, I had to make a painful choice between carrots and broccoli. Sadly, the eight-dollar bottle of wine wasn't even in contention.

It's 10:04. She should be here soon. Penelope "Pip" Stone. My new roommate, and my solution to the problem of a desperately dwindling bank account. A bank account so close to being in the red, I've had to stop checking it.

I can't sit still. My mind is churning, my pesky knee throbbing with the anticipation. I know this whole situation is the definition of hasty. We've literally never met in person, have only conversed via screen. But the reference letter she sent me—glowing praise from a former landlord—was the last piece of the puzzle for me. I emailed the address listed on it and got a prompt response back, with reassurance that Pip was a great tenant. I could almost cry with relief. Even our discussion of our living preferences had gone smoothly. She told me she was dying to be more plant based, could I teach her my ways? I confessed to her that I was struggling for work. Being a yoga teacher with an injury had left me no support system, no backup option, no safety net. It's why I was looking for a roommate in the first place. I didn't mention the other reason, which was that I had unceremoniously broken my previous roommate's, and ex-fiancé's, heart.

She understood, she told me. "Not the injury part! I can't do sports for shit," she clarified. "But the lack of a safety net. What's it like for people who actually have that? Must be nice. I just need a safe space to land for a while, you know? Maybe a few months. Maybe longer— you'll tell me, I guess!"

She seemed perfect. *Seems* perfect.

Of course, her perfection, or lack thereof, is irrelevant. I had few to zero options in inviting her to live with me. I *have* zero choice. No time left to spare. Not now.

I pray silently to the universe that I am not making a mistake.

I feel ridiculous for even checking the time, again: 10:07. I have so little going on in my life that I can only wait, like an eager kid on Christmas morning itching to tear open her presents. She isn't standing me up. That's not happening. Besides, Pip said ten o'clock, but she's bringing a lot of bags and boxes, which is the obvious reason why she's running late. She said she was borrowing a friend's car to load them up. "Not too many!" she told me genially. "I live pretty light. Won't be in your way at all."

Good, because this place has a high cute factor but is inarguably low on space. Don't get me wrong. By San Francisco standards, this condo is practically spacious. A medium-size one-bedroom in a five-unit building. My aunt bought this unit thirty years ago when her romance novels hit the bestseller lists and she churned out three a year and managed to make bank. Back then, it cost $200K. Now, it'd be worth a cool $1 million. Not that I'd ever sell it.

This place is too much in my bones. Threaded through my DNA. I'll never move.

They'd have to drag me out, kicking and screaming.

If you're imagining a gorgeous Victorian exterior like you've seen on *Full House*, kindly pivot away from that wholly inaccurate image. The condo building I live in, at 351 Elizabeth Street, is plain and boxy, the teal paint over unembellished siding more "uninspired" than "historic gem." Sandwiched between two beauties, 351 is a mildly offensive sore thumb. Not the worst home on the block. Definitely not the best. To the north: a navy-and-robin's-egg-blue Victorian boasting original nineteenth-century details and dotted with gold paint, not a bit of it flaking. To the south: a pure-white Edwardian two-story home, the perfect size for a young family, complete with original hardwood floors and vaulted ceilings. (I stalked the Redfin listing when it sold for $3 million and changed hands—who wouldn't, in my position?)

The interior of my home is a different story. Every square inch of 3C contains multitudes, and it's been that way since Aunt Viv was living here, solo. Once I arrived, we upleveled our efforts, made decorating it a kind of church. Over the years, it became an oasis full of all our treasures. Vases, street-fair finds, threadbare rugs in vibrant hues, splashy pop art. It's not a house that everyone in the world would love. But it's home. My sanctuary. The only place I feel 100 percent like myself. I'm a homebody, yes, but also—this place is my own personal museum. An ode to my past and the people I loved here. Maybe that's dramatic to say, but it's the truth.

The bell rings downstairs at the gate. It's 10:13. She's not even fifteen minutes late. Pretty punctual, all things considered.

I press the talk button. "Pip? Hi! Come on up! I'll buzz you in."

My nerves tingle, sending a jolt of worry up and down my spine that causes my knee to throb. Stupid meniscus, will you ever stop reminding me of your existence?

I'm anxious, and for the first time, my empty belly is a godsend. Nervous stomach on top of everything else would be stressful right now, even embarrassing. I want—no, I need—to exude confidence. My new roommate needs to like me for this to be as smooth a process as possible.

The truth is, I need her a lot more than she needs me.

It was never my plan to take in a roommate, never my plan to be single, and near broke, and living here by myself, mortgage payments looming and with an uncertain future.

You're fixing the problem, I remind myself. I don't have funds for expensive therapy, but I can give myself an old-fashioned pep talk. *You're adulting. Suck it up. Channel that Zen. Everything happens for a reason, doesn't it?*

That last platitude's a hard one to swallow. Aunt Viv getting dementia and having to move out to an assisted living facility . . . What meaning is there in that, besides pain and loss? My unfortunate breakup three months ago. I can't find anything to mine there except heartbreak. Hard as I keep trying.

A knock at the door. A second rap.

I move to open it, overeager, but why shouldn't I be? This is the person I'll be cohabitating with. Who'll be sharing my sacred space. I have to do it for Aunt Viv, so we don't lose our home. I have to do it for myself.

I wrench open the door, plastering on a smile that feels like it belongs to the Emily of yore. New Emily is not so smiley. But New Emily will try damn hard to appear that way.

Standing on the threshold of my home, Pip looks exactly like she did over FaceTime. Dirty-blond hair, smile lines around her eyes. She's my age, or somewhere in that ballpark, wearing high-waisted jeans that could be thrifted but are very on point. Clean white sneakers, a tank top, gold bangles on her wrists, and a constellation of studs in her left ear. One stud in her right. A diamond. Cubic zirconia, I'm guessing, because what Craigslist seeker owns the real thing?

I breathe out a sigh. She is what I was expecting. She's better, even, because the vibe she gives off here, in person, is a friendly one. Her face is warm, her expression authentic. This is someone I can live with. I know it.

Gripped in one hand is a rolling bag, next to her a wheelie duffel. A box rests behind her, labeled BOOKS.

None of that is surprising. The books are a plus—who doesn't love a reader?—though I don't know how much space we'll have for them. I put that thought out of my head. We'll manage.

Everything is in order, I think. Everything about Pip, so far, is as expected.

What I was not expecting is the girl standing a few paces behind Pip. She looks about eleven, maybe twelve. With giant brown eyes, glossy auburn hair, and white teeth behind a hundred-watt smile, she is the picture of adorable.

But who the hell is she?

"It's sooo good to be here!" Pip exclaims, peering in behind me at the apartment. "And the place is just magical. I can already tell!"

"Great," I say, my smile still plastered on. "Let me help you with all this!" I reach for her wheelie bag, eyeing the tween girl as Pip surrenders her suitcase to me. Is this girl a friend who came to help her move? But she's so . . . young. That hardly makes sense. Why do I feel a low-level sense of panic rising in my gut?

"Thanks. Oh, and by the way—this is my twelve-year-old daughter, Sofie," Pip says breathlessly, flashing her own pearly-white teeth. "I mentioned her when we chatted. Didn't I? Surely I told you . . . she'll be living here too."

Chapter 2

It's like a tornado hit my historically peaceful apartment.

Pip's duffel is splayed open on my faded pink overdyed rug, and she's forming unruly piles of clothing, both hers and her daughter's, across my floor. The way they barged in here, hardly letting me think. Hardly letting me breathe. I am scrambling for my footing while they unpack and make themselves shockingly comfortable in *my* home.

"I did a full Marie Kondo before we moved," Pip's explaining. "Completely chucked all my threadbare underwear because it didn't spark joy—sorry, is that TMI?" She looks up at me from her kneeling position, perched beside one of her numerous growing piles, her white sneakers kicked to the corner and pieces of her blond hair falling out of her topknot. I catch a glimpse of her broad smile, and for a moment, I almost forget that she has dropped a bomb on me, one that is detonating in my formerly calm and cozy sanctuary. "Emily?" she prods.

I answer, because I can barely think. Responding seems like the path of least resistance until I figure out what the heck I'm going to do. "Nothing is . . . TMI."

"Great, because I'm a bit of an open book. Can't help it. Always been wired that way." Pip laughs, and Sofie rolls her eyes.

"Ugh, Mom, you overshare like it's your job. Can you at least *try* to stop?"

Pip ignores the question, which I take to be rhetorical, the kind of mother-daughter ribbing that must be a daily occurrence between these two. These two . . . Since when is Pip a *mom*? Now she yanks a flowery dress from the top of a stack of clothes. "Is this out of style? Are long-ass dresses squarely 2017, or could this count as cottagecore? Emily? What's the verdict?" Pip's staring at me, her eyebrows furrowed.

"I . . ." I'm at a loss for words. Cottagecore? The TikTok aesthetic glorifying country life? Is she serious right now? My chest tightens, almost like a scream is trapped there that would love to escape, only I won't, can't, let it.

I train my eyes on Sofie, who must be a dancer—she's so lithe and sprightly—as she rips open the box labeled **BOOKS** and scans the room, assessing my very full bookshelves with a discerning eye.

"We could get an IKEA KALLAX," Sofie suggests, spitballing, not to me but to her mom. It's almost—almost—like I'm not even here. "If we put it there, by the TV . . . I think there'd be room. I've seen them on the Buy Nothing groups. I can get us one for free, easy." I watch them work, feeling invisible, aware of my increasingly fast-paced heartbeat and the dread bubbling up in my chest.

Pip absolutely did not mention a daughter.

It's not a detail I'd forget, like the fact that she asked to bring her special coffee maker with her, or that she offered to install blackout shades in the living area.

It's also not a detail you could accidentally leave out. "Hey, I'll be moving into your smallish apartment and sleeping on your futon. By the way, I have a kid, a nearly full-size one—we'll need to triple our occupancy!"

There is absolutely no way to interpret this omission as anything but a deception. And look, I get it—she wanted the spot in my apartment. Really wanted it. More than I even realized.

I'm sure she knew that suggesting three people live in this space would be a deal-breaker.

I'm sure she figured, no, *counted* on, me falling in love with her daughter. She banked on asking forgiveness later, not permission first.

But still. A kid? Three of us living here, in my home? Where will Sofie sleep? With her mom, on the futon? No one's even mentioned that. No one's mentioned it because it doesn't *work*. It's called a one-bedroom for a reason. This condo was designed for a single person, a couple at most. My aunt and I made do, barely, because I was a teenager by the time I moved in and accustomed to small spaces, and because I was family, and it was the only choice that made sense at the time. After my parents died, I didn't want Aunt Viv to have to sell her place to find us something more fitting for our situation. She loved this apartment. It was a piece of her. More than a house. A true home. Anything she could have bought or rented for the two of us, with two real bedrooms, would have left so much to be desired. Generic, boxy condos without any history to them, without any roots. I already felt like a burden, didn't want her to make any more sacrifices for me. So I made the living room nook my own by stringing sparkle lights from the ceiling, hanging a shimmery beaded curtain as a pseudoseparator from the rest of the space, and curating a gallery wall, including a pinboard where I collected bits and bobs, torn-out yearbook pages, poems from friends, old-school Polaroid snapshots we'd taken at Ocean Beach. If my aunt invited friends over, she lent me the bedroom for the night so I'd have peace and quiet, and privacy.

But the bedroom is mine now, obviously, not Pip's. I made that very clear from the start. The mortgage payment on this condo is $3,500 a month. I asked Pip to pay only a fraction of that—for the futon. I figured it was a fair price for what she'd be getting. A room share, essentially. A bedroom that, for all intents and purposes, is basically an extension of the living room and kitchen, with no barrier dividing her from the common areas.

Two of us in this house wouldn't be ideal, but it would have to work.

Three is . . . untenable. Three is . . . not what I bargained for. Not cool. Not what I planned.

Is any of this what you planned?

Of course not. A twelve-year-old?

It's not workable. It's not practical. It's not even suitable. This kid should have a real room, not a fraction of a condo she shares with a total stranger.

They probably can't afford any place with a real room. Housing in this city is astronomical, I know that more than anyone. Still—it doesn't mean I have to accept this. It's my condo, and it's my life. Any sane person would ask them to pack up their things and leave.

But then what?

I remind myself that I got no other responses to my Craigslist ad. No viable ones, anyway. It's still posted. I never closed it out, keeping it live as an insurance policy of sorts.

For exactly this situation.

Aargh. I haven't gotten even a single nibble on it. There's only the air-conditioning-obsessed guy, and the dog owner. I can't have three dogs living here. It's not even allowed . . . besides, they'd take up the entire condo.

I should kick Pip and her daughter out. I should stop this charade right now and tell them this was never the deal, never the plan.

But then it could take weeks to find someone else. Weeks I simply don't have.

Am I a monster for feeling like this is a complete disaster? For not wanting to share my home with two warm bodies instead of one? I watch them, my brain whirling, desperate to figure this out. I have nothing against this child. It's the furthest thing from personal. I *like* kids, generally, and she seems sweet, like a really well-behaved and thoughtful kid . . . and she's undeniably cute. She seems smart, precocious even.

What if . . . Is there any way her presence here could be considered a plus? Or am I simply reaching for any justification I can think of to let them stay? It's not like I'd want some partier living here. Sofie's mere existence is proof positive that Pip is responsible. A mother, of all things.

If I'm being honest with myself, this new wrinkle—Pip as a mother—actually makes me like Pip even more than I already did—in spite of this huge omission of the truth on her part. I'm exasperated by what she's done, and more than a little annoyed she's complicated this situation so unnecessarily. But the mother development . . . it paints Pip in a totally different light in my eyes. A mother is automatically serious, responsible. A mother would want to provide her daughter with a stable place to live. A safe home. Children need stability and routine, don't they? I'm not a mother, don't know if I ever will be. But I can imagine this duo may have faced hardships. Obstacles that I could push out of their way by offering them this opportunity. How many Craigslist ads did Pip respond to before this one? Perhaps she tried taking the up-front route. I can only imagine how many dings she got if she started with the unvarnished truth. "My daughter and I need a place to crash . . . we're quiet. Easy. We promise!"

I wouldn't be surprised if every other poster said no. I would have said no, I'm sure of it. But now . . . now. What do I do now?

"I need a soft space to land," Pip said on our FaceTime. What did that mean? What had they endured before this? What road had they traveled to get here? The idea of losing my home is so painful, the mere thought of it cuts a trench in my chest. And here are Pip and Sofie, a mother and daughter—a family—without a real home. That realization cuts me to the core. How easily that could have been me, as a child, after my parents died of cancer within months of each other. I'm no stranger to the school of hard knocks. And it's none of my business, of course, but Pip's my age, maybe a year older. Early thirties, no more. I do a quick calculation while I watch them work, side by side. Sofie's twelve . . . which means Pip had her when she was somewhere around twenty.

I think of myself, back then, of how immature I was, how unready to face the world. I was a junior in college, learning to navigate beyond my life with my aunt. I can't even imagine a pregnancy, how I would have dealt with raising a child.

They continue unpacking, strategizing. Testing the coat closet to see how many of their clothes will fit on the hanging rack. Sofie suggests another DIY IKEA hack. Pip agrees it's a good idea.

My heart sinks for Sofie, watching her shove her sweaters and jeans into that tiny closet, when she should have her own room, one she could wallpaper with fairies and cover with BTS posters. But she doesn't have that. She barely even has this. This third of a condo.

Still. This is my life. My house. Three of us living here, that's . . .

How did this even happen? I tiptoe over to my comfy swivel chair in the corner and curl up there, folding my arms around my legs, so I can think. Mercifully, they don't seem to notice *what* I'm doing at all. Which is strange, and unnerving. They've made my house their house in mere minutes, and I . . . What about me?

What about you? You did this, Emily. Your choices got you here . . .

More specifically, my choice to leave Seth before our wedding. To wait until he came home one day after work, to this very condo, and blindside him by breaking off our engagement.

I hurt him. God, I hurt him. I never intended to, never wanted to.

I didn't do it because I don't love him. Quite the contrary.

I did what I did to protect him. To *save* him.

From me.

I'm a broken person. Not just emotionally, though you could argue I have a lot of work to do on myself.

It's my DNA. I'm certain that if I tested for the BRCA gene, I'd get a positive result. Both my parents died of cancer within *months* of each other. Those aren't good odds.

Because of my extensive risk factors, I've been urged by doctors for the last decade and a half to get tested. I just haven't been able to bring myself to do it.

I know what they will find. I *know*—and I guess I've been too afraid to know it empirically. To see it written out, so starkly, and then . . . What then? Would I take the next drastic steps? Remove my uterus and ovaries, freeze my eggs, and have a prophylactic mastectomy? Even then, it might not be enough.

Even then, I'd pass my genes along to any children I might have. And what if I didn't live long enough to raise them—like my parents didn't?

Seth deserves more than that, whether he knows it or not.

It's why I had to do the impossible, myself, and end our relationship. So that he could have something, someone, more. Someone who could give him the whole life he wanted. The picket fence, the kids, a chance at growing old together.

I might only have ten years left, maybe less. My parents were in their forties when they died. I'm only a decade behind.

It's a thought I carry with me every day of my life.

My decision to break up with Seth had radical implications for my life, my future. But it had a practical one too. I no longer had anyone with whom to share the rent.

I clamp my eyes shut, attempt some pranayama breathing. The breathing I teach—no, taught—my students every day at Roll and Flow, back when I had a steady job there. Now I only have one shift, and sometimes not even that. Constrict the throat. Inhale . . . exhale . . .

"Emily?"

I'm shaken out of my self-care moment, open my eyes to find Pip standing in front of me, seeming concerned. And not only that. She looks anxious, stressed. I wasn't sure if she was the type. She's projected such a chill, carefree vibe so far.

"It's Sofie, isn't it?" She sits down on the floor dejectedly, hunching over her crossed legs in a posture that screams defeat. "You're not okay with it. With her. You feel like I tricked you. I . . . I'm sorry."

"Sofie's great . . ." The but is on the tip of my tongue. I know it, and Pip knows it even more. I let out my yogic breath. "This really isn't going to work."

There. I've said it. I don't know what I'm going to do if they leave and I have to go back to the roommate drawing board. But this situation is nuts, and there's no point in dancing around it anymore.

"I know I glossed over the whole daughter thing, but you have to understand. We're a duo. A team. We're like *Gilmore Girls*, except we aren't super preachy, and I don't talk too much!"

"You completely talk too much," Sofie groans, not even looking up as she flips through a graphic novel she's unpacked from the **BOOKS** box.

I try to center myself. Breathe, Emily. Breathe. I hate confrontation, avoid it like a root canal. But I must be honest with her. This is my life, my home, after all.

"I'm going to be transparent with you." I gather up every ounce of courage I can muster. "I knew I was making this decision much too fast. But I liked—*like*—you, and I had this feeling when we were chatting . . . like maybe we wouldn't only be roommates, but actual friends . . ."

"Me too!" Pip smiles, this wide, contagious smile that makes it hard for me to hate her for what she's done.

"I'd like for this to work, and the truth is that if you leave, I'm going to have to live with a guy with three dogs."

Pip laughs, and there it is again, dammit: that smile that spans her whole face and is hard not to appreciate and gravitate toward.

Still, I have to not be taken in by how charming she seems to be, how nice. This is not a matter of liking her or not. It's about our living situation, and whether it's viable. I take in another breath, feeling my chest start to tighten. "I know I'd be well within my rights to rip up our lease and tell you to pack your bags. But I don't want to have to do that to you."

Am I doing this? Am I going to . . . actually let them stay?

"I can give you twenty-four hours," I add. "And then, if things are really not working out, we'll call it. Let's think of it as a trial period, for both of us. Either one of us can renege by noon tomorrow." This seems reasonable. This seems safe. It gives us both an out. It feels like the smart way to handle this. It feels . . . right.

Pip's eyes widen, and she grins so big now you could see her teeth sparkling from outer space. "Thank you." She clasps her hands together. "Thank you, Emily, I mean it. I think this will work, I honestly do. I've had this really good feeling from the get-go, and you haven't even spent time with Sofie yet, but she's the best of both of us. Truly, you will love her as much as I do."

"I'm fun," Sofie pipes up, not looking up from her book. I try not to smile, though it's hard. Sofie's deadpan sense of humor is adorable given her age, her size. These two are so aggravating, and yet I want so badly for them to live up to their potential. I can't believe I'm giving them a chance, but I need that $1,200 yesterday if I'm going to make my mortgage payment. Waiting another few days, even a week to seek out new candidates, isn't an acceptable option.

I try to think positively . . . screw positivity, but right now I need some. Sofie's cute, Pip's a mom, and the two of them need a home. Kids bring joy to the spaces they inhabit, don't they? Is it possible this all happened for a reason, that these two landed on my doorstep because they were the thing I needed to boost me out of my funk—and not just financially?

"Okay," I say, feeling my chest tighten one more turn, like a screw being fitted. I may regret this later, when three of us are competing for the one small bathroom.

Twenty-four hours, I remind myself. That's all I've agreed to.

Pip is leaping to her feet, pulling me into a hug that surprises me. Are we at the hug phase of our arrangement already? "You are a lifesaver. Truly. You'll barely even know we're here."

Chapter 3

I wake up the next morning to find myself sprawled on top of my covers in my bedroom, harsh light streaming in the windows. I exhale. This room is my oasis, filled with so many of the objects Aunt Viv and I collected over the years. On the wall across from me is a framed black-and-white charcoal drawing by a local artist. In it, a woman stands on a beach, looking out at the waves, and the way it's all drawn, so simply, but sparking so much emotion . . . we knew the instant we saw it hanging in a coffee shop, for sale, that it would occupy this exact spot in the bedroom. Some might have walked right past it, deeming it plain, but we knew it was The One. I smile at the memory of how we high-fived at learning it was only $300. The Bernal Heights artist was up and coming.

I check the time: 10:43 a.m. Shit. I bolt upright in bed, then wince, feeling my knee tighten with the quick movement. I never sleep this late. But then again, I usually don't stay *up* so late. Ever since the breakup, I've found myself in bed as early as 9 p.m. every night. I sleep a lot these days. Nine or ten hours. Sometimes that's easier than facing the world awake.

Last night, Pip and I stayed up bingeing *White Lotus* and drinking the bottles of wine she'd brought in her rolling bag. I began laughing when she unearthed them from the depths of her suitcase. She assured me that she didn't usually tote alcohol around like this, but she hadn't wanted them to go to waste. A friend had given them to her, and she'd been waiting for the perfect time to open them.

"Think of it as a housewarming gift." She filled my glass to the brim.

"Housewarming? But it's *your* new house . . ." I laughed. "That's a little unconventional, but I like it."

I hadn't drunk wine in ages. It's not in my current budget. Plus, I had surgery only a few months back, and wine isn't great for recovery. But yesterday felt celebratory. I was finally solving my problems, picking up the pieces of my broken life. Assuming we don't call this whole thing a mistake in a few hours . . . I'll admit, it felt premature to celebrate with Pip before we'd made it official, but I refused to think that way. Positivity was going to be my new motto. I would give this living arrangement every opportunity to work out if it killed me. Better dead than without my home, right?

Sofie fell asleep on the futon, behind the beaded curtain, around 8:30, and I watched as Pip lovingly covered her with a blanket and removed the iPhone from her hand. One episode turned into the next, and by the time I looked at the clock, it was 1 a.m.

I get up gingerly, now, and assume a few yogic stretches—easy ones like bird dog, cat-cow, and a gentle downward dog. My knee keeps complaining, but the rest of my body is itching for more. Harder poses, more challenging workouts. I'm three months post-op, and my doctor gave me the go-ahead. I can even teach again—if I can secure some more shifts. But I'm cautious, still worried I'll tear something again and be back at square one. This surgery isn't a "forever" solution, and I know people from my meniscus Facebook groups who ended up tearing ACLs and other ligaments because they took things too fast, too soon. A few even tore the meniscus again months after surgery. Most were skiers, not yoga teachers, but still. I can't weather one more injury; I'm already teetering, and that would ruin me. I slip on yoga gear and crack open my door, padding out into the kitchen. It's cold. I'm thinking I should crank the heat up when I emerge into the common space and stop in my tracks.

My apartment is barely recognizable.

Pip and Sofie's things are spread out over every available surface. Sweaters, jackets, knickknacks, schoolwork, art supplies, even a panini press. It's like their bags and boxes exploded all over my house while I was sleeping, and they made no attempt to clean up the resulting mess.

"Morning!" Pip calls from behind the kitchen island. She's standing at the griddle making pancakes, and I notice her oversize coffee maker next to a huge jug of orange juice. That's not what startles me. Every single item from my pantry appears to have been taken down from its spot on my shelves and deposited randomly. Cereal, oatmeal, nuts, seaweed snacks. My food is everywhere. "You like pancakes, right?" Pip asks, her back turned to me while she completes an impressive pancake flip. "Don't worry, they're protein pancakes. Full of eggs and super low in sugar. I know you're into healthy." She spatulas two on a plate and slaps it down at my bite-size breakfast table. "Go ahead, eat up! We wanted to do something nice for you. Since you've been such a lifesaver. Right, Sof?"

Sofie nods from her perch on the couch, where she's scribbling in a notebook. "Yep." She doesn't look up.

I sit down, tentative. "Thanks," I mutter. I take a bite. They *are* tasty. But—what the hell is happening in my home? I didn't even realize they'd brought this much stuff . . . they only had two suitcases yesterday, and the book box. Was there more down in the friend's trunk? Did they bring it all in this morning while I slept? "We'll have to find places for all your things . . . ," I say weakly. I feel bossy, inflexible. Surely they're going to figure this out on their own and not force me to do it? And if their stuff doesn't fit . . . I assume they'll find somewhere else to store it, or give some of it away? This place is small, there's no getting around that. But I was clear about that from the first day we talked.

"Oh, we'll get to that," Pip says, waving me off. I feel dismissed, but I tell myself she'll get on it. Why wouldn't she? No one would want to live with all this stuff . . . everywhere.

"We had to throw out all your coconut," Sofie pipes up from the couch, finally looking up from whatever she's working on. "I'm allergic."

I stare at her, uncomprehending. "Oh," I finally say. "Everything containing coconut?" That was a lot of potential foods. As I'm a plant-based eater, coconut's a staple of a lot of my dry goods.

"Yep," says Sofie. "Every last item. That's why your other stuff is all here on the counter. We had to be really thorough and sift through it all. Otherwise, I could die."

Shit, I think. I mentally swipe through the large inventory of items I usually eat that contain coconut. "Would you mind giving me the bag? Of items, I mean. I could take them to the yoga studio. So they don't go to waste."

"Sorry," Pip says, looking grave. "We already took them to a dumpster. I couldn't risk having them in the house any longer. You know, just in case."

I stare at Pip. "You threw it all away? Without asking me first?"

"We had to. It was a liability."

I can't believe what I'm hearing. The allergy, I get, but why wouldn't they at least have bagged up the items and put them out in the hall or in their car and let me take them from the building? "I really wish you'd checked with me. All that food was kind of expensive." I silently mourn my protein bars and coconut shavings, at least fifty dollars' worth of items.

"Oh, shit!" Pip claps herself on the forehead. She grabs her purse and roots around in it, coming up with some cash. A couple of twenties. "Here." She pushes the money to me across the table. "I should have led with that. That should cover it, right?"

I accept the money, let out a breath. "Um, yeah. Thanks." Why do I suddenly feel like the unreasonable one? I feel heat rising to my cheeks.

They're the ones who threw my food out. I didn't do anything wrong. So why do I feel bad for asking to be compensated?

"There's something else we should talk about," Pip says, sitting back down across from me. She's wearing a bright-pink tank top and wide-legged black pants. Her toes are painted pink to match her shirt.

"Right," I say, taking a bite of pancake. Her security deposit. On our first phone call, we chatted about this, briefly—she agreed to pay $1,200 right away, to help me catch up on last month's mortgage payment. We both thought it was fair for me to have some kind of reassurance that she wouldn't live here rent-free for a month, then bolt, so I included some wording about it in the lease we both signed. I feel a sense of relief that she's bringing it up so that I don't have to. I need to get that check deposited in the bank ASAP. I glance at my phone. It's 11:15 a.m. Technically, we have forty-five minutes before we discuss how the trial has gone.

The truth is . . . I'm feeling less certain about it. Far less certain than I did last night when I fell asleep, buzzed, on top of my covers.

The throwing away of my food has unnerved me. Sure, Pip compensated me for it, but it feels *odd* that they did it all while I was asleep. Like they were counting on me not waking up until it was all gone and out of here, and too late to retrieve it. For a half second I wonder if Pip suggested we drink late into the night so they could guarantee I wouldn't wake up early, giving them time to do whatever they wanted in my house.

Including bringing in all this extra *stuff*. But that sounds like some kind of conspiracy theory. It's hardly likely.

My eyes land on the panini press. "Are you going to find places for everything? I know the condo's small, but . . ."

Pip waves me off. "Don't worry. We will. And if we can't fit things, I have a friend who can keep some stuff for me, no problem. She has a storage unit out in the burbs with extra space, so I can drive it out there this weekend."

I feel myself relaxing a bit. That makes sense and is reasonable. They want to see how much they can fit before ditching some of this stuff. I can understand that.

I swallow before speaking. "So, the trial period. And your security deposit. If we're going ahead with it, that is."

This feels anticlimactic. I'm not sure what I thought would happen at the twenty-four-hour mark—some kind of sign from the universe? Barring that, I guess we have to go on our guts. I'm still not convinced this will work out, but I need the money, and so far, they aren't terrible roommates. I could do worse . . .

When Pip doesn't answer, I decide to be more direct. "Did you decide on a check, or Venmo, or . . . ?"

"Oh!" Pip raises an eyebrow. "That's funny, the security deposit isn't what I wanted to talk to you about, but yeah, sure, I'll get that to you soon. This is, well, it's a bit awkward to bring up, but . . ."

"I'm all ears," I say, shoving another bite into my mouth. It's been a while since I ate a full meal. I'm always conserving so I don't have to make another trip to Mollie Stone's.

"Well, it has to do with the futon. It's right next to the window, and . . ." Pip shoots Sofie a look. Sofie nods at her mom. Pip mouths something back to her, and Sofie shrugs.

I set my fork down on the table, trying to ignore the pounding of my heart in my eardrums. "And?" I prod.

"It's really freaking loud," Sofie says. "I didn't want to have to tell you, but a bus runs by this place at all hours. Can you believe it?"

I can believe it. I know that bus intimately. That futon used to be mine, after all. I slept on it from age sixteen until I left for college, then returned to it after I graduated. Once Aunt Viv left for assisted living, I took over the bedroom. But that futon was my bed for a good eight years of my life. Which is why I have an easy fix. I get up and head to a corner console. I fish around in the drawer. Inside is a pair of earplugs. I hold them up satisfactorily. "I've got you covered. These worked great for me when I lived here with my aunt."

Sofie stares at me. Shoots her mom another look. Pip sighs, folds her arms over her chest.

The pounding in my ears resumes.

Why do I suddenly feel like I'm in the middle of an intervention? That I'm being cornered by the people I just invited into my home? Who just went through my cabinets and discarded my food. I shake that feeling off. Whatever the issue, we will find a work-around for it.

"We actually wanted to ask, well . . ." Pip clasps and unclasps her hands. I brace myself for whatever is coming. "If this is going to work, really work, then we're going to need to take the bedroom." Her words come out in a rush. "There are two of us, and only one of you, and the bedroom has a queen but the futon is only a full . . . the queen's really more suitable for two of us, don't you think? Plus, Sofie has school. She's in sixth grade now, and she really can't be tired during class, or she'll be penalized, and I worked so hard to get her this spot. It was a lottery to get her into a good public middle school, you know? But I guess you don't, not having kids. Not that that's your fault!"

I stare at Pip. Can she even be remotely serious? She wants to take my bedroom from me?

"I thought we agreed on the futon. Didn't we?" My words are shaky. I am shaky.

"Well, yes, but now that we see the conditions, we need to pivot. You understand, I'm sure." Pip stands up from the table, grabs my empty dish and fork. "Look, we really appreciate it. More than you can know. You're the absolute best. Right, Sof?"

Sofie nods, once again absorbed in her work.

I don't know what to say. My limbs feel weak, and I feel destabilized, like I did when Pip first showed up here yesterday with Sofie in tow. But say something I must.

"You can't—no." My brain whirs as I try to make sense of this. "That won't work for me. Look, I know we both want this to be viable. All three of us. But I'm not sure it's going to. I think, maybe . . ." I hate to say it, but I feel I have no choice. "Maybe we should call it. Time of death"—I check my phone again—"11:57 a.m. I'm sorry, Pip. And Sofie. I really like you. But you can't take my bedroom. That's not an option."

Pip stops doing the dishes long enough to look at me with a face full of regret. "I'm sorry, I know it's a lot to ask, and I wouldn't, except we've had such a shit time. I hate talking about it, and I *really* don't like talking about it in front of you, Sofie."

"It's fine, Mom. I know more about it than you think."

Pip sighs. "We've stayed with some bad people over the years. Which I feel terrible about. The last thing I'd *ever* want is to put Sofie in that kind of situation, but there was this one landlord . . . I don't really want to get into it, it's too triggering. And then there was the boyfriend . . ." She wipes a tear from her eye, and I feel myself waffling. Am I really going to kick this family out of here? Isn't there *some* way to make it work, for all of us?

"You can take the bedroom if you pay more," I blurt. As soon as I say it, it starts to feel possible. "I could make that compromise. And it's only fair, anyway, since there are two of you, and one of me. The twelve hundred dollars I was charging was rent for the futon, specifically. If you take the bedroom, I'll have to ask you to pay . . . two thousand. I think that's perfectly reasonable, and it's honestly less than the bedroom's worth. A deal for you, really. I'd still be paying a lot—the mortgage is thirty-five hundred. But I'm willing to agree to that."

This proposal isn't a disastrous idea. Much as I don't want to give up my room, $2,000 per month, in my bank account, would go a long way toward climbing out of my financial hole. I'd be able to settle my debts a whole lot sooner, and I wouldn't even need roommates as long. I'd be speeding up the whole process. Looking at it this way—it would be a win for me, not a loss. "I'd need two thousand for the security deposit too."

"Deal," Pip says, without even blinking.

I meet her eyes. "Really?"

"Yes, really." Pip picks up a dish towel, smooths it, sets it down again. "That's fair, as you say. And I can give you half the security deposit tomorrow. The rest by the end of the week."

I'm so relieved, I could cry. A thousand dollars I can deposit right away. The rest coming in a few days. If the bedroom is what they need to be able to make this work, then I will relinquish it to them—for the right price. My old futon was sufficient for eight years of my life, and it will be sufficient now.

I don't stop to ask myself if she and Sofie can afford it.

Chapter 4

Two days later, still no sign of the security deposit. Either the first $1,000, or the second.

Pip hasn't brought it up, and neither have I. Our first twenty-four hours were fraught with so much drama, and I'm cognizant of not wanting to seem *too* desperate, or *too* strident. I also get what it's like to have to gather funds together, and I'd rather give her the courtesy of an extra day or two. She promised it, so why shouldn't I assume it's coming, albeit a little late? I've prepared a jaunty note to leave for her with a short scrawled-out message.

Sorry to bug but if you can get me that security deposit today—the whole thing if you can!—that'd be great! My Venmo is @EmilyH56890. Thank you!!

I have underlined the word "today" twice. No room for vagaries here. I fold the piece of paper and scrawl "PIP" on the outside, in large Sharpie letters. I'll leave the note for her on the kitchen counter, where she absolutely cannot miss it. And then I'll go, and pray it's the impetus to get her to pony up.

I'm tidying up in the kitchen, relieved the condo looks vaguely back to normal. Pip and Sofie have returned all my dry goods to the pantry and found spots for most of their things. Of course, some of those "spots" are in the space formerly known as my bedroom. I have to tiptoe in there, when they aren't home, to grab clothes from my dresser, or my yoga mat from the corner of my closet. I realize how absurd this is, but

I remind myself it's only temporary. I need Pip's deposit if I ever want that room to be mine again. I pour myself a coffee—might as well use their fancy-ass coffee maker!—and scan the living area, taking stock. Categorizing my things—mine and Aunt Viv's—gives me a sense of comfort and peace. Overall, the place feels mildly altered, but still like my home. Our art is on the walls, and the furniture pieces that accent the living room are all still here. The worn violet-hued pouf that I always put my feet up on. We rescued that from the Alameda flea market. The heather-gray throw blanket, made of buttery-soft cashmere, is folded over the back of the couch. The throw was Aunt Viv's gift to herself after her first book had been published.

I'm stirring my coffee, trying to go about my day unobtrusively, because Pip is sprawled out at my breakfast table, in the middle of a tutoring session. I'm certainly not complaining. I'm happy to see her hard at work. She sits with a boy, aged nine or ten, hunched over a writing assignment, discussing his topic sentence. I don't mean to eavesdrop, but it's tricky not to hear them while I grab an apple from the fridge and add a splash of almond milk to my mug.

"Let's break down this part about baseball, Desi," she's saying, leaning over his paper as he fidgets in his chair. "But you'll have to explain the game to me. I'm an idiot when it comes to sports!" Pip laughs.

"You seriously don't know how baseball is played?" Desi looks at her askance.

"Nope, I don't have a clue. Is that the one with goalposts? Like Quidditch!" I can see the mirth in Pip's eyes; she's obviously fibbing to get this kid to open up to her. It's a good tactic. I make a mental note of her natural teaching abilities as I creep to the door, snagging my athletic shoes as I go.

"No," Desi is saying, without humor. "Quidditch isn't a real sport, at least not in my opinion. And you're thinking of soccer. Or *fútbol*, which is what they call it everywhere besides America. Here, we have American football. But you really don't know this? Are you from, like, Mars or something?"

"You found me out," Pip answers, deadpan. "I'm full-on martian. Now, what if we started the first paragraph like this . . ."

From the exterior hallway, I close the door behind me, feeling calmer than I did yesterday when I went to bed worrying about the security deposit. Pip's working. That's a good sign. It means there's some form of a paycheck coming her way, even if it's not the full $2,000 she owes me. Pip told me originally that between her tutoring and consulting gigs, she'd have more than enough to fulfill her end of the bargain. She's obviously good at what she does. Hopefully, there are a lot more clients like that kid.

I slam my feet into my sneakers, quickly tie them, and head for the stairwell at the end of the hall. My knee is creaky, so I go slowly. Down, down, down, both feet on each step. I reach the second floor. One more level to go . . . I pause for a second on the landing to stretch my hamstrings, leaning over in a nice, gentle posture, when the stairwell door opens, and Nathan almost knocks me to the ground.

"Oh! Crap! Emily, you okay?"

I straighten to find myself staring into the eyes of my downstairs neighbor. His hand is on my shoulder, steadying me. I'm in no hurry for him to remove it.

We're standing in this cramped space together, neither of us making a move to extricate ourselves from it.

My heartbeat quickens, and I feel an involuntary thumping in my chest. There's no denying it . . . Nathan is hot. And we've slept together—twice. We're not an item. We aren't even dating. But . . . we're something. Something extremely undefinable. And the sex was *good*. More than good. In fact, I'm sort of in love with him. But not like that. Absolutely not like that. It's too soon, way too soon, after Seth . . .

Nathan is fun. Nathan is a distraction. Nathan also lives directly downstairs from me, meaning I have to tread carefully. The last thing I need is drama in my condo building because a one-night, *two-night*, stand went awry.

My heart is drumbeating, and Nathan's still holding on to me, even though I'm clearly not wobbly, and we both know he could have released me at least twenty seconds ago. Be chill, Emily. Be chill.

"I'm fine," I say, finally answering him, hoping I sound breezy. *Hand still there. His hand is still THERE.* "But where are you going in such a hurry? There are speed limits in these halls. I'm reporting you to the HOA president." It's an inside joke, because Aunt Viv was the president, and I have taken over the job in her stead. It's not much of a role. I collect HOA dues, and if anything needs repair, I contact this woman named Celeste who manages the building. Twice, we've voted on whether to paint the building's exterior, and what color. And once a car actually ran up onto the sidewalk and caused damage to the building's foundation. That required a big insurance battle. But luckily, I didn't have much to do with it.

"Ha, ha." Nathan finally releases me—too bad—and I shift my feet, trying to determine what to say next.

"I—" I blurt, right as he says, "Maybe we should—"

We both laugh. "Want to get a drink sometime?" I try again.

Nathan threads his fingers through his hair, which isn't long but is beginning to curl past his ears. When he lifts his hand like that, his shirt rises up, revealing a sliver of his toned stomach. He's a good foot and a half taller than me, and his face is striking, a bit Adam Driver–ish in some of the oddness of it, but the full package of Nathan is universally attractive, with his broad shoulders and crackling smile, and I know I'm not the only one who thinks so. An ex of his, Serena, also lives in the building. There are only five units, total, so when I do the math on the odds of that . . . I remind myself I'm not special to him—we barely know each other. But he's been the one thing these past few months that's made me feel like getting out of bed. He even brought me chicken soup after my surgery, before we ever slept together. When a dude like Nathan brings you soup, well . . . it's hard not to fall for him, at least a little.

"Hey, so I'm in a rush, I'm late for a meeting, which is why I almost mowed you down. But I'll text you. A drink would be great."

"Sure, you know where I live." What a dumb, obvious line. So not clever. But he doesn't seem to mind. He grins, then pulls me toward him unexpectedly, grabbing the small of my back, and kisses me on the lips.

Short, sweet. *Hot.*

Why am I so attracted to him? I'm not getting into another relationship. And neither is he—he told me. He's a no-strings kind of guy. We agreed: Strings just become nooses. I literally broke up with Seth *because* he wanted strings. Lots of them. I clearly can't be with anyone else who's into commitment.

So it's no wonder I like Nathan. A little bit more than I want to admit.

He lets go of me, again, smiling. I'm sure I'm grinning giddily back, in spite of my efforts to be cool. He turns his back to me, starts down the stairwell, taking the steps two at a time, and waves his hand in the air as a goodbye.

I can't help it; I'm still beaming. Shitty as things have been lately, and they have been seriously shitty, Nathan has been my one pick-me-up. The pain in my knee is all but gone as I gallop down the stairs, feeling, for a second, like my old self again. My chest feels more expansive. I can breathe.

That ebullient feeling fades forty-five minutes later when I return from my walk, step inside my now-empty apartment, and see that the note I wrote for Pip is still on the counter.

It's exactly where I left it. Still folded, with those three letters visible on the top. "PIP." Impossible for her to misunderstand. The note is clearly for her. And if she didn't see it, well, I doubt that's even possible. She cleaned up from her tutoring session, put all her supplies away. The note is at eye level from where she was sitting. She might have even seen me place it there, during her session.

Which means . . .

She either read it and, somewhat infuriatingly, put it right back where she found it, in the same exact position, leaving me completely confused as to whether I need to follow up with her.

Or she ignored it, never opened it at all.

Alone in my home for the first time in what feels like too long, I take my time making a wrap for late breakfast and step into the bathroom for a much-needed shower. It's so quiet, I can hear the traffic outside.

I have no idea what to do.

What a lousy plan, leaving it there like that so passively. I should have had the guts to say something to her, in person, to her face, but I was too worried about dealing with her reaction. I've always hated telling people things they don't want to hear. It's a flaw I've been working on since I was a kid. In this case, it's understandable, isn't it? I've already had to lay down the law, demanding money for my pantry items, and insisting they pay me more for the bedroom. It's more confrontation than I usually face in two years, much less two days. And we're stuck here together. I left the note in an attempt to give her some space to process my message without me standing there, nagging, since physical space from each other is the one thing we don't have.

After drying off, I'm throwing on a fresh pair of yoga pants, the bathroom door cracked open to let some steam out, when I hear Pip come in.

". . . waiting for checks to come in. I've only got one more session scheduled this week. If you know of *anyone* looking for tutoring, let me know, okay? I'm good. And I do all subjects."

I can see through the crack of the door that Pip's on the phone. I freeze, half-dressed, standing right where I am, not wanting to make myself known. Not until I hear everything she's about to say.

"Of course I've posted on all the forums . . . Maybe you can blast it on the school networks?" She pauses, as if listening to the person on the other end. "Thanks. It's just my consulting work has completely dried up lately, and if I don't get at least a few more kids, I'm not gonna be able to pay for Sofie's ballet lessons. And definitely not my rent."

She hangs up, and I slink to the closed toilet, sit down on it in the steamy room, trying to think. *Think.*

Pip's basically admitted to this person, this friend, whoever it is, that she's flat broke.

She doesn't have the security deposit for me—not even the first $1,000 she promised me—which came after ballet lessons in order of importance, because she doesn't have the funds. It's what I suspected yesterday as I waited, and waited, to no avail, for a Venmo or check that never surfaced. Her bank account's even emptier than mine.

Chapter 5

After Pip went into the bedroom—*my bedroom*—I sneaked back out of the apartment without crossing paths with her, closing the front door behind me as quietly as possible in the hope she wouldn't hear me leave. That she wouldn't know I had even been there.

I needed, *need*, to think.

I stand now at the corner of Elizabeth and Noe Street, in front of a rainbow row of Easter egg–colored homes, the clear blue sky visible above the peaks and valleys of the shingled roofs. This city has been home for my entire life. Some don't understand, from afar, why San Francisco is worth the trouble. The high rents, the even higher prices. But live here for a day, a month, a year, and you'll never get enough of the natural beauty or the stunning pastel-toned vistas. But for me, this city is so much more than that. To leave it would mean abandoning myself. My memories. My childhood, my dead parents, my aunt—my very existence. I breathe in, channeling the Headspace meditation app I used to subscribe to (no more, too expensive) as I try to regain some sense of composure.

How broke is Pip, truly? I know she's not flush with cash. I realize that no one with a cushy amount of funds, a high-paying job, or any kind of safety net at all would move into my small one-bedroom with me, especially not with their kid in tow.

Pip's down and out.

Just like you are.

It's not like I could expect her to be some gloriously generous benefactor who would swoop in and solve all my problems. And the truth is, when I first hatched the plan of taking in a roommate, I talked myself out of it five times before posting that ad. Because I figured I'd be in real danger of attracting a bunch of weed-smoking drifters who'd steal my shit or invite strange dudes over at all hours. I needed someone solid. Stable. Pip and Sofie are exactly that, at least on paper. Of course they're not swimming in cash. Otherwise, they'd have their own place and never would have been looking for a room share.

That still doesn't mean I have time to wait, or waste. She agreed in that lease to pay me something up front. She's going to have to find a way to get it to me—or move out.

It's just past noon, and I'm five minutes late to meet my friend Alli at Martha & Bros Coffee. I jog the three blocks, my knee aching, and remind myself it's good to use it to full capacity and not hobble around all day, tentative. The surgeon warned me not to let the surrounding muscles grow weak from inactivity. I wrench open the glass door to the shop and spot Alli inside, already seated at a tiny café table. She's texting furiously, her head down, her brown hair falling across her face in soft waves.

I slip into the chair across from her. "Sorry I'm late."

She looks up from her phone, her brow furrowed. "Are you? Late, I mean. Not sorry. I know you're sorry." She looks down at her phone again. "Oh. You are late." Then she surveys me. "You look skinny. Are you doing another cleanse?"

I shift in my seat, pulling my flowing yoga cardigan around me. Shoot. Is it that obvious? I don't answer. No point in Alli suspecting the whole truth. A cleanse sounds . . . more upbeat. Better to let her think I've been sipping bone broth and chowing on pricey kale.

Anyway, the odds are she'll see right through it. I've never been able to keep much from Alli. She's been my best friend since college. We met there, at UC Davis, where I managed to get a full scholarship (dead parents help with that). Then she and I both settled back in San

Francisco after graduation. Me with my aunt, Alli with her then boy-friend, now husband, Josh. They live in a fancy condo in Pac Heights. Josh is in tech, and Alli does freelance consulting. But I know they've spent a small fortune on fertility treatments. So much so that I suspect it's taking a toll on them, not only emotionally but financially too.

"You okay?" I stare at her. I, too, can play this game. I know this girl well enough to tell when she hasn't been sleeping. When dark circles pop up under her eyes. Which is the case right now.

"It's the IVF," she says, sagging, releasing her phone to flop it onto the table. "We failed. Again."

Crap. That is not what I was hoping to hear. Alli and Josh have been trying to get pregnant for, what now? Three years? Four? They were the first of any of our friends to tie the knot. They'd always wanted to be parents, so they went for it pretty early, hoping to pop out a couple of kids before they were thirty-five. Now, Alli's thirty-two, and . . . nada.

"Shit, I'm so sorry, Al."

She's crying now, sniffling and trying to hide it. "It's fine. I mean, it *isn't*. We've used most of the embryos. I think the doctor said we have, like, two left? Which means we could try one more time, and maybe just implant both of them and try for twins. I know, I know. I said I'd never have twins because the idea of breastfeeding two bloodsuckers at once sounds like my worst nightmare, but two for one would definitely be a lot more bang for our buck. And anyway, I think I can only go through this process one more time. It's too awful, it's bankrupting us, and the hormones make me a monster. I don't even know if Josh wants to be married to me anymore. I'm only half-kidding. The other day he actually said we should pivot and start breeding show dogs." She sniffles, and I hand her a napkin to blow her nose on.

"Shit," I say.

"Yeah. Shit."

"Can I do anything?"

"Unless you can impregnate me . . ." She laughs. "Then no. Not really."

I reach across the table and grab her hand. She lets me. "Alli Cochran, if I could impregnate you, I one hundred percent would. Right now. Here in this coffee shop."

She snatches her hand away, laughing even harder now through the vestiges of her tears. "Thanks, I know you mean it too. How are you? We don't have to be all sad and mopey just because I'm going through it. How's your knee?"

"Okay," I fib, repositioning my legs under the table. I haven't told her exactly how hard recovery has been. And that I'm still not back to my old self—physically or mentally. Or financially.

"And . . . Seth?"

I stare at her, taken aback. "What about Seth?"

"Please tell me you've talked to him." She isn't laughing anymore. She looks very stern, and very serious.

"About . . . what?" My voice comes out hollow. I really don't want to know where this is going.

"About reconciling!" She crosses her arms over her chest. "Come on, Em. Whatever happened between you two—*if* anything even happened, which I don't know because you never confided in me—you can't just throw that away! You guys were *happy*."

I feel branded, like someone's shoved a hot poker in my back.

"How do you know that? You don't know if we were happy."

"You were happy." She stirs her coffee violently with one of those wooden sticks, I assume so she won't have to keep looking at me.

"Well, sure, we were happy, but he's not happy with me now that I dumped him. So, no, we haven't talked. He probably has a new girlfriend by now. So, unless you know something I don't know . . . I think you should drop it."

Alli sighs, looking put out. "Fine. How's work going? How's Aunt Viv?"

"Aunt Viv is . . . the same." I shrug. "And work isn't really happening, not yet. You know, because my knee has still been hurting, so . . ." I hesitate. Am I really going to tell her about Pip? I hadn't meant to. I thought I wouldn't bring it up, because I didn't want to have to answer uncomfortable questions. But now I find myself needing, wanting, to share. There are so few people in my life these days who I feel I really can share things with. Maybe I won't tell her the whole story. Definitely not the whole story. But a smidge of it. "I took in a roommate."

Alli drops the wooden stick. Coffee splatters on the table. "You what?"

"A roommate," I say, daring her to criticize. "Her name's Pip. She's great. You'd like her. It was the financially responsible thing to do, now that I'm . . . alone. It's only temporary, till we both get back on our feet. Me, literally." I laugh lightheartedly, hoping to up the mood in the room.

"Jesus, Em! What the hell is wrong with you?" She drops her head into her hands and groans.

"Um, that's not really the reaction I was hoping for, but thanks for the vote of confidence."

"You and Seth would be married right now. Settling down. *He'd* still be your roommate, for God's sake, if you hadn't—"

I'm instantly on edge. "Hadn't what?" I'm tense. Rage is bubbling up inside my chest. "Hadn't thrown it all away?"

Alli stares at me. Says nothing.

Finally: "I'm sorry." She sighs. "It's the IVF talking. The drugs they put me on, you wouldn't even believe how many at once, and I'm pretty sure it's all probably killing me. I'm so cranky from all these hormones pulsing through my body. I screamed at Josh this morning for making my eggs sunny-side up instead of over medium. I felt terrible about it. Meanwhile, I'm just an empty vessel, so . . ."

I hold back my tears. "I get it, Al. Maybe you should head home. Take a nap."

"Yeah. Okay. Look—"

"It's fine."

"I feel so out of control," Alli goes on, and now I see she's fighting tears. "I would give anything, anything to fix myself, but I can't, and you—"

"You think I had a choice, and I chose to screw up my own life." She doesn't answer, which is how I know that that's exactly what she meant.

I stand up, abruptly, telling myself not to say something I'll later regret. I push my chair neatly into the table. "I love you, Al. Will you text me later? And for the record: you'd be a great mom of twins."

I scurry out of there, tamping down my emotions. I didn't want to admit it to her. But everything that's happened these three months . . . she's right. It is all my fault.

———

Thank God I didn't confide in Alli any more than I did. If she knew that my new roommate hasn't paid me a cent so far . . . I don't want to think about the ensuing lecture. It's hard enough facing my reality. I don't need my best friend judging me about my financial life too.

I tread lightly as I walk up to the exterior gate of my condo building. I'm feeling the need for an Advil. Swelling is an unfortunate side effect of the surgery, and even though the interwebs tell me I shouldn't be experiencing this symptom anymore, I still am.

I'm met with a dude in a motorcycle helmet, holding up a paper take-out bag. He's buzzing 3C.

"Excuse me." I intercept him. "I'm 3C. Is that . . . for me?"

He looks at the receipt stapled to the bag. "DoorDash delivery for Emily Hawthorne. Two salads from Souvla, plus frozen Greek yogurt?"

I stare at the bag, perplexed. "I love Souvla. But, no, I didn't order that. Sadly, takeout isn't in my budget these days."

"It says Emily Hawthorne." The dude looks annoyed. I'm sure he's ready to get on to his next delivery, and this snag is holding him up. But the thing is . . . it's not mine.

"Maybe my roommate ordered it?" I offer. "Does it say Pip Stone?"

"Nope. Emily Hawthorne. 3C. Would you mind checking your app? I need to know what to tell my boss. I can't just leave." He's impatient, and I don't blame him, but I know checking my phone isn't going to help. I didn't order this.

I pull out my iPhone anyway, because I don't want to be rude, and I scroll to the DoorDash app. I have to log in, since it's been months since I've used this. The food on here's so pricey, and I can make my groceries last weeks longer for the same amount of money.

"Look, right there." The guy's standing over me, a bit closer than I would like. He points to my screen. "See, it's a Souvla order. Under your name. Your phone number's there, the whole thing."

I breathe out. What the hell?

"Just take it," he says, thrusting the bag in my direction. "Complain to customer service. If you ordered it, I have to deliver. Pro tip: you might as well eat it. It's gotta be thrown out, either way. It's contaminated now, and they won't ask for it back."

I humbly receive the bag from him as he walks down the steps.

Five minutes later, I'm at the door of my apartment, still churning about the salad order. My phone's been with me all day. I guess I could have butt-ordered this, if that's even a thing . . . but mostly I'm consumed by worry. If they don't take this charge off my credit card bill, it's a whopping fifty-seven dollars I'll owe on top of everything else. I can't weather another hit, not even a single extra cost, not now. That's practically a whole week of groceries . . .

I quickly type out a message to customer service, explaining that under no circumstances did I order this and they must make the charge go away. I sound desperate, but oh well. I am.

My head is spinning from everything that's happened today. And worst of all, I still have to confront Pip about the security deposit. And the fact that I know she's paying for ballet lessons and considers those more important than her actual rent. I open the door to my condo, giving myself the mother of all pep talks. I can do this. I can be an adult, talk to her calmly about what I'm rightfully owed.

When I walk into my home, all thoughts of the security deposit, and DoorDash, and all the rest of it, leave my head when I see him standing there in my living room.

Seth. My ex. Not just ex-boyfriend, but ex-fiancé.

The person who used to share this apartment with me, who I thought I'd be spending the rest of my life with.

The person I still love, whom I haven't seen in many months.

I freeze in my tracks, unable to comprehend. Ice curls around my heart, and I feel mounting dread. "What—what are you doing here?"

Pip smiles at me from the kitchen, where she's pouring tea into mugs. "Emily! Hi! Seth's here! I guess that's obvious, huh." She plunks one of the mugs down on the table, presumably for Seth. "Hope it's okay . . . I let him in."

Chapter 6

I thought this day couldn't get any worse. That my life couldn't get any worse.

I was dead wrong. I'm sitting at my breakfast table across from Seth, and if that isn't bad enough, Pip is hanging around, standing behind us, acting like this is the most normal situation in the world, when in reality, it is awful.

It's almost like she knows how painful this is going to be for me and is excited, her mouth watering, in anticipation of the forthcoming train wreck. But that can't be right. She'd have no reason to want to put me in such an awkward position. She barely knows me. And besides, Seth's the one who showed up here unannounced, at my house. He started this. Pip probably answered the door and didn't know what else to do but let him in.

The only silver lining in all this is that I actually put on real clothes to meet Alli, so I don't look like a total slob. Under my yoga cardigan are some high-waisted, wide-legged jeans I found at a local consignment shop that look straight out of the seventies, and I'm wearing a couple of the jewelry pieces Aunt Viv left here. It makes me wistful to think about the evenings we spent trying on all the chunky gem-studded pieces she'd collected from estate sales over the years. This morning, I slipped on a ladybug ring and a pendant necklace featuring a scalloped, oversize gold heart. None of it's particularly valuable in the monetary sense. But to me and Aunt Viv, it was part of our quest. To find beauty in the world wherever we could, and seize it. Wearing them, now, makes me feel close to her.

"So, you lived here before me, huh?" Pip breaks the tense silence, leaning on the counter in the most casual of poses, like she's got nowhere to be, like we're having freaking tea together. Well, we are having tea—because she freaking brewed it—but we are most definitely not "having tea" in the normal, hospitable sense.

Seth looks good. I hate admitting it, because I've been trying for the last three months to convince myself that I'm over him, that I never really loved him, et cetera, et cetera, et cetera.

It's all a big lie.

"Yeah, we were roommates," he explains, answering Pip's question but looking at me uncomfortably, like he doesn't quite know what's happening. That makes two of us. "Roommates who slept together."

"Ha," I say. Seth always had a great sense of humor. Good to see that hasn't changed.

"You look . . ." He trails off.

"Thin?" I say pointedly. I haven't taken my eyes off his constant hazel ones. It's unsettling looking at them. Like gazing at an image of my future, the one I lost irretrievably and cannot, for the life of me, ever locate again.

"I was going to say good. You look good."

"Thanks. You look scruffy."

Seth reaches up to massage the stubble on his chin. He was always clean shaven when we were together, kept his electric razor plugged in precariously on the edge of the sink, and I always nagged him to be careful not to let it fall in . . . I wonder what's caused this change in his hygiene paradigm. "Just something I'm trying."

"So, I'm your replacement, then," Pip interjects, piping up as she slips a plate of cookies onto the table. I don't know who she thinks is going to chow down on those. Not me, and definitely not Seth. No one besides her has food on the brain right now. I can vaguely appreciate that she's acting as a buffer, of sorts. Things can't get too weird between me and Seth with Pip right here in the room. But her presence is also off-putting, and I wish she'd have the sense to go in the bedroom and close the door. Or, better yet—leave.

"You didn't tell me you got a roommate," Seth says, his foot tapping the floor in a rhythm I remember as his nervous tic.

"I don't tell you anything anymore, do I?" I reply. I don't mean to sound harsh. It's simply the truth. "But yeah. Pip's great. She and her daughter moved in a few days ago."

Seth raises an eyebrow. "Daughter?" He stares at Pip like she's an alien. I know what he's thinking. This is beyond bizarre. Even I can't really explain it . . . Can I?

"We're all getting along smashingly," I answer, forcing a smile. Dammit, what a dumb word choice. I've never said "smashing" in my entire life, and Seth probably knows that. Shit. The last thing I want is for him to figure out that things are not going as planned. And I really don't want Pip to think I'm worried about our . . . situation. "But truthfully, I have a lot to do, so . . . What did you need, exactly?"

"Oh. Right." Seth stands up from the table, wipes his hands on his jeans. Damn, he does look good. As fit as always, but his clothes seem more stylish than when we were together. Maybe it's because he's back in the dating pool so he's making more of an effort. That realization stings. "It's my hard drive. I think it's in a bin in your bedroom closet. I completely forgot about it until recently, and . . . Can I take a quick look?"

"Sure," I answer, eyeing Pip sideways. I pray she doesn't mention the fact that my bedroom is *her* bedroom now. The idea of explaining that to Seth . . . it's humiliating.

Thankfully, Pip doesn't say a word as I lead Seth back to the bedroom and show him to the closet. Unnecessary, since he lived here for two years and knows this condo like the back of his hand. He starts rooting around the top shelf.

"Got it," he says after a couple of awkward minutes. "It's my crypto key," he says a bit sheepishly, holding up a chrome-colored external drive. "I can't believe I left it here, festering . . . if I ended up like that dude who buried his millions of Bitcoin in a dumpster in Wales . . . I'd never forgive myself."

"Glad you came back for it, then," I say tersely. This stings, on so many levels, but mostly because I know, now, that he truly came here for transactional reasons. Not to see me. He really wanted that hard drive back. It could be worth a small fortune.

He could have asked you to UPS it. Or drop it off in his mail slot.

Maybe he *did* want to see me.

But that's irrelevant now. Even if he came here to connect, to say hi, using the hard drive as an excuse, I know we'll never get back together. What I did—it was too hurtful. Too cruel. I don't regret it, because I know I was protecting him. Doesn't mean it's not agonizing, seeing him again. Remembering how much I loved—love—him. I hustle him to the bedroom door, eager to vacate before he notices Sofie's stuff all over and gets suspicious.

"I'll let you go . . . ," I say as his eyes meet mine one more time, and I look away.

I walk him through the apartment to the front door.

When we reach it, I open it for him, and he steps out into the hall. No hug, no wave. It's too messed up between us for those niceties. I won't make the gesture. That could open up old wounds that might never begin to heal. They're barely scabbed over as it is.

"I guess we'll see you around, Seth. Want your tea to go? Cookie?" Pip asks brightly.

"Um, no. Thanks. I gotta run. Thanks, Em, for this," he says, stuffing the hard drive deep in his jeans pocket. "And nice to meet you, Pip."

Then he's gone, and I shut the door securely behind him, feeling a throbbing sense of loss. I thought that the last time I saw him would *be* the last time. Sure, I had the vague understanding that we might run into each other, someday in the distant future. But this was so soon. So fresh. It's like there's this outstanding balance of emotion in my life that I can't pay off, like all my other bills. I don't know what to do with it. Stuffing it under my mattress isn't an option. And I can't ignore it.

"Seems nice. Too bad you broke up. Was the sex not good?" Pip plops down on the sofa and hugs a throw pillow to her chest.

"The sex was good." I wish she'd drop it.

"I'm a really good listener, I've been told. I've got nowhere to be, if you want to talk. I've also been through it with a lot of shitty guys."

The last thing I want to do is discuss Seth with her. Maybe in some other context, she'd be a good confidante. I can see that about her. But now, this living situation, my ex—just, no. "Seth actually isn't shitty. That's the worst part of it. But thanks. And sorry you had to deal with all this. I can't believe he didn't text first, or anything . . ."

"Emily, it was no big deal. I'm here for you. Seriously." She checks her watch. "Sofie's not back from school for another hour. You sure you don't want to veg with me? We could finish *White Lotus* . . ."

"Question," I say, then spin to face her, not even considering a TV session. I have way too much on my mind, and for some reason, Pip has an irritating way of distracting me. I'm beginning to think this is one of her many quote unquote talents. "Did you accidentally order food from DoorDash, from my account?"

Pip stares at me. "DoorDash? What kind of food was it?"

"Souvla. You know, the Greek place. It was two veggie salads . . ." I walk over to the console, where I'd deposited the take-out bag before I got waylaid by my ex. "Also, a frozen yogurt. I definitely didn't order it, but the delivery guy insisted. And it's showing up on my account, which is so, so weird." I show her the bag, which she takes and inspects, and then I check my app. No response yet from customer service. Dang. I'm going to have to write them again. I can't add this charge to my already teetering balance of unpaid bills.

"Emily, I've heard about this happening," Pip's saying excitedly as she studies the receipt. "It's just never happened to me before! But it's all over Reddit. Look it up. Somebody out there is trying to set you up for identity theft. They start small, and it's confusing, because why would they order food and then send it to you? But I think that's how it begins. Change your passwords immediately—all of them. Good news, though—we get to keep the food."

"That's what the delivery guy said too. That they wouldn't want it back."

"Of course not. It's got our germs all over it. Lucky us." Pip starts opening one of the salad boxes and roots in the bag for a fork. "I can have this one, right? Nice of this fraudster to send us two," she's saying, and I'm staring at her, my head starting to pound.

This day feels like I've deep dived into *The Twilight Zone*. Never to return.

"Yeah, you can have it . . ."

"Cool, I'm starving. Do you want the frozen Greek yogurt? If not, I'll save it for Sofie."

"No, I don't want it," I hear myself saying. "Give it to Sofie, that's fine. I think . . . I need to lie down for a bit."

"Oh shit, of course. I bet seeing Seth was hard. Especially if you still have feelings for him . . . ?"

Damn, she doesn't let things drop, does she.

I'm not going to fall for it. I'm not telling her the tragic story of me and Seth. It's none of her damn business. Being here, being my roommate—if you can even call her that, given she's yet to pay me a cent—doesn't give this woman unfettered access to my private thoughts. My history, my *life*.

I'm about to escape to my corner of the room when Pip sets her fork down and starts walking toward me. Before I even know what's happening, she's enveloped me in a tight hug. And she doesn't let go.

Chapter 7

I have no appetite for the suspicious DoorDash food, so I slip it in the fridge for later, then pop an Advil. My knee is aching, but more aggravating is the pain in my head. When I think back on today, I can't even wrap my brain around it.

Hanging over me like deadweight is the fact that I haven't broached the subject of the security deposit with Pip. But I can't do it now, not with this mounting headache that feels like it could be a migraine in the making. I need to confront her, to tell her I know about Sofie's ballet lessons and her own lack of clients. But it can wait till morning, till the pounding in my head subsides.

I lie down on my futon and am drifting off in minutes, even with the traffic rushing past. I don't need the earplugs—it's like my body is shutting down, knowing a dreamless sleep will be far preferable to being awake and forced to confront the reality of my situation: A roommate who hasn't paid me. An ex who popped back into my life, unexpectedly, who completely squeezed my stomach in knots. Several months of lurking mortgage payments . . .

The truth is, I have no idea exactly how long I have until the bank seizes this place. I've willfully avoided doing the research because I don't want to know. Instead, I've been blindly scrambling to make my payments any way I can. I know there's some grace period, but in the last two months, I haven't paid them a dime. Soon it will be three. Surely they won't let me get away with this for much longer, and then . . .

I can't think about it. I won't. I'm a master of denial. I know this about myself; it's why I can't bring myself to do the genetic testing, to find out my risk profile for cancer. And now, because of that, here I am. No fiancé, no money in my bank account, no yoga shifts to speak of. No life.

It's 5 p.m. when I force myself up from the futon and pad into the kitchen. My body feels like lead, but at least my headache's gone. Thank you, ibuprofen. I'm going to force myself to eat a few bites of the Souvla salad before it gets soggy. It would be foolish to let something so pricey, and healthy, go to waste.

I stop short when I find Sofie in the living room, performing a ballet routine. She's as graceful as I imagined when I first met her, and I'm genuinely impressed by her arabesques and pirouettes. I watch her for a minute, unobserved, until she senses me standing there and stops abruptly.

"Oh!" she says. "I didn't know you were there."

"Sorry," I say, curling up on the couch. "I didn't mean to scare you. You're really elegant. That's hard stuff."

"Thanks." She shrugs. "I love ballet. My mom used to work the reception desk at a dance studio, back when I was, like, two. I started taking classes there and kind of never stopped. I do all the styles. Modern, tap, jazz. Even hip-hop. I love the dance studio I go to, now. I have so many friends there. Katie, Abby, Clementine, Izzy. Way more than at school. That's because my school is new, so I don't really know a lot of the kids yet. It's hard starting over, but this school is ranked higher than my old one, and my mom, you know. She's always trying to give me the best things she can. If I do well in middle school, I can get into a better high school. Then maybe get a full scholarship to college. The UC schools are good *and* cheap, so maybe one of those."

I don't know what to say. This is the first time Sofie's shared anything like this with me. She's been living with me for days, and I haven't stopped to really consider her as a distinct person. She's been merely an extension of Pip, piping up here and there with a witty remark. This feels different, like a real attempt to connect. I register a guilty twinge in my gut. This kid's smart. And insightful. I should have paid her more attention . . .

"Your mom loves you," I say. "You're her kid. Of course she wants the best for you. I took dance when I was little too. But I wasn't as graceful as you. Now I only do yoga. When I'm not injured, anyway."

Sofie leaps onto the couch and folds her legs beneath her, looking up at me. Those brown eyes really tug at the heartstrings. It makes my chest ache, a little, recalling how Seth and I talked about having kids. That feels like such a faraway, lost dream.

Sofie's staring at me. "How'd you get injured?"

"I twisted my knee during one of my classes, and . . ." I make a ripping motion with my hand.

"Ouch." Sofie grimaces, as if in sympathy for the pain I endured.

"Yeah. It's almost better now, though."

She seems to be considering something, then: "I wish my dad could see me dance. But he lives in Florida, or maybe Montana, and I don't ever see him. I've never even met him."

Shoot. It hadn't even occurred to me to think about Sofie's dad. Or to wonder if she even had a dad in her life, at all.

"So you don't ever . . . visit him?" I have so many questions but don't want to overstep.

"Nope. My mom says it's because he's busy, but I think the truth is he doesn't really want to be a dad."

Oh. That sucks. Now I really don't know what to say. I'm not used to hanging around kids. Sometimes a few show up for my yoga classes with their moms. But not often. I was an only child, and I never babysat. Kids are a little bit like foreigners to me. I know only a few of their words, am still learning their language.

"I don't think he even sends child support," she goes on, thoughtful. "My mom works so hard to have money for my dance lessons and clothes for school . . . groceries. And rent, obviously. I'm pretty sure it's illegal for him to not send us any money, but what is she going to do about it, take him to court?"

I'm instantly uncomfortable. Where is this coming from?

Her mother. It's obvious, isn't it? Kids repeat what their parents say. Pip must have mentioned child support on multiple occasions. And Sofie picked up on it. Of course she did—she's an observant kid.

"She wouldn't want some messy custody battle. Or, like, to sue him." Sofie traces the edge of the rug with her toe. "That would be awful, and she probably doesn't want to put me in the middle."

I hate that Sofie's heard this so many times, she's parroting her mother's words. But clearly that's what's happening here. The only question is . . . Why is she sharing it all with *me*? "I'm sorry, Sofie. That sounds . . . hard." It's all I can muster.

"She'll get you the security deposit." Sofie looks up at me, releasing her toe from the rug's edge and folding it back under her again.

I'm suddenly on edge. "What?"

"I heard her say she has it. She was talking to a friend about it. I think she was waiting on one more tutoring payment to come in, but it did. I bet she gives it to you really soon."

I despise myself for putting Sofie in this position. Discussing the rent money with her. She's a kid. She should be focused on dance, and friends, and schoolwork, and crushes. Not . . . this.

"That's great, Sofie. Thanks." More than anything, I want to change the subject. "Shoot, I have to run to the store if I'm gonna have food for dinner tonight." It's a complete fabrication, an excuse. But it's the only way I can think of to extricate myself from this conversation. "Do you need anything from the outside? Ice cream? Cereal?"

"Nah, I have to do my homework." Sofie grabs a notebook and settles in at the breakfast table. I let out a breath. I need air. I slip out to the hall and down the stairs, outside to the street.

My bike is here, locked to the rack on the street, collecting dust. I don't own a car. It's too expensive, and anywhere I need to go I can either walk, ride, or take public transit. For a moment, I consider unlocking it and taking it out for a spin, but then I remember my knee.

I'm not ready.

So I walk, appreciating the crispness of the day. San Francisco weather is predictably unpredictable. Layers are key. You never know if temps will rise to eighty or dip unexpectedly to fifty.

The security deposit. Shit. Now Sofie's asking me to be patient. Ugh!

In fifteen minutes, I'm at Roll and Flow, the yoga studio where I've been working for the past ten years, ever since I returned from college. Aunt Viv first introduced me to yoga after my parents died. We came here every day for an entire year. It was Viv's way of connecting with me, giving me something—*anything*—that might be a source of comfort after what I'd endured. I knew then that I wanted to teach it.

Only problem is, there's no safety net for yoga teachers. No health benefits—I have to buy mine through the open market. No job security or disability benefits. My meniscus tear meant I couldn't work for more than three months, and I wasn't compensated at all for the shifts I missed.

I approach the studio and push open the glass door, bells jangling, to find Wren, the owner, behind the desk going over paperwork.

"Emily!" She looks up, pulls off her reading glasses. Wren is about fifty, now, and has owned this studio for more than twenty years. She's like family to me, or she was, anyway. Now, I don't know what we are to each other. Her smile fades to something like confusion. "Do I have you on the schedule for today?"

"No," I'm quick to answer. "Not till next week. Have any of your teachers called in sick? Or do you think you might add that slow flow class back on the schedule? I'm free anytime, and slow flow is about my speed right now." I give a watery smile, doing my best to sell myself.

Wren looks tense, her lips pursed. "Sorry, Emily. No. We don't have the numbers right now for an extra class. I promise, you will be the first to know if I add any shifts."

I transfer my weight from one foot to the other, looking around the studio space with an ache in my chest. This place was my second home, until it wasn't. I know these wood benches, and shoe cubbies, and used yoga-mat bins like the back of my hand. I used to wipe them down every evening with a Clorox wipe. And deposit any lingering items in the lost and found bin.

"Wren, look. I'm asking this more as a favor than anything . . ." I pause, not sure if I can do this. Asking for help is not in my DNA. "Is there *any* way you can get me on the schedule for more than one class per week? I could really use the cash."

She sighs, sits back in her chair. "Ashlee took over all your shifts when you were out, Em. And she's good. The customers—"

"My customers," I can't help interrupting.

"They love her. I can't fire her. She's got kids. And there would be no cause to let her go. She's doing a great job."

"I did a great job."

"Of course you did! Your injury sucked, Emily, but I'm running a business here. The numbers are barely adding up as it is. My own girls are off to college next month, which is pretty much going to bankrupt me. They didn't get much financial aid, but now I have to tell them they can't go?" She looks like she's on the verge of tears.

"I get it," I say softly. I feel like climbing under a rock. "It's okay, Wren. Really. Please don't worry about me."

"Well, I am worried."

"I know, but I'll manage. I applied to a bunch of other jobs." It's humiliating admitting this. "I can't do cashier, or barista, or waitress. Too much standing. My knee, you know, it would never hold up. I found a couple of office positions I might qualify for, but it's a brutal market out there, even for someone with a college degree. My only experience is, well, yoga. But look, I'll see you in a week for my shift. Thanks. And nice sweatshirts." I indicate the wall full of retail items. Yoga pants, yoga mats, hoodies bearing splashy inspirational quotes like KEEP IT ZEN. "Those will fly off the shelves."

"Here's hoping."

I turn to go, not looking back. Bells once again jangling as I open and close the door behind me.

I bite back the tears on my walk to my condo. I haven't had time to process. Seeing Seth again. Losing my bedroom to a couple of strangers who haven't even paid me. Wren basically telling me I have no job anymore, that she can't help me.

My life is beginning to feel like it's gone so far off track from where I started, it's hardly recognizable as my own.

Why did Seth have to show up like that? I don't think he did it to rattle me, though a small part of me wouldn't blame him if he did.

I hurt him first, after all. When things were good with us. Alli was right. We were happy. So why couldn't I let us be? I know why. It's because of my defect, the hole my parents' death left in my chest, along with some seriously faulty DNA.

I run up the steps to my home. All I want to do is curl up under the covers and make this awful day disappear.

When I step inside, there's no sign of Pip or Sofie. The bedroom door is shut. Maybe they're both in there. Who knows? Who cares, honestly? I grab my laptop and head to the couch, telling myself I must do the thing I've been avoiding for months: tally up what I really owe. To the bank. To the utility companies. Make a plan to pay it all off. That plan will include confronting Pip about her unpaid security deposit.

The next time I see her. No excuses. I must.

I'm logging in to my email, gathering up the courage to visit my bank's website and check the exact amount in my dwindling account.

The page loads . . . and loads. One of those spinning dots that never seems to reconcile itself.

That's unusual—unless the internet company cut me off. But, no, that's the one bill I've managed to consistently pay. I couldn't let that one slide, it's too critical. I'd pay it before buying food.

I hover my cursor over the top, right-hand side of my screen where the little curved bars are, the ones that indicate you're on Wi-Fi. I click on my known network—Vivian0524, Aunt Viv's birthday and what our account has been called for years—and go to input the password. Weird, because my laptop always remembers it. But maybe I got disconnected, somehow.

fivefourthreetwoone

It's been my little inside joke with Viv for years. We couldn't come up with a good password when we first got internet service, so we thought this was perfect—we'd think of one in "five, four, three, two, one" seconds.

I type in the letters now.

But when I hit return, I get a message back.

password invalid

Chapter 8

I didn't change the internet password. Why would I?

Only a few days ago, I gave it to Pip, so she and Sofie could log on to their devices.

There's no reason I would have had to change it. It's been the same for *years*.

Which means *someone else* changed it.

In my house.

I slam my laptop closed so hard, the screen almost cracks.

I'm instantly regretful. The last thing I need is a broken computer on top of everything. Then I'd really be screwed, with no way to job search or connect to online bill pay. I stand up from the table, all the emotions of the last week bubbling up from my belly to my chest and threatening to explode.

Something is not right. I didn't change the Wi-Fi password, which means it must have, somehow, been Pip. But why? And how? How would she even do such a thing, unless she had all my credentials?

Her explanation about the DoorDash order was fishy. I knew it right when she said it but didn't want to argue. Sure, as a one-off, it was believable. Weird shit like that can happen. I once had an Uber arrive for me that I never ordered. But now . . . this.

Pip owes me. She's taken over the place. And now I'm locked out of my own internet connection.

I'd be angry as hell if I weren't so freaked out.

Is she messing with me? Trying, somehow, to put me off balance so that she can stay in this apartment without ponying up the cash? Is that what this is about? Some twisted tactic to mess with my head, play mind games that make me doubt myself, gaslight me so that I'll stop nagging her for the security deposit?

It sounds so far fetched. So . . . unlikely. But when I add up everything that's happened the past few days: the way she deceived me about having a kid, the way she and Sofie threw away my food and manipulated the situation to take my bedroom from me, the food order, the password . . . Could all those events simply be a string of odd coincidences?

Or is there more going on? Some kind of exploitation on their part? I have to find out.

I knock forcefully on the bedroom door. "Pip? Are you in there? If you are, please open up."

"Just a second!" I wait, impatient, until she yanks the door open a few seconds later. It's a quiet scene inside. Sofie's wearing headphones and reading a book, which she doesn't look up from.

"We have to talk," I say, too worked up to waste time on pleasantries.

"Is this about Seth?" Pip looks appropriately contrite. "I never should have let him in, or opened the door at all. If I'd known how much it would hurt you to see him again . . . I should have texted you. Warned you in advance—"

"No! It's not about Seth." *Stop changing the subject on me!* "It's about the security deposit you owe me. I don't have any time left. I need it, now. All two thousand dollars." I'm boiling, so angry that it's come to this. Why am I having to hound her for what she owes me? What we *agreed* on?

Pip doesn't answer. She turns and steps back to the nightstand, where she grabs a piece of paper, holds it up so I can see it. "Perfect timing." She's grinning. "I wrote this check for you not five minutes ago. And I included half of next month's rent in there, too, since you've already been a superstar landlord."

She hands me the check. I study it. The name on the far left-hand corner says "PL Consulting."

"That's my consulting company," Pip's quick to explain. "I incorporated a few years ago. Better for taxes."

My eyes land on the amount. Pip's not lying. She's made the check out to Emily Hawthorne for $3,000.

I exhale. Thank God.

I clutch the check to my chest like a lifeline and am about to pull her into a spontaneous hug when I think better of it, stopping myself and hanging back. Pip may have paid me, but there's still the matter of all the other stuff that's transpired since she came into my life. I need to set boundaries. No more hugs, or girls' nights bingeing shows. This relationship has to stay strictly professional from here on out.

"Thanks," I manage to say coolly, though inside I'm screaming with relief. "I really appreciate it."

"Course." Pip smiles. "It's what I owe you."

I start to go, then remember. The internet. "Wait." I turn back to look at her. Her face is the picture of concern. "Did you notice that the Wi-Fi password got changed? I can't log on."

Pip stares at me for a beat. "The password?" She claps herself on the forehead. "Yes! I am so sorry about that. Sofie and I were working on a project for school, and it got all messed up, and I had to actually call the internet provider, if you can believe it."

"But . . . How? It's my account. You're not authorized." I'm trying to remain calm. I have the deposit, and half of next month's rent. That's a whole heck of a lot more than I had twenty minutes ago. I'm still in debt up to my elbows, but I can rest a little easier tonight. And that's because of Pip. Because I did what I had to and invited her to live with me. Whatever she might have done to screw up the internet . . . it's worth it.

"Right, well, about that." Pip speaks methodically, like she's weighing her words. Or afraid of how I'm going to react to them. She grabs a scarf from the top of my dresser and winds it around her neck, playing with the ends. She's staring at her reflection in the mirror over the dresser, not looking at me at all. It's odd and off-putting. Can't she look me in the eye while she's talking? Is there a reason she isn't? "So, I basically had to tell them I was you, and give your birth date. Which is listed on our lease. Remember, we both attached copies of our IDs? You weren't home, and I didn't think it would matter, long as we got it fixed. I didn't want you to come back and have it still be unresolved. It was easy, we just had to make up a new password."

It doesn't all add up. Don't you need some kind of phone password to get AT&T to talk to you? Maybe she guessed mine?

"So, what is it?" I prod.

"What's what?" She finally turns to look at me.

"The new password! What did you change it to?"

"Oh! Of course." Pip flops down on the bed and kicks her feet up. "Ourhouse. One word. No spaces."

Chapter 9

I can't breathe when I read the notice from the bank the next morning at 9. Transaction canceled says the text from Chase. Insufficient funds.

My mobile deposit, the one I made last night after snapping a photo of the $3,000 check from Pip and uploading it on the Chase app, did not go through. And they've charged me a thirty-five-dollar returned check fee for their troubles.

Holy shit. I went to bed last night, exhausted after such a long, shitty, ass-kicking day, finally feeling some sense of relief—and release. And hope. Pip had finally paid me. I'd even received a quick text from Nathan, asking if I wanted to do something this week. Maybe catch a movie at Alamo Drafthouse. I'd sent him a flirty reply:

Sure but you're buying the beers

It was a joke, a way to signal that I was playing a little bit hard to get, that I wasn't the girl living upstairs who would make herself infinitely available to him for booty calls whenever he liked. But there was more truth to this text than he would ever realize. No way I could shell out for movie tickets and beer. I had no right to, not now.

I fell asleep feeling a peace I hadn't in weeks. I was still in the hole, majorly so. But Pip's check was a start. Enough to convince me that things might work out.

It was also validation that I had not made a massive error in judgment by taking Pip and Sofie in.

Morning light streams in my north-facing windows as I sit cross-legged on my futon, in my tiny corner of the condo, the beaded curtain pulled across my space so that I can, for the moment, at least pretend I have some modicum of privacy.

I feel hot tears threatening to come.

What game is Pip playing? Did she know this check would bounce? Did she even look at her balance before writing it to see if she had the appropriate funds available? Or did she simply dash it off, knowing full well it would get me off her back for a night, intending it as a stall tactic? Was she already prepared with her cover story?

A question enters my mind that is even worse than all those others: Is Pip ever planning to pay me?

Because right now . . . I'm smelling a pattern. It's beginning to feel like I am the target of a very cruel scam.

I let the Wi-Fi incident go. I still think Pip did something highly unethical, and I don't know how, and I definitely don't know why. It's not like I hadn't shared the password with her. She had what she wanted: working internet service. Yet she pretended to be me on the phone with AT&T. Which is suspect. And dishonest. But let's face it: she's been dishonest from day one. When she showed up with a *child* she failed to mention.

This is all unsettling in a way that I don't want to admit to myself. Unsettling . . . and disturbing.

I have no choice now. I have to confront her, and this time, I cannot let her manipulate me. I am allergic to confrontation, but this is my life. My house. This is a must.

I make my way into the kitchen to brew a cup of coffee. Stupid fancy Breville that I'm pretty sure retails for $1,000, with its touch screen, grinder, and milk frother. She could sell this puppy for at least a couple of hundred dollars. We don't need elaborate espresso when we are soon not going to have a roof over our heads. Where did she even get this thing? I smack it to get it working, knowing I'm being petty, but I might as well get a decent cup of joe out of it if I'm going to have to deal with her.

I hear the door opening and brace myself. If it's Pip, and she's alone, then I have to talk to her. No way around it.

". . . it's so weird. Like driving around in a video game."

I freeze, setting my empty coffee mug down. Is that . . . Nathan's voice?

"I haven't ridden in a Waymo yet, but I'm dying to." It's Pip. Nathan is talking to Pip.

In my hallway.

Right outside our—my—door.

"Half the time you're gripping the seat thinking you're gonna die. I mean, there's no driver. It's so weird!" I can't see either of them, but from the tenor of Nathan's voice, it sounds like he's smiling. "And the other half you're realizing we're all screwed. AI is taking over. We might as well give up and go on a living wage. Quit while we're ahead."

Nathan is talking to Pip. *Nathan is talking to Pip.*

Well, fine. They are neighbors now, technically. It's not like I could expect them to never meet.

"Hey, idea." I hear Pip's upbeat tone, and my stomach curls. I am so angry at her now, all I can think is how fake she sounds. How phony. "Let's ride in one together. I'd be too afraid by myself. Maybe this week sometime? My schedule's pretty flex."

"Sure. Give me your digits."

This isn't happening. It can't be.

But it is. Of course it is. Pip is charming. Pip is attractive.

And Nathan, who texted me not twelve hours ago that he wanted to hang out . . .

It's his prerogative. We aren't a couple, aren't even in that zip code. But still . . . Pip, of all people. They're flirting. And I'm wishing I could crawl under a rock.

I make myself as busy-looking as I can when Pip strides in, closing the door behind her.

"Ooooh, coffee," she says, skipping the greeting. "Isn't that machine a godsend? Make me one, will you?"

I place my shaking hands on the counter, my back to her. Inhale, exhale. I am going to need all my yogic-breathing tricks right now if I'm going to refrain from throttling her.

I spin to face her, trying my best to forget what I heard moments ago, between her and Nathan. That was upsetting, but it has nothing to do with her security deposit bouncing, and it's neither here nor there in terms of my current predicament. Nathan is a distraction, a dalliance. She has no way of knowing that we've slept together or that he means anything to me. This is about the check. Her deception. Her tricks.

"It bounced," I say, finally looking her in the eye. "Your check bounced."

Pip sets down the grocery bag she's carrying.

"What do you mean?"

"I mean, the funds didn't go through!" There, I've said it, and I've lost my temper too. I feel my cheeks burning with rage as I pull out my smartphone and show her the text that came through from Chase. "See? It says 'Insufficient funds.' Did you make sure you had the money before you wrote me this?"

"I—I did check," Pip says. She sinks down onto the couch. "But I can explain. There were three different payments I was expecting from three different customers. Tutoring clients. I deposited those two days ago, and one was a Venmo, which should have been automatic, but maybe, maybe . . ." She wipes at her eye, as though brushing away a tear.

Now Pip's crying? Why do I feel like this is one more ploy to manipulate me?

Because it probably is.

"I will fix this," she says, gritting her teeth. "I knew I should have given you two grand and stopped there. I just really wanted to make things right. Stupid me, overshooting and trying to pay you more . . . please, Emily. Give me a day to correct this. I swear, I'm good for it."

I am so furious, I could scream. The excuses. The gaslighting. Making *me* feel bad for asking for what I'm rightfully owed. How long can she toy with me like this? She's even got me feeling guilty about *her* situation. When she clearly doesn't give a crap about mine.

"You could cancel Sofie's ballet lessons."

Pip looks up at me, an expression of shock on her face that feels about as genuine as a counterfeit handbag. "You were listening to my conversation with my friend?"

"It's a small apartment." I don't move my eyes from hers.

"You aren't seriously suggesting I pull Sofie out of dance, are you? It's her life. Her passion. She's only a child. It would crush her."

"That's all well and good." I shrug. "But the rent has to get paid. What's the point of ballet if none of us have a place to live anymore? The bank isn't going to care if she can pirouette."

I sound harsh, but I know I'm in the right. It's time to make her understand the gravity of the situation. Either she's in stubborn denial herself, or she does get it, and she's trying her best, scrambling to get me the money. I'd like to give her the benefit of the doubt . . .

Somehow, I don't believe it.

I grab on to the counter so I don't throw something. Like her stupid coffee maker. "This is serious, Pip. If I can't pay my mortgage, we can't stay here. Do you understand?"

She nods, looking appropriately chastened. "Of course I do. Emily, I'm sorry. I'll get you what I owe you."

She grabs her grocery bag, walks into the bedroom, and shuts the door.

———

I could kick them out.

I should kick them out. Anyone in my position would. They've done nothing but mess with me since they arrived, and with each increasingly frustrating move they've made, I've come no closer to actually getting any funds into my bank account, which was the whole point of taking them in, in the first place.

Do I believe Pip's sob story that she had sincerely meant to pay me, she simply needs more time to gather the money together? I might have, had she not tried to defend Sofie's ballet lessons straight to my face.

I'm outside on my street, intending to tour the city by foot. My plan is to walk into every yoga studio listed on Yelp and leave my info at the front desk. It's humiliating, but . . . if Wren has no loyalty left for me, then I must do what I have to do.

Before I can get too far, Nathan bounds out the front door of the condo building.

It's too late to pretend I don't see him. Too late to double back and head down the street, wait until he leaves. He's spotted me.

"Emily!" He flashes that goofy yet disarmingly handsome smile of his. "Want to hang tomorrow? I heard there are a couple of eighties movies playing we could watch ironically while getting stupid drunk."

Why do I like this guy so much? He is nothing like Seth. Seth, a warm blanket you want to wrap around you and settle into. Nathan is . . . fuckable. Sweet. Not even in Seth's area code.

"Tomorrow?" I'm blindsided. How can I think about seeing a movie with this guy when every other part of my life has gone to absolute shit? Besides, I'd be thinking the whole time about that conversation. Between him and Pip.

The truth is, I'm too broken to make a fun date with a fun guy.

"Can I text you? I have a lot going on."

"You have my digits!" he calls out before heading off down the block with a wave.

His digits. That's almost exactly the wording he used with Pip.

I feel such an overwhelming pang of disgust and sadness, it almost doubles me over.

I fight it off, pulling out my phone.

What are my options, truly? I can walk inside and tell Pip that I've changed my mind. She and Sofie can't stay. This whole thing was a big mistake, and they can get their stuff out of here as quickly as possible and leave.

I'll be back on Craigslist, searching for a new roommate, but at least I'll have some prospect of making my mortgage payment. Right now—that seems like less and less a possibility, the longer these two stay in my house.

It's what I'll do. It's what I have to do. I pull up Safari and google "evicting a tenant San Francisco." I should be prepared, since I know Pip will be armed with a whole host of excuses. I don't expect her to leave willingly—everything I've learned about her since she moved in points to her digging in her heels. But if I have talking points, and if I can scare her with them a little, only enough for her to know I'm serious . . . I'll feel more confident.

I click on the first few links that pop up and almost lose my shit over the search results. "Tenants' rights . . . Just cause . . . Penal Code 418 . . . Cannot lock a tenant out without a court order . . . Relocation fees . . . Protections for families with children."

This is not good.

I knew, vaguely, somewhere in the recesses of my mind, that evicting a tenant in San Francisco isn't the easiest process. Still, I assumed nonpayment of rent would be a no-brainer. Pip's paid me nothing! But as I scan a few more articles, I start to feel dread creep up my spine with each and every line I read.

I never should have signed that lease. Because according to these links, the lease makes it all official—no matter how unofficial that document actually was that I found on the internet. It hardly even matters what the lease *says*. The fact that both parties signed it, and Pip has established *my* home as her and Sofie's home . . .

That gives them all these tenants' rights. And me, as their "landlord," hardly any.

I keep scrolling, hoping I'll find something positive to counter everything I've just seen. There it is, at the bottom of the page: the number for a legal hotline, one specializing in helping landlords. My stomach jolts. This could be one of those creepy Saul Goodman type of places that advertises on billboards and scams you out of your money. A place targeting actual jerk landlords who are trying to kick out nice families. But that's not what I'm doing! Pip's the one who's been using *me*.

I make note of the phone number as I head toward Dolores Park. No way I'm walking into yoga studios right now trying to snag a job, but I'm also not ready to go home, see *her*. I need to think. I consider calling Aunt Viv. It's not the same anymore, talking to her. Half the time she doesn't remember anything we've previously said, and each phone call breaks me a little more in two. Maybe hearing her voice would help. It will be the pick-me-up I need. Remind me what this is all for. Why our home is worth salvaging.

But when I call the assisted living, they tell me she's napping.

I stay out most of the day, letting my feet carry me around the Mission, stopping every now and then to people watch and lie in the grass at the park. I can't get that lease out of my head. I can't get *Pip* out of my head. When I do finally return to my house and trudge up the stairs, I'm curious about the noise coming from inside. Sofie and Pip must be watching TV. I slip my key in the door and open it to find a shocking scene.

There are five women in my living room, plus Pip, and they're all drinking wine, at 3 p.m. There are platters of bread and cheese and a full-on charcuterie board—one that looks like it cost a fortune—spread out on the coffee table, and several empty bottles of vino that they've clearly already demolished.

"That's what I said! I *told* the school, we are done with field trips! Finito!" A mom wearing a flowy cardigan over leather pants, her shoes tossed to the side, is brandishing her wineglass. "We don't *want* to chauffeur other people's kids all over town, and we definitely don't want them going to the freaking zoo when they should be learning math.

They're twelve! They've seen animals before. They need geometry, not a bunch of monkeys and giraffes!"

The other moms laugh, and Pip clinks glasses with the speaker. "Here, here," Pip adds. "Jennifer, I will back you up with the PTA if necessary . . ."

Her eyes meet mine across the room.

"Oh! Emily!" Pip claps her hands together like she's thrilled beyond words to see me. "Have a glass of wine! Join us. These are the moms from Sofie's new school!"

They all turn to look at me. "No thanks. I—can't."

They go right back to talking, chattering away as I move past them, through my living space, and straight to my bedroom.

I have never needed to be by myself more in my entire life. I open my bedroom door . . .

And find Sofie inside, her headphones squarely on her head. She looks up at me, questioning.

This isn't my room anymore.

Chapter 10

Pip is holding court with the moms. She's a complete natural, a born entertainer. An extrovert in the most literal sense.

She keeps their glasses full to the brim with wine. Wine that had to have cost an arm and a leg. From the looks of it, these are overpriced bottles. The cheap ones clearly wouldn't do. I hope and pray one of these other moms contributed them. Because if Pip bought all this . . .

No. I can't even consider that possibility, or I'll lose it.

Pip urges the moms on, to dish about the school, to gossip, and share their struggles.

My tiny apartment has become uninhabitable.

"What I think," Pip is saying, holding up her stemless glass of bloodred wine in her hand. She swirls it around, a prop she's using for emphasis. I'll bet she isn't even drinking it. It's all for show, and the other moms are getting drunker while she stays completely sober, and in control. "Is that the PTA needs a complete overhaul. We don't want things done the way they've always been done. It's 2025. This is not our mothers' PTA."

"Run for PTA president," one of the women pipes up. "You clearly want the position . . ."

"I literally have never considered it, Amanda, until right now," Pip says, placing a hand dramatically over her heart. "Scout's honor."

"Well, consider it, Girl Scout," says another mom, a surprisingly tall woman with a long braid running down her back, who looks like she belongs in a Nordic ski catalog. "Because the current president is phoning it in. You'd run circles around her."

I am steaming as they celebrate Pip's finer points.

If only they knew what I suspect . . . that Pip is a liar. A master manipulator.

After everything I have done to try to keep this place. After Pip gave me a faulty check . . . I can't believe she had the gall to invite these women over, take up every square inch of space, and act like she hasn't got a care in the world, when she is putting me through hell.

I have nowhere to go. Pip and I never discussed social gatherings or made any kind of agreement about how we'd handle them. But now that my room is, for all intents and purposes, *in* the living room, I literally have no choice but to sit here, enduring their banter. Or go behind my sad little curtain. Or leave. If she had paid me, it would be a different story. If she'd done her part . . . but this. This is outrageous.

I'm invisible here. These women aren't acknowledging me, and Pip is either ignoring me because it's easier, and because she knows I'm angry, or being thoughtless enough to not even care. Or, worse: my anger amuses her.

I have never felt this unseen, altogether disregarded, in my life. As I scan the apartment, watching these women drink, and grow rowdier, and continue to dish to each other in a way that feels so catty and wrong . . .

I spot it. Pip's laptop. Right there on the side console. She must have set it there when she first walked in. Then she started prepping for this fabulous little gathering and left it there, without another thought.

I don't even feel a bit guilty as I walk straight to the console, pick up Pip's laptop, slip it in my bag, and leave.

When I sneak back into my apartment at 2 a.m., I feel like a criminal.

I have stolen goods in my purse. Well, Pip's laptop, if you can count that.

I took it for nefarious reasons. I visited my old friend Jack, the closest thing to a hacker I could think of, and asked for his help in cracking it.

Even comparing Jack to a hacker is somewhat laughable. He's just a brilliant dude who lives with his partner, Mark, in the Mission and makes ends meet by taking the odd IT job here and there. Needless to say, Jack was surprised when I showed up at his doorstep, asking for his help. But after a minute's explanation, he was all in.

"You sure you're okay doing this?" I asked him. Pip's laptop was in front of us on his coffee table. I'd taken him up on his offer of a glass of wine and a hot meal. Over fifty-cent packets of ramen, I spilled everything to him: How down and out I was. How Pip hadn't paid me a cent. How bad things were for me, financially. How much I missed Seth.

I had never told a soul any of this.

I know why I chose Jack to confess to. He's considerably older than me, by about fifteen years, at least, though he's never disclosed his actual age. We met at a party a decade ago, right after I'd graduated from college and moved back home. He was the crotchety gay guy at the gathering who'd been brought there against his will. At the time, he'd briefly broken up with Mark and had been dragged to the party by a friend.

A few vodka tonics in, we ended up hitting it off, doing our best impressions of the other guests (stiff British dude, clueless hippie chick), and going back to my aunt's place to watch campy movies all night. There was obviously nothing romantic between us. But a friendship had been born.

"Pop that baby open," Jack said, indicating Pip's closed laptop. "This isn't a crime. It's not like we're doing insider trading or hacking into the DMV. We're simply . . . investigating. Get your detective hat on, Nancy Drew, 'cause we're going for a riiiide."

I cracked a smile. This was exactly why I'd gone to Jack for help. Well, first, for his technical prowess. But second, because I knew he wouldn't judge me. We were old buddies, the longest-running kind. He knew no one else that I knew. I couldn't let Seth see me like this, air all my dirty laundry to him. It would kill me a little, inside. And I couldn't confide in Nathan. I wanted him to see me as confident, breezy, cool.

There was absolutely no way I could reveal all this to Aunt Viv. And Alli . . . I couldn't bear to be on the receiving end of her judgment. She'd try to fix things for me and treat me like a child.

But Jack had done his fair share of questionable things over the years. Dabbled in coke. Shoplifted once, on a dare. I was there when he stole two beers and a bag of Lay's potato chips from a 7-Eleven. He's a good person, the best. And he's forgiving. And I knew he wouldn't think less of me.

Jack tore into Pip's computer with the enthusiasm and precision of a professional who hasn't had a chance to practice his craft in many years. Truthfully, I couldn't follow a thing he did. He threw out words like "admin" and "remote desktop" and said something about a bug in the current operating system that most people seemed to know about, a work-around that allowed you to unlock the whole device by going into System Preferences, Users and Groups . . . I drank my wine and gobbled up the ramen while he worked, performing operations that looked difficult but that he assured me were nothing more than basic hacking commands. Two hours later, success. All he'd had to do was get past the first lock screen, and the rest was not password protected. Why would it be? I don't lock my emails beyond that first screen. I definitely don't lock my texts.

We were in. Logged in as Pip. All her texts, available to me. All her emails.

I sat in Jack's living room for hours, going down, down the rabbit hole. Sipping more pinot than I should have and not giving a rat's ass. Jack eventually said he had to turn in, but he encouraged me to stay as long as I wanted.

I scanned over texts to friends, emails she had sent to acquaintances. All manner of group text chains with the moms from the school, about social dynamics, sports, puberty, book clubs—everything under the sun. An email to Sofie's music teacher about her cello (what cello?), and friends who seemed to be in Pip's life for transactional reasons, like they provided her with help, or status, or gossip.

Now, in the quiet hours of the night, returning to my house, I feel only mildly guilty about what I've done. And mostly justified. Because there are a few gems buried in there. A few smoking guns.

I found exactly what I'd been looking for. Incontrovertible proof that Pip doesn't have the money to pay me. According to several emails to someone named "Frank," Pip's consulting business hasn't made her money in years. And the tutoring—well, you can't make a solid living off helping a few kids a week with their math homework. It doesn't add up. I couldn't get into her bank accounts. That would have required a whole other level of know-how and probably could have put us in jail. We didn't even consider it, and anyway, Jack said his skills were limited to basic-level stuff. But I don't need the bank accounts. She all but admitted to several friends that she's broke.

Then there was "the one." The text that filled me with murderous rage.

roommate situation handled so far. She's pretty naive. I think we'll be good for a while

A one-liner from Pip to someone named J. Someone who only wrote back, simply, with a thumbs-up emoji. That was it. The whole exchange.

Good for a while? She can only mean one thing by that. Good living rent-free.

She called me naive. You only point that out about someone if you plan to screw them over.

I slip into my house, empty now of the PTA moms, and deposit her laptop back where I found it. Empty wine bottles litter the coffee table, and Pip left the charcuterie board out, not bothering to even clean up, or save the prosciutto and cheese, which now looks warm and inedible.

I will call that legal hotline tomorrow.

I will see what rights I do have. After all, I'm not a shitty landlord. I'm just a person trying to save my house. My home. From a scam artist. Those tenants' rights exist in San Francisco for good reason. But I'm not someone trying to make a retaliatory eviction, or screw Pip over by kicking her out of her longtime home. Surely that will count for something. And even if it doesn't, I will make sure I have some appropriate language to use when I talk to Pip. There's no reason to think she wants me to take her to court . . . I hope.

I crawl into my futon, feeling the warmth of my blankets and wishing I could hide in here forever. But I lie awake, my mind churning. I feel bad about Sofie. It's not her fault. But I'm not the one making up stories, giving faulty checks. I'm not the one trying to live rent-free on someone else's dime. I didn't put a twelve-year-old in this untenable situation. Her own mother did that.

The thing I can't stop thinking as I shut my eyes and attempt to sleep . . . and it's the thing that makes me the most furious. Even more furious than the fact that I'm bankrolling all three of our lives.

The thing that sets my teeth on edge is that I've been totally played. That ends now. I'll use what I know now about Pip to my advantage. I will beat her at this game. I'm nobody's fool. Not anymore.

Chapter 11

Usually when people say they barely slept, they mean they tossed and turned for a good part of the night, passing out for increments in between. The time feels like it slogs on, endless, but ultimately they wake up at seven and realize they finally conked out at 3 a.m. and slept for four hours straight.

Not me. Not last night. I lay awake, listening to the bus that runs past my apartment every twenty minutes. Taking strange comfort in it. That number-47 route is a part of me, of Aunt Viv, and of our lives together. The bus is part and parcel of apartment 3C. To wish it away would be to wish my home away.

It's 5:30 a.m., and I feel like I've been hit by a train. I'm tired but wound up. The worst of both worlds. Dragging myself to the bathroom, I'm grateful that Pip and Sofie are in the bedroom, door closed. I can't face either of them right now. I don't know what I might be pushed to do.

I brush my teeth to banish the old-sock taste in my mouth, then open the medicine cabinet, bracing myself to confront all the shit Pip's crammed into my once-tidy space.

There it is, right in front of me, squashed between the Q-tips and my face cream: a bottle of Tylenol PM. It's Pip's, of course. I'm a big believer in holistic living, and with the exception of the Advil I've taken for my knee, I shun most pain medications. But if I don't sleep . . .

I'll go mad, living here with those two.

I open it up and swallow one dry, then try to smoosh the bottle back into the cabinet. Pip's stuffed it full of so many toiletries, they've now consumed the space where it just sat. I'm pissed, shoving the bottle back in. Band-Aids and lip balms fall out into the sink. My cheeks getting hot, I give up, pry the top off again, and take another of her pills. Then I stick my head under the faucet to wash it down with a gulp of water. I leave the bottle out—I'll let Pip deal with it—before returning to my futon and praying for unconsciousness.

——

At 11 a.m., I wake to the sounds of Pip and Sofie arguing. I'm groggy from the pills I took but relieved I got five hours of shut-eye. At least now I'll be able to think clearly. And think is what I must do.

"They were awful to me, Mommy. They're bullies." I sit up, squint between my beaded curtain to watch these two. If they realize I'm here, listening, they don't seem to care. It's not like I'm even remotely hidden.

"So you, what—up and left?" Pip shuts the front door behind them, grabs Sofie's backpack from her, and sets it down, forcefully.

"I told you, they were awful! They kept saying that I never should have come to this school. And that there's a reason I have no friends. It was so mean." Sofie looks about near tears.

Pip walks to the kitchen, starts pulling food items out of the fridge. Bread, cheese, turkey. I'm confused. If she's upset this happened to her kid, she isn't showing it.

"So I walked out of the school onto the sidewalk. And there weren't any teachers there to stop me, so I kept walking." Sofie trails her mom into the kitchen, grabs a piece of bread, and takes a bite.

That's when she meets my eyes through the curtain.

Pip follows her daughter's eyes to mine. Something about the look on Pip's face unsettles me. She seems . . . stony, in a way I haven't seen from her. She's usually so effing perky. I look away, pretend to be focused on making up my futon. I'm obviously crashing a private discussion between these two, and I wish heartily that I weren't. I'm seething at Pip, but I can't possibly say anything to her right now. Not with Sofie here.

"You can't leave school like that, honey," I hear Pip tell Sofie as I grab some clothes from a pile and take them to the bathroom to change. "I'm sorry that happened. They sound like real mean girls. But you still need to learn and go to class. You'll fall behind."

She sounds a bit more empathetic now to her daughter's struggles. Maybe before she was trying to hold in her frustration. After all, Sofie did completely walk out of sixth grade, without notifying anyone in charge. That can't be allowed, no matter what the circumstances.

I'm closing the bathroom door when I hear Sofie promise she knows exactly which work to do and will spend all day catching up. Pip seems to accept that and tells her to pull out her schoolbooks. "You need to focus. No video games. No reading unless it's for school."

I splash water on my face, then steel myself to call that lawyer and prepare to confront Pip. This has gone on too long. I will tell her that I know: she doesn't have the money, and if that's true, she must leave. I don't know what she will say to that, how she will react. But I will no longer be her victim.

I emerge from the bathroom to find Sofie doing schoolwork at the breakfast table. Pip is gone.

"I'm sorry, Sofie," I say, choosing my words carefully. "About the mean girls. I overheard."

Sofie shrugs. "It's okay."

I consider my options. I need to speak to Pip, but I don't want Sofie in the middle. "Where's your mom?"

Sofie indicates the bedroom. "In there."

I'm going to have to go in, tell Pip I know for a fact she's got no plans to pay me. That she will have to move out if she can't pony up. I'm about to, when there's a knock on our door. Then another.

Surprised, I walk to it. We don't get packages up here. They go to our lobby. And I'm not expecting anyone. But maybe Pip is. If it's a PTA mom, I swear, I will lose it.

I open the door to find Nathan standing there. He looks rattled. That's new. Usually he's cool as a freaking cucumber.

"Is your roommate home?" he asks. Any sign of his usual affable smile is gone. "I need to talk to her."

I am overcome with such ire that it's all I can do not to scream. He starts to come in, but I physically block him with my body. "In the hall," I tell him. "Now."

Nathan's clearly surprised by my intensity but does as I instruct. He backs into the hall, where I follow him. Then I firmly shut the door behind me so Sofie won't be privy to any of this.

"Sofie's inside. Her daughter," I add for emphasis. I'm not holding back. Nothing in my life is going the way it should. But I'm done being everyone's punching bag. "You can't come in."

"Um, okay." He looks distressed. By me? Or by . . . something else entirely? I'm sure he didn't expect easygoing Emily to go all ragey on him. Too bad.

"Look," I continue in a half shout, half whisper. "I heard the two of you. Flirting." Nathan raises an eyebrow, starts to talk, but I cut him off. "It's fine. It's *whatever*. You and I were a two-night stand. If we'd gone to Alamo Drafthouse, we could have made it three."

"Emily . . ."

"I don't know what's going on with you two," I say, indicating the condo behind me, and clearly I'm referring to Pip. "And frankly, I don't care. But I am not her broker, or your liaison, and I'm definitely not her friend. Did you know she hasn't paid me yet? Not a cent?"

Nathan looks like he's really regretting his decision to come up here. I don't blame him. "I . . . did not."

"Yeah, well, it sucks, because I'm pretty sure she's a conniving bitch. Stay away from her," I practically hiss at him. "Seriously. Nathan, you're a nice guy. One of the good ones, as far as I can tell. Stay away. Don't get involved with her, I'm begging you."

He lets out a massive breath. "Well, it's a bit late for that."

I stare at him, my heart plummeting to my feet. "What's that supposed to mean?"

"It means . . ." He sighs, looks down at his Nike Dunks. "It means what you think it means."

The two of them . . . Jesus Christ. It's not like I'm surprised, but that was . . . fast.

"We're over, for what it's worth." I know it's a harsh thing to say, and a complete overreaction, but I'm on the verge.

Nathan looks pained. "We weren't really together? But listen, Emily. I didn't—are you mad at me for some reason? I thought we were cool. Chill. Just hanging out."

I grip my hand into a fist. *Don't lose it. Don't lose it.* "We were, Nathan. You're right. We totally were."

I walk down the hall, down the stairs, and outside, taking what's left of my pride with me.

———

Four hours later, I return.

That's how long it took for me to speak to three different lawyers. I felt humbled by the experience: One was so fancy their assistant said I'd have to make an appointment four months out (thanks, but not helpful). One sounded like he operated out of his truck and probably never passed the actual bar (also, no thanks). The one who finally gave me some free legal advice started with the words, "You sound like a nice girl, and I'm sorry to tell you this, but . . ."

It went downhill from there. He basically confirmed what I'd already discovered in my Google search: the process to evict someone in this city is so gnarly, and so time consuming—not to mention, expensive—I'd better get ready for an extended legal battle. With funds I don't have.

That hit me hard. I couldn't spend *more* money on lawyer's fees to get Pip out—that would literally put me in a worse position financially than I'm already in!

He did leave me with one helpful nugget. "Forge a letter from a lawyer, on fake letterhead," he told me, confidentially. "It might be enough to scare her off."

Forged letter in hand—it hadn't been too hard to find a logo online and put this together at PO Plus—I return to my house, fired up and ready to confront Pip. I won't lead with the letter. I'm still hoping I won't need it. But something must happen, a reckoning, of sorts. I won't live this way any longer. A prisoner in my own home. If she can't pay up, she will have to leave.

I slide my key in the door, and as soon as I step inside, I notice it. An intoxicating smell that makes my stomach rumble. The table is set. There are platters of food on the kitchen counter. My house is sparkling. The floors have been mopped. There are even fresh flowers in a vase on the side console.

The rage bubbling inside me threatens to take over. And I might just let it.

Pip greets me, wearing a striped apron I've never seen before. "I know, I know. The flowers were unnecessary, but don't worry, they were practically free. Carnations."

I stare at her, unhearing. What is she going on about right now when I am this close to throttling her?

"Sit!" She smiles. "Eat. I made everything vegetarian. I hope the lasagna's okay. I've never done it without beef before. I'm just going to bring Sofie a plate. She's in her room sulking. Those mean girls suck, but I'm hoping she can find a way to stay out of their path."

Pip scoops lasagna onto a plate and pushes her way into the bedroom, closing the door behind her.

I stare at the food, feeling like an alien in my own home. This has gone too far. She has gone too far. Acting like we're friends? After everything she's done . . . Is she certifiable? A sociopath? How can she continue to act like everything's fine when she has done nothing but lie to me, manipulate and gaslight and scam me—and, on top of that, sleep with Nathan? Cleaning the house, making me this meal . . . I am on to her tricks now. If she thinks I'll fall for it . . . that I'll be lulled into thinking she is a nice, normal, upstanding roommate . . .

She's insane.

I pull out a chair and sit squarely down at my breakfast table. I'll eat her food. I'll show her I'm not some gullible sucker she can take advantage of. I will lay claim to this place. To my house.

Pip returns to find me spooning food onto my plate. I take a deliberate bite of the veggie lasagna.

"Delicious," I tell her. "I had no idea you were such a good cook."

She stares at me a beat . . . then grins, taking a seat across from me. "Self-taught. I don't even use cookbooks, just YouTube videos, you know, for recipes."

I set my fork down. This is it—moment of truth time.

"You still haven't paid me." I say it lightly, airily. This conversation will likely only go one way—down. So why start there? I'll be the bigger person, at least to start.

Pip freezes. Was she not expecting this? Too bad. It's happening. "I thought I told you. Didn't I tell you? I'll get you the money. Cross my heart and hope to die, and all that jazz!"

I don't react. I'm certainly not amused. "The thing is, Pip, and I say this generously . . . and respectfully." Stop being so nice, Emily! "I don't think you actually will get me the money. I don't think you intend to get me the money even a little bit. Which means . . . you have to leave. I'm sorry. I really wanted this to work, but it isn't. You and Sofie need to be out of here by morning."

Pip slides her napkin between her fingers, toys with it, avoiding my eyes. "I don't think you want to go down that road. Do you?"

I stiffen. "What road do you mean?"

"Court. A hearing. That's going to cost you. A lot." She finally looks up at me. "You're the landlord. I'm the tenant. It's all very clear, really. I have a daughter. A minor. The lease we both willingly signed establishes this as our home, and all those moms who were here for the happy hour, they all saw me here, *living* here. They saw Sofie's bedroom. They'd vouch for me. Especially if . . . if it came to some kind of trial."

I feel like I could scream. Sofie's bedroom? She means *my* bedroom . . .

I reach for the letter in my bag and slip it out, slide it across the table at Pip. "I didn't want to have to do this, but you're not giving me much choice. Either cough up the funds, or start packing, Pip." She glances at the paper. Poker-faced.

"That's a nice letterhead. Did you find it on Google Images?"

I feel branded on the back of my spine, as though by a hot poker. She's seen right through me.

I worried this would happen, feared she'd be seven steps ahead of me. I prayed it wouldn't be the case. But fighting her on this . . .

It's like sparring with a professional. And I'm a mere amateur. And we've only just begun.

I can't eat the food. How could I, after that?

I need a plan B. I need to get better at this game, and I resolve that I will. But for now, I will claim some physical space. I get up from the table, leaving my plate. I'll let Pip take it to the kitchen. She made this huge mess, cooked this ridiculous meal. For what—so she could try to distract me, gaslight me, hope I wouldn't bring up the money she owes me? I turn on the Roku, to the episode of *White Lotus* where we left off. I will not go hide in my nook. This is my house, my TV, my living room. I sprawl on the couch, leaving no room for her. I turn the volume up way too loud, ignoring her request that I turn it down because Sofie is studying.

I turn it up even more.

When Pip perches on the small sliver of the couch I've left empty, I can hardly contain myself. Are we really doing this?

I won't leave. I can't. I'd be relinquishing the living room to her. The whole goddamned house. And I won't. Absolutely not.

I make no room for Pip, and she doesn't give up her fraction of the sofa, either. When she adjusts her butt so she's practically sitting on my feet, I give her a small push with my toes.

She reacts by repositioning herself more forcefully this time. Her eyes fixed solidly on the TV.

Neither of us is budging.

We watch, barely acknowledging each other. Me sprawled across the sofa; Pip squeezed in at the end. Pip does eventually get up to check on Sofie, fetching her water, bringing back her empty plate. When she returns, she wedges herself back into her eighth of the couch, grabbing the remote to turn the volume down. I let her, but only because it actually is too loud, and my ears are ringing. Sofie emerges thirty minutes later to go to the bathroom, then returns to her room. My room.

One episode turns into the next, and I'm not even registering the plot. All I can think is, How has Pip managed to make my beloved sanctuary a battleground, full of land mines?

She is not going to leave willingly, is she. And if I'm going to have any chance of reclaiming my house, my life, I am going to have to find a way to outsmart her.

The obvious question is: How?

It's 10 p.m. when we hear the sirens.

Chapter 12

The strange thing about emergencies is that until you know what's happened, they feel oddly impersonal. Until you have any real grasp on the situation, on what's transpired, you wonder if maybe you should go and investigate . . . or simply continue watching TV.

Pip's instinct appears to be the latter. She barely looks up from the show, even as I follow the screaming sounds of emergency vehicles to my beaded curtain, parting the incandescent beads of my boho makeshift room divider and heading to look out the bay window at the street below.

Rapidly spinning red-and-yellow lights fill the night sky, and for a moment, my rage subsides. Or, rather, I force it to. I push my simmering resentment of Pip and all she has done to the back of my brain.

"Something's happened." I say it to myself, but I suppose Pip is privy to my words. She's here, isn't she?

"No kidding," Pip breathes. I want to throttle her. How dare she be snarky with me. Can't she for one minute be grateful, or at the very least, civil, after all I've put up with?

I press my hands to the glass of the window, forcing myself to focus on the street, on what's happening down there. My brain whirls with the possibilities. Has a car struck a building or, God forbid, a pedestrian? I pray not. I hope no one's been mugged or assaulted. I hope it's only a small fire that's put out, quickly, before anyone gets hurt, or better yet, a false alarm, precipitated by some smoke from an overzealous cook in an underventilated kitchen. Even an old person requiring oxygen, I could accept. But would those scenarios require this kind of response—by my count, three fire trucks and two police cars? I know the answer, much as I don't want to acknowledge it.

"Should we . . . ?" Pip asks, and I turn to face her.

"Yes, let's go down," I answer. I could strangle her, but right now, all that matters is this emergency, whatever it is. I feel compelled to find out, and as soon as possible, if this crisis involves someone who happened to be walking down the street, or if it's coming from one of the houses on my block. One of my neighbors. I think of Wanda, the eccentric lady who's lived across the street in the tiny yellow house for decades, since long before Viv got here. Or the families on this block with kids. One with toddlers, another with teens.

Pip peeks in on Sofie, confirms she's asleep, her headphones firmly in place. The blaring of the sirens hasn't woken her, amazingly enough. I gather my keys and phone, and head for the condo door, Pip close on my heels. We keep an intentional pace, hurrying but not running, as we head down the interior stairwell together, the emergency lights still throbbing under my eyelids like an afterimage and the sound of those shrieking sirens in our ears. It's muted by the insulated stairwell walls, but we can still make it out.

We burst through the front doors of the building, and now the flashing lights fill our vision with an artificial sun so bright, I have to blink it away. At least now the sirens have started to die down. Only one still wails. I can begin to hear myself think.

A crowd has gathered on the sidewalk, mere feet from our building's entrance. It's unsettling, seeing this group of strangers gathered here, outside my home, appearing like one pulsing entity in the man-made light. I blink again, as though I could close my eyes and reopen them to a different scene.

I'm alarmed by how still these people look. Frozen in time, like they've witnessed something that makes moving past the scene unimaginable. No one is talking, scarcely moving at all. I notice, with a feeling of dread I can't place, that a mother is shielding her teen son's eyes with her palm. She pulls at his arm in a futile attempt to yank him away. He's not budging.

And now I see why. I see it—what *they* all see.

A body, splayed out on the sidewalk. It's partly obscured by the crowd but still visible. Visible enough. I spot a foot clad in a Nike Dunk, black and gray, a high-top. The pant leg—black jeans.

I recognize the shoe, of course.

He was wearing that pair today.

I stumble two paces back, almost toppling to the ground, but my body slams into a man's torso, breaking my fall, as the sickening realization hits my system. As my brain begins to make sense of the information in front of me, laid out as a fact I can't ignore.

It's his shoe. Nathan's.

Which means Nathan must be dead.

His body has somehow ended up on the ground, unmoving. Lifeless.

Oh, God. Oh, no.

Nathan, who for two singular nights, I teased about his shaggy-ass hair. About how he insisted on opening a can of beer with one hand, awkwardly spilling a third of it on his jeans. About the sheets on his king-size bed that seemed like they hadn't been washed in half a decade. Nathan, who for twenty-four hours transferred to me a kind of lightness I hadn't felt in months. Nathan, who spooned me after we hooked up, in spite of us being near perfect strangers. Who was hot to the touch, whose fingertips on my own skin felt as comforting as warm rain.

I begin to shiver and shake, and I can't stop.

Can this be happening? It can't, can it? I am going to be sick.

Pip grabs my arm, jolting me out of my thoughts into a present reality that feels like the stuff of nightmares.

"He must have fallen," she whispers. "From up . . ." She points above our heads to the rickety metal fire escapes that line the exterior windows of our building. "Up there."

He fell. Of course, he fell. It's obvious, isn't it? A body on the ground, bent like that into a grotesque, unnatural shape? The limbs stuck at odd angles? Gravity did that to him. Pip's right.

A male voice pipes up, startling me. "You think he fell?"

I'm surprised that someone's addressing me. I turn, noticing the bystander mere inches from me. We're all packed tightly together, a motley crew of rubberneckers. I recognize this guy vaguely from the block. He's a twenty-something who grew up here. I've seen him around, first as a teen, years ago, and now as a full-grown man. I reach for his name in the recesses of my mind. Austin. Austin Marks.

"What if he was pushed?" Austin goes on. "Look how the police are studying the body. Taking photos and measurements. Documenting."

"Third possibility." Pip shrugs. "He jumped." Her face is emotionless. I can't help but register how calm she seems. A lot calmer than I am. Maybe she's levelheaded in a crisis. Who the heck knows.

Shaking. Must stop the shaking. I stare down at my trembling hands, surprised by my body's reaction, by how unmoored and out of control I feel. Sure, I knew Nathan . . .

You slept *with Nathan.*

True. But it's not like we were close. We were neighbors. People destined to feature in each other's lives for only a short while.

Short—but not *cut short.*

"Wouldn't the police investigate, regardless?" I turn to Austin, knowing I'm grasping at straws. Almost pleading with him, this random neighbor, as though he has the power to change this situation, this horrific outcome. "We don't know how he died. We don't know anything about it!"

I feel dread flooding my body. I can't believe I'm saying these words. It's surreal. Too awful to be true. No matter how Nathan died. If he jumped . . .

Could Nathan have jumped?

Chill Nathan, who seemed perfectly content with his life, clocking nonstop hours for a start-up, earning little cash but putting all his faith in a big exit and some valuable equity that might or might not pan out . . . Nathan, whose apartment was littered with empty pizza boxes he swore he was going to recycle, "one of these days." I told him not to bother. You can't recycle cardboard if it has even a smidge of grease on it. Believe me, I'd tried, and been chewed out on multiple occasions by Recology. I gathered up the boxes for him, tossed them in our building dumpster after we'd slept together that first night.

The truth is, in my gut, I don't think Nathan plummeted from that fire escape on purpose. Sure, I only went on two dates with him and certainly can't claim familiarity with the inner workings of his mind. But something deep within me tells me his death wasn't a suicide.

"Everyone, back up! This is a crime scene!" A detective approaches, stern and intimidating in a standard-fare police uniform, trying to control the ever-expanding crowd that has gathered here.

"See?" Austin says under his breath. "He said 'crime scene.' Not 'accidental death.'"

"You watch too much *Law & Order*," Pip tells him.

I can't think. Can't *breathe*. Constrict the throat . . . inhale, exhale. *Maybe it isn't him.*

It's a hopeful thought that enters my mind, a way out of this, and I'm grateful for it, grabbing for it eagerly. Could this all be a terrible mistake? I haven't seen his face. I don't know for sure the body on the sidewalk belongs to Nathan, do I? How many men own sneakers like that?

Come on, Emily. Wise up. Those other men wouldn't be lying directly under Nathan's fire escape.

"I haven't watched *Law & Order* since 2012," Austin says, defending himself to Pip. "Now it's all podcasts, all the time."

"True-crime podcasts," Pip riffs back. Is she . . . flirting? She's bizarre enough to do that. Uncaring and selfish and opportunistic—ugh.

It's so effed up, I almost can't stand it. I can't stand idly *here* next to these two, while they discuss this like it's a reality TV show. Pip having the nerve to say anything at all about Nathan's death makes my skin crawl. After she slept with him. After this last week from hell . . .

I sneak away from Pip and Austin, too caught up in their armchair-detective work to notice, then edge around the back of the crowd, pushing myself between pockets of bystanders in an attempt to see things for myself.

I have a primal urge to see it—the body.

It's a monstrous thought, and the last thing I want: to witness that, to really observe it, up close with my own eyes. But how can I know, otherwise? How can I make my brain understand without internalizing the evidence firsthand?

I elbow my way past a few people, who shoot me aggravated looks. I want to scream at them, rail at them for even being here, for loitering around taking some sick satisfaction from a man's death. If they didn't know Nathan personally, and I bet most of these people didn't, then what are they still doing here? I know I'm being unfair. I'm sure if I were them, I'd be standing here, shamefully curious, doing the exact same thing. Perhaps some of them genuinely knew him.

Like I do. Did.

Heart pounding, sweat collecting on my forehead, I keep pushing my way through until I'm finally at the front, or as close to the body as I can get.

With my view unobstructed, I can see it now clearly. A sight that I will spend the rest of my life trying to erase from my mind's eye.

His lanky, athletic body is mutilated into an unnatural form, face down on the sidewalk with his arms spread out in a dead man's float position. His left knee juts out, bent the wrong way. I can't see his face, and thank God for that. But I recognize his hair, that too-long, scraggly hair. And his cracked leather jacket, soft from decades of wear . . . he had it on both nights we hooked up. I know unequivocally that it's him—I know now, as surely as I've ever known anything. And I wish I didn't.

I watch as the police draw a chalk perimeter around his frame. Blood has seeped from his body onto the pavement, formed a pool around him that's larger in diameter than I would have imagined possible. How that much blood came from one body, I have no idea. A camera clicks with the finality of a forensics investigation, of photographic evidence being shot and stored for later use. An officer shouts for us all to move along, as a beeping ambulance backs up to the body, which it will likely transport—in a bag—straight to the morgue. There's no chance he's alive, I can see that plainly. EMTs won't bother to crowd over him, performing CPR or other vital acts to save his life.

Chapter 13

Pip putters around my kitchen, brewing tea, while an officer perches at my bite-size breakfast nook, notepad and pen in hand, appearing oddly comfortable in my house.

"Just doing my due diligence," he said ten minutes ago when he approached me in the crowd, asking if I resided in the building from where the deceased had fallen.

I don't know how Pip is functional enough to prepare steaming drinks. My hands are still unreliable, shaking uncontrollably. I wouldn't trust myself with a hot liquid right now. I'd scald myself.

"We're chatting with all of the residents," the officer explains, accepting a mug from Pip, as well as one of the cookies she attempted to force on me and Seth.

The memory of that jolts me. The visit from my ex feels like centuries ago but was only two days prior. How is that possible?

Pip and the officer continue talking, but they sound far away, like they're in a wind tunnel, or at least another room. I'm right here, on the couch, mere feet from both of them. How are they functioning, calmly conversing, when Nathan is no longer alive? After what we all just witnessed?

The feeling of dread that's been rising from my feet to my chest this last hour is beginning to morph into something more visceral, and uncomfortable, the longer I sit here: full-on panic. I try my yogic breathing—in, out, in, out—but it's failing me. There's a fifty-pound weight sitting on my rib cage.

I am no stranger to death. I watched cancer take my mother first, reducing her body to a skeleton before she finally told me she was ready to go, and she no longer wanted to live in pain. My father died shortly after her, cruelly of cancer too. I squeezed his hand in the hospice-care center as he took his final breaths. All this before I turned seventeen.

But a mangled body—a crime scene—a possible *murder*. That is not within the scope of my lived experience. Because it shouldn't be. Because it's too sick, too unnatural. Too *wrong*.

I know Nathan and I weren't anything besides a distraction for each other. We wouldn't have ever been together, beyond our no-strings arrangement. I'm not deluded enough to think our two-night stand meant enough to either of us to turn into something lasting. But the idea that he's dead—and not only dead, but that someone might have killed him . . . pushed him off that balcony . . .

"Emily?" I hear my name once, then repeated, by this officer. I turn to look at him. He's tall and hunched over, almost like he's aware he's taking up too much space in our—*my*—small home. If that's how he's feeling, he's right. He is. "Your roommate has stated, on the record, that you were both home today, between the hours of three and ten p.m. Do you concur? Or would you like to make a statement of your own? We have no reason to believe that either of you had anything to do with what happened. I'm purely fact-finding, and I appreciate your full cooperation."

In spite of the anvil weighing on my chest, and my still-shaking hands, a voice in the back of my head tells me to answer. I'm being questioned by a cop. Not because he thinks I did anything wrong. Because I might be able to help. If someone really did murder Nathan . . . this is the least I can do. For him.

"I—" My eyes flit to Pip's. She looks unbothered, chill as always. What is wrong with this woman? Has she no emotion at all? A man she just had sex with might have been murdered, and she's passing out cookies? Brewing lavender tea? No wonder I can't suck air into my lungs. Nathan is dead—but that changes nothing about my feelings toward Pip. I still want this woman out of my house.

And yet. And yet! Now I must look to her for cooperation. We are a *we*, suddenly. This officer perceives us as a duo, a team, simply because we live together. If only he knew.

"Um." I find my bearings, turn to address him, ignoring my seriously restricted airflow. "I agree. We were home. Not doing all that much, really. Pip cooked us a meal. A lovely meal." I bite back the sting of those words. Lovely, it was not. Nothing about her is. Twisted and bizarre and manipulative? Check, check, and check.

I notice the platters are still out. Pip never bothered to clean up before sitting down to binge *White Lotus*. This officer must think we're slobs. But at least the dishes back up my version of today's events.

I go on. "We ate, and Sofie—that's my roommate's teen daughter—had her dinner in her room. We watched TV, for a long time—"

Pip cuts me off. "She's twelve. My daughter. Really a girl more than a teen."

Is she contradicting me for some reason? Or is she just being Pip? I hold back an urge to slap her.

"And it was three episodes," Pip continues. "I remember because we were on episode four, and now we're about to start seven. Jennifer Coolidge is about to go to that weird island . . . sorry, have you seen the show yet, Officer? I don't want to spoil it."

The detective sets down his pen, cracks a minuscule smile. "No, I haven't."

"Oh, well, forget I said anything about Jennifer Coolidge. She's a national treasure, but you'll see what I mean when you watch it. It was three episodes, which makes sense, because we ate around six and started watching TV around seven. And ten p.m., that's when . . . well, when it all went down."

I stare at her. What game is she playing? Joking around with this cop . . . acting all goody two shoes, like she wants to get the details right as much as I do and impress this officer. Maybe she does. I suppose that's possible, but . . . I can't trust a word she says. It's hard to believe she's hoping to help this detective out of the goodness of her heart.

I refuse to let Pip run this show. I was here, too, and this is my house, after all. I should confirm what she's saying. I feel a responsibility to do that. For Nathan. "We both sat here the whole time, Officer," I say pointedly. "We probably each got up once or twice to pee."

"And to check on Sofie," Pip is quick to add. "She was in her room the whole time, trying not to lose it. Some girls at school had bullied her, you know how that can be. So I let her eat dinner in her room. She was on her computer for most of the time, working on a group project on Google Docs. But also playing Roblox. I could show you the setup, except she's sleeping . . ."

"That won't be necessary." The officer scribbles something down. Pip shoots me a look. I stare back at her, stony.

"Actually, can I add something?" I interject. The detective looks up at me.

"Go on."

"Well . . ." I scan the recesses of my mind for the chronology of the evening. It's foggy, mostly because I spent all of it seeing red, trying not to let Pip get the better of me. I barely processed the show. "What Pip says is true. She did check on Sofie. I can't recall for how long, exactly, but at one point she was in there for quite a bit. Maybe even as long as ten minutes."

"That's right," Pip is quick to add. "My daughter was upset, Detective. Like I said. I sat there with her, comforting her while she told me what those mean girls said to her. That's hard to hear, as a mother . . ." She reaches for the plate of cookies. "One more?"

"No, thanks," he says, then scribbles something. "And what about earlier in the day?"

"We were here. Both of us. And Sofie was here once she left school, around eleven. After the bullying incident." Pip sets the plate down, goes to sit directly across from the cop. "I work from home, although

95

I didn't have any clients. Not today. Emily was home too. She's . . . unemployed."

I wince at the term. That's not this officer's business. And anyway, Pip's the one who hasn't paid her rent. Not me.

Pip strains to get a peek at the officer's notepad. "Are you getting all this? It might be important. You know, for later." She widens her eyes, looking every bit like the sweet, helpful neighbor, playing that role to a T. But more important than how she's acting is what she just said. I wasn't home *all* day—though she only said I was "home," not that I never left at all . . . she was vague. Purposefully so? I have no idea. My head spins. Should I speak up? But what does that tiny detail matter, if we aren't actually suspects? Besides, I left far earlier in the day than when . . . when he died. And I'd rather not have to tell this police officer I called lawyers and went to PO Plus to put together a forged letter. I can't tell him that in front of *her*. Besides—how would that even be relevant?

It wouldn't be, because I didn't kill Nathan.

Still, I wonder: Why did Pip answer so affirmatively about *both* of us when the officer asked her about her own whereabouts earlier in the day? "We were here. Both of us," she said. Is it because I made a point of telling him she went into Sofie's room—my room!—for ten minutes? Was she somehow trying to mess with me, like she's done ever since she landed in my apartment?

The officer closes his notebook. "I think I have enough for tonight. But here's my contact info." He sets a business card on my table, nudges it toward Pip with his index finger. "If you think of anything else, please call me. Day or night."

He stands up, pushes his chair back politely under the breakfast table, and heads for the front door.

"Wait," I yell out impulsively. "What does this all mean? Are you absolutely sure that Nathan's death wasn't an accident?"

The officer stops, turns around to look at me. "Nothing is off the table at this juncture."

I feel my whole body tensing. He must really think foul play was involved, or suspect it, anyway. Otherwise, why would he even be here? They don't investigate if they're sure someone fell by accident.

Which prompts the question . . . If Nathan was murdered, who could have done it?

Who would have wanted him dead?

Pip thanks the officer and promises to follow up if anything else occurs to us. She's the picture of graciousness as she shakes his hand and closes the door behind him.

Once he's gone, she returns to our messy kitchen, begins tidying up.

I stand there, frozen to the spot, watching while she works, placing platters in the fridge and rinsing out some of the bowls she used to cook this meal. She's actually *humming*.

I've so beyond had it with her. I want to grab those plates out of her hands and scream that a man has died! Remind her that she's living here illegally! But I won't.

I can't.

And that's when the realization hits me.

For the past hour, I've been so busy processing the shock of Nathan's death that it didn't occur to me until this minute. Pip and I may not be suspects, not yet anyway. But we are two of the people, two of very few people, who were in the vicinity of his condo tonight. She's my nonpaying roommate, and she slept with Nathan. After me.

All that would be bad enough, would look bad enough, if not for the one piece of this puzzle that is far worse. And almost too unbelievable to bear.

We are also each other's alibi.

Chapter 14

All I can think about as I stand next to Pip in my kitchen, drying the mixing bowls after she rinses them in the sink, is that over the course of a few days, everything I thought I knew has been turned upside down, like I'm peering into a fun house mirror that threatens to erase the image of who I once was.

Pip is silent, except for her continued, incessant humming. Infuriating, this way she has of perpetually taking up space. How can this even be happening? This woman shows up less than a week ago, lies to me, uses me, takes over my condo, takes over my life. I've got to get her out of here.

Only, how can I? She saw right through my attempt to fake her out with that phony letter.

I am so screwed. Undeniably. Unless I can outsmart her. Get her out of here, out of my life—

I hate thinking it—I really do. Nathan is dead, was quite possibly murdered. My life is peachy compared to what he experienced, the hell his family will suffer learning that he died. Nathan was kind. Nathan didn't have enemies, did he? He hardly left his room, was a workaholic, typing out code till the wee hours. Both nights we slept together, I woke up in the early hours the next morning, 4 or 5 a.m., to pee, and found him coding away. The man lived for his work. He was a nerd, albeit a cool one, an unexpectedly attractive one, one women dug . . .

He did seem to be a magnet for romance, for sex, for fun. He slept with me, and Pip, and Serena. That's three women all from the same *building*. How many others out there did he also date? Could an ex have done this to him? Pushed him off that balcony in a fit of rage, or hurt, or betrayal?

It's as likely as any other explanation. Maybe more so, given who Nathan was. Not someone out there in the world stirring up trouble.

Unless he had a whole identity I know nothing about. The reality is, I don't know that anything he told me about was actually the truth. He could have been a drug dealer, and I'd have been none the wiser . . .

But is that likely? Or simply my imagination running wild, searching for any possible explanation when there seem to be none at all— none that make sense, anyway?

"Pip," I say quietly.

She puts down the plate she's rinsing—I don't have a dishwasher, so it's all by hand, here—and looks at me. "What's up?"

I brace myself. Saying this out loud is going to be downright painful. But what choice do I have?

"You and Nathan . . ." I exhale.

Just do it, Emily. Say it, for the love of God.

I take in a breath. "You two were, well, from something Nathan told me this morning, before . . . it seems like you slept together."

Pip peels my yellow rubber gloves off her hands and sets them on the counter, where they lie clumped in a soapy, slick heap.

"You talked to Nathan today?" She glances at me, and I can't read that stony expression on her face. Is it accusatory? Curious? Or is she simply asking a straightforward question? With Pip, it's impossible to know. Though I assume the worst, at this point. How could I not?

"Yeah," I answer her, prickles dotting my spine. Why do I feel like she's interrogating me? Even the officer didn't do that . . . "I talked to him. For about two minutes. In the hall. Right outside the front door." I don't say "our" front door. This is not Pip's house.

"Oh. Interesting." She takes her eyes off me, wanders to the fridge, from which she grabs a beer, pops it open.

"What's that supposed to mean?" I can't help it. As hard as I'm trying to keep my cool, continue forcing down my rage at her, I have my limits. Soon, I will not be able to hold back.

"Oh, nothing." She sips her beer. "Just that you didn't mention that to Mason."

Mason? Who the hell is that?

"Detective Mason?" Pip holds up his business card. "Says his name right here."

Oh. I stare at the card as she wiggles it between her fingers. Almost like . . . but no. She's not waving that in front of my face to taunt me, is she? Or scare me?

She's certainly capable of that. And probably far worse.

"I didn't mention it because he didn't ask," I say, quick to defend myself.

"Did he have to?" She takes another sip of beer, plops down on the couch. "Want to watch episode eight? It's a juicy one."

I'm so beyond incensed I can barely see straight. "How do you know?"

"Know what?"

"That it's juicy. We haven't watched it yet. We're on episode seven, by your own account, right?" I'm doing everything I can to keep my voice level, all while attempting deep breaths that feel impossible. If only I could get out of here, away from her. But now more than ever, I can't leave.

Can't leave her here in my home.

"Oh!" Pip laughs. "I've watched this whole series before. I thought you knew that."

Of course. She thought I knew that. She thought I knew she had a daughter. She thought I knew that she was broke, that her check would bounce. She thought I knew she was never intending to pay her fair share . . .

"No," I answer, my voice sounding hollow. "No, I didn't."

"Don't be mad!" Pip is smiling now, acting for all intents and purposes like we're nice, normal roommates having a congenial spat, and that our downstairs neighbor hasn't died today under suspicious circumstances. "I didn't spoil it, did I? Kept all the twists to myself? I'm a pretty good secret keeper. It's sort of a talent of mine. I could definitely keep secrets for a mob boss if I had to."

I cannot believe her. I don't know if I've ever met anyone more infuriating in my entire life. All I can do now is try to hang on to this apartment and find a way to breathe again. Even if only for the night. I shove a stack of dried dishes into a cabinet, then turn to face her. I'm going to ask it. I must. "Who do you think . . . Who do you think killed him?"

"I just told you—I don't do spoilers!"

I suck in a breath through my teeth. "I'm not talking about the goddamned show, Pip."

"Oh. Got it. You don't have to yell." She crosses her arms over her chest, appearing hurt, like *I've* done something to *her*.

"I'm talking about Nathan. Obviously."

Pip sighs. "Gosh, I have no idea, Emily. I mean, I just moved in. Barely knew the guy . . . Do you have any clue?" She pats the couch next to her, inviting me over. I consider for a moment. Could I run out of here, into the chilly night? Hop an Uber to Jack's? Get out of Dodge until I figure out what I'm going to do?

I don't even have the energy to make it three feet to the door. Between the throbbing in my knee and that feeling that my chest is a cylinder being pumped too tightly with air every time I take in a breath . . . I don't have the strength to go.

It feels like surrendering, but I plunk down on the couch. My couch, mine and Viv's. The love seat we used to inhabit, together, watching everything from *Friends* reruns to classic films. And where Seth and I . . .

I push the memories away. Too painful. Too hard.

Last I checked the clock, it was close to 2 a.m. Pip and I should both be in bed. Sofie's been asleep for hours, since before Nathan died.

It strikes me that this day will always be imprinted on my brain as the day everything changed. A man was killed, likely murdered, in the building I've called home for the last sixteen years. Thank God Viv isn't here to see it. I won't mention it to her when I talk to her next. It's true she'd probably forget about it twenty minutes later, but still. Telling her something so gruesome about her home would hurt her, if only momentarily.

I move to the edge of the couch, curl my legs under me, and hug a throw pillow, careful to keep my distance from Pip.

"Look," I tell her, shutting my eyes—both from fatigue and because looking at her makes my blood boil. "We should probably make sure we get our story straight. Just in case, you know."

Her eyes go wide. "What are you saying? You think they're going to call us in for more questioning?"

"Cut the innocent act, Pip."

She raises an eyebrow. "I'm sorry, did I do something to piss you off?"

Inhale and fucking exhale, Emily. Don't even answer that. It's beyond insulting. "We have no idea what the cops are thinking. I know you were here, with me, except for those ten minutes you were in the bedroom. And you know I was here, with you. But the police have no way of verifying that, unless we vouch for each other."

"As alibis," Pip clarifies.

"Yes. As alibis." Ugh. How did I get myself into this extraordinarily screwed-up situation? I can't trust this woman. Can't trust her to tell me the truth about having a child or paying her portion of the rent. How can I trust her on this? She could tell this Mason anything about me. Am I really going to have to find a way to make sure she's on my side, because I can't risk pissing her off? Is that even possible, given who she is? "And look, yes, I did see Nathan today, and he did imply that you guys, umm, you know. Got together. And it's fine. I'm an adult. I can deal with you hooking up with him and not get jealous because we . . . you know. Went out." It's not fine, but I will lie through my teeth. "But that means you must have seen him early this morning. Or late last night. Or . . . *sometime* before he was killed."

Silent for a long moment, Pip finally speaks. "Emily, you have to believe me. I honestly didn't know you two were a thing."

I grip the pillow tight so I don't reach out and smack her. "We aren't. Weren't. He's dead, Pip! It doesn't matter if we were a thing, and we definitely won't ever be a thing *now*! But he was somebody's son. He had a brother, did you know that? A younger one. He kept a framed snapshot of the two of them on his desk, from a white water–rafting trip they took a couple of years ago. Grand Canyon." The tears start to stream down my face, unabated. I'm so sad it physically hurts, and so tired I feel my eyelids scratching at my eyeballs. All I want to do is lie down on my futon and sleep. Make this go away. But Nathan . . . all this . . . it won't. I'll wake up, and he'll still be dead.

"It's really sad," Pip agrees. "He seemed like a sweet guy. I'm sorry, Emily, really. He flirted with me, and some stuff happened. It was meaningless. Look at me. Emily! For real."

I wipe the tears from my cheeks, force myself to look her in the eye.

"It was nothing between us, okay?" She looks earnest now, her blue eyes shining, and for half a second, I put my hatred of her aside. It's irrational, I know. I do hate this woman to my core. But right now . . . it's too hard to even access those emotions. Besides, she's a human being, after all, and in spite of everything she's done, and how undeniably terrible she is, I don't actually believe she slept with Nathan to hurt me. Besides, I had no claim on him. None at all. "I thought you were still into Seth," she goes on. "I didn't even know you and Nathan had hooked up. How would I have? You never told me, and he certainly never did."

She's right about that, of course. It was on him to let her know he'd been involved with me. It seems obvious he didn't do that, but if he did, and she's lying about that, he clearly didn't care what I'd think, or he wouldn't have gone through with it in the first place.

I stand up, feeling my knee throb with such intensity it's like it's channeling all the awfulness of this day. "Let's go to bed," I hear myself saying as I shuffle across the room to my futon. "It's really late."

I climb under my covers without brushing my teeth, while Pip pads over to the bedroom, opens the door and disappears inside. It's just before I pass out completely that I think I hear a lock on my bedroom door click.

But wait! I think, as sleep overtakes me. I don't have a lock on my bedroom door.

Chapter 15

Pip and Sofie have barricaded themselves in *my* bedroom.

Which means I can't access any of the clothes in my closet. And, more pressingly, I can't get to the bills stuffed under my mattress.

I tossed and turned all night, waking up nearly every thirty minutes with the desperate hope that I'd think of a way to get Pip and Sofie out of here.

I haven't found it yet. I'm more concerned than ever—as I climb out of my futon to face the day, the sun slamming at my eyelids through the wide bay window, and the reality of last night smacking me in the face: Nathan is dead—that getting these two permanently out of my home will require a combination of some sort of miracle and superhuman strength. And until I can kick Pip out, my only option is to show her how truly dire things are.

I must tear open those bills, every last one, and reveal to her the cold, hard truth: that we are close to being evicted.

But first, coffee. I bang around the kitchen, revving up Pip's stupid-ass fancy Breville and clanging my spoon on the counter in hopes my overly noisy process will lure her from the room. It's already 10 a.m. Sofie must have left quietly for school already. I don't see her bag by the front door, where she normally stashes it. But where is Pip? Holed up in there, doing whatever she does in her free time that is clearly not gainful employment?

I walk straight up to the bedroom door and knock.

"Pip?" I give it a beat, then louder: "Pip!"

Nothing. Is she even home? I try the handle. It's locked.

When did she install a *lock*? And how? What did she do, put up one of those cheap slider bars you can get for two dollars at the hardware store, or something more substantial? I shake the handle, turning it aggressively, or trying to, anyway, but it won't budge.

Either she's in there, ignoring me, or she's left and shut the door, locked it behind her. But how would she get back in, then? I study the knob. It's the same one that's always been there. At least, I think it is. An interior one, basic and chrome and round, without a key slot. She must be inside, then. There's no other explanation, unless she *did* lock it before shutting it . . . but that wouldn't make sense. She'd be essentially locking herself out too. I search in the recesses of my brain for something I read once, online, about a tool that can open a door no matter how it's locked. That wouldn't work with a slider, but it would work if she'd somehow replaced the knob with one that has a locking mechanism.

Would Pip go to such lengths? And why the hell would she even bother? I gave her the room and haven't made even the tiniest fuss about leaving all my clothes and personal items in there with her. I've given her carte-fucking-blanche. She has no *need* to lock me out.

Unless there's something in there she's hiding.

Well, I'm not getting this door open right now, so I might as well be productive.

Obsessing, I shower and change, locate a clean pair of underwear and Lululemons that don't smell and will be workable for today. Then I pour coffee into my favorite mug, the one with the corgi butt on it that Alli gave me for my twenty-fifth birthday, and sit down at the breakfast table with my laptop.

Today is a new day. A dreadful one, when I consider everything that's happened. Nathan has died, the police are investigating, and I will never again feel my heart flicker with nervous anticipation passing him the halls. Never curl up next to his warm body after one of those nights that makes you remember why it's good to be alive. I think of his brother. Does he even know yet?

My chest constricts. I don't want to google him—the fall, the crime, his name—but I'm morbidly curious if it's been reported in any online publications. So I type his name into my search engine. Nathan Wills.

I get his LinkedIn profile and Instagram page but nothing else. It's too soon for an obituary, apparently too soon for any news on what's happened to him. Maybe the police don't want it reported yet, until they know more. Can they even control that? I have no clue. It's strange, though, not seeing any evidence of his death on the web. It almost makes it possible to pretend it didn't happen.

Almost.

I'm about to shut my laptop and stand up—I need air, and some gentle exercise for my stiff knee, and to think about what I can possibly do about Pip—but I log on to my email first, thinking I'll delete all the spam and promotions for clothes I can't afford, check for any messages about the jobs I've applied for. I stop short when I notice the first message, on the top of my inbox stack.

It's from my bank. "Notice to Accelerate" it says in bold in the subject line.

Panic races through my already too-tight chest as I click to open it. I skim it through half-closed eyes, wincing when I read some of the words and phrases that jump off my screen at me. "Formal demand letter" and "30 days to bring mortgage up to date." And the final, painful one: "foreclosure."

I slam my laptop screen shut, my breaths accelerating, tears brimming in the corners of my eyes, threatening to deploy. I don't need to read the fine print to know exactly what this says.

It's finally happened. My due date has come and gone. The bank is no longer going to let me fail to pay, and if I don't cough up the funds in the next thirty days, it's game over. I'll be homeless.

Viv and I will lose this place, and I'll have to tell her that it's all my fault. Because I didn't have a plan B. Because I hurt Seth, when I loved him more than I've ever loved anyone. Because I ran.

My chest starts to constrict so much that it doubles me over. I am sweating all of a sudden, whereas seconds ago I was cold. I stand up, placing my hands on the breakfast table to brace myself, feeling a pounding in my chest that's so much worse than the weight I felt bearing down on me last night. This is different. This is unbearable.

I've had anxiety all my life. Since my parents died within months of each other. Who wouldn't? I've never asked myself if I'm actually wired to be anxious, genetically speaking, or if it's some form of PTSD . . . who knows. Losing your mom and dad, both, as a high school student, is enough to wreck you for life. I always figured I'd gotten off easy. My moderate symptoms were nothing compared to the stories I'd read online, from kids who couldn't move past a trauma like that. Who couldn't get out of bed, or worse, no longer wanted to live.

But this . . . this is not my old friend anxiety, who motivated me to keep up my yoga practice all through college and ultimately pursue it as a career. No, this is something else entirely.

It feels like it's going to kill me.

My stomach roils. I'm dizzy, and so lightheaded I almost can't stand. I lean over the table, trying to force in air through what feels like a completely cinched tube. It's not working. I won't make it out of this unless it's on a stretcher. I feel sure of that now.

I do the only thing I can think of. I stumble toward the bathroom, bang into a chair on my way, and knock it over before reaching the medicine cabinet. I don't know how I got this far . . . the room is spinning, and I'm so woozy, the floor feels like it's melting under my feet, like I'm trapped in a distorted Disney ride. I yank open the cabinet and rifle through Pip's disorganized mess of toiletries, all larger than life and screaming into my view as the rest of the world falls away. I pull out an orange prescription bottle, then another, squinting at the names. Amoxicillin? No. Fluconazole? Also, no. It's like a truck is resting on my chest, parked there, unmovable, and I'm desperate to get my hands on something that can yank it off me, that can relieve this oppressive feeling of the walls closing in. Tubes, lip-balm pots, serums, and bottles of pills fall from the cabinet and clatter into the sink as I continue to ransack Pip's items, at last clasping my hand around a final prescription canister. Please, let it be something that can help me.

I read the label. Xanax. Thank God.

I choke one down, not bothering with water.

Within minutes, I'm back in the living room, having found my way to the couch, where I now lie, eyes shut tight, inhaling and exhaling and praying this drug works as advertised. I've only ever once taken an Ativan, before a medical procedure. I have no clue what this particular pill will do to me. I'm also quite sure I had no choice. It was the Xanax, or call 911. But the potential cost of emergency services . . . no way I could afford that.

"Emily?"

I open my eyes, carefully, my breathing slowing as I take stock of my body. The truck-on-chest feeling is abating. I feel slightly better. Newly drowsy. It's not an unpleasant tiredness. It simply . . . is.

Pip's standing over me, her face the picture of concern. Her blond hair is down, and she appears both monstrously large and oddly angelic at the same time. Must be the Xanax, because angelic she is not. "Em, are you okay? I heard weird noises. And the bathroom's a mess. What happened?"

"Panic attack," I tell her, not mincing words. "Did you install a lock on my door?"

"Oh!" Pip smiles. "Yes. Meant to tell you—I got it this morning. Sofie will feel safer at night that way. She's . . . not reacting well. You know, to the murder. It will help her sleep."

I stare at her, my mind growing foggier by the minute. For which I'm grateful, but I'm also wary. I can't lose control around Pip. She could do anything. Say anything. Stupid email from the bank. If only I had a solution that could get me out of this . . .

The thought of it causes my heart to flip, but the action feels muted, thanks to the drugs. I can ponder my fate but still breathe. I have thirty days to save this apartment, and myself.

"Pip," I say, gritting my teeth. The Xanax is making me soft. Unworried. Rationally, I know I hate this woman. But right now, I feel less like smacking her and more like napping. "I got a foreclosure notice from the bank. I need you to come up with your portion of the rent, or all three of us are gonna be out on the street. Oh, and also: don't install a lock on my fucking door without asking me first."

I feel the couch under my splayed-out legs slump as Pip collapses next to me, nearly sitting on me in the process. "About that," she says, leaning back against the cushions. "I have an idea. I know you're struggling financially, and we are too. But it's not going to be a problem anymore." She smiles. "I thought of a way out, for both of us!"

"Okay," I answer. Where the hell is this going?

"Just pay us a relocation fee!"

Deep breaths, Emily. Deep breaths. At least I have that pill on my side right now. Otherwise, I'd scream.

"A relocation fee."

"Yep, I've read of this happening. You know, when a landlord wants a tenant out, but all the laws favor the tenant." She shrugs. "Like our situation. I think fifteen thousand would cover what we need to find a new place. Normally I'd say forty K. This is San Francisco after all, but fifteen would make it doable for us. I'm willing to work with you."

Chapter 16

Thank God I took that Xanax, because otherwise I think I would have sat up and put my hands around her neck, and squeezed.

A relocation fee? Fifteen-fucking-thousand dollars? It was the most absurd thing I'd ever heard in my life. Thanks to the medication, I refrained from screaming at her, and instead started laughing. And laughing. And it wasn't until there were tears cropping up in the corners of my eyes that Pip realized she was not going to win that round. She slinked away, and I felt my laughter morphing into sleep.

It's 3 p.m. I've actually managed to sleep most of the day. It wasn't the good kind of rest. The Xanax knocked me out, sure, but I wake up now, groggy, feeling like someone's stuffed me with cotton.

Pip isn't in the living room, thankfully, because if I had to face her right now, I'd probably punch her. I pad over to the kitchen to make myself a coffee. I'll drink it black, try to get my head on straight.

The idea of losing my home—truly losing it—it's a sobering thought.

But I must face my demons. Make a game plan. Step one: the bills under my mattress. It's time to excavate them, to tally them up, face whatever death march I must if I'm going to get any control of my finances. I will keep this condo if it's the last thing I do.

Step two: deal with Pip.

I have to get her and Sofie out, without paying them magical unicorn money I don't have. Without a formal eviction. It's now clear:

they won't be leaving willingly. If anything, Pip's digging into her claim on this place, which is laughable by any standards, but I have to hand it to her—she's an evil genius. She played me like a fiddle. Setting up camp here, putting down roots. Taking the bedroom and leaving me the futon so it looks like *I'm* the squatter. Asking for a relocation fee from someone she's been gaslighting and manipulating from the minute she stepped in the door. I'd compliment her ingenuity if I weren't so murderously angry.

I can't take her being here for one second longer. Even if the bank seizes this place in the end. Even if I'm doomed to end up sleeping on Alli's couch for the rest of my life . . . I want whatever time I have left in my home to be mine.

I plunk down my coffee mug and walk toward the door to my bedroom. I jiggle the handle—it's unlocked. The door opens, and I walk into my once-familiar room to find it empty. The bed, which still feels like it's mine, is made. My mint green ceramic lamp rests on the nightstand, my worn white duvet hugging the bed. My bookshelves are still full of all my favorite novels. The dream catcher Aunt Viv and I got in Arizona dangles over my rattan headboard. Pip hasn't moved or messed with my things, which is good, because that would absolutely be the last straw. Not that there are truly any left.

I'm flooded with thoughts of Seth. Caught off guard by the tightness in my throat as my body is inundated with memories of how happy the two of us were here. How content, in a way I'd never been in my life, not since before I lost my mom and dad. In a way I fear I never will be again. We'd lie here on Sunday mornings with the shades open, not bothering to get dressed, not bothering to do much of anything at all but enjoy the serenity of each other's company, each other's bodies.

I shut out the memory and turn to face the door, searching for the lock. There it is, the slider bar I imagined in my mind. Brassy and cheap, probably under five dollars at our local hardware store, the one down the street that boasts everything from Halloween costumes and body glitter to Spackle and tools. The bar slides across the crack of the door, allowing whoever's inside to lock it whenever they want. I toggle it back and forth a few times.

So that's what she did. Installed one of these puppies without telling me. Well, of course she didn't tell me. It's not like I own the place or anything.

Gone are the sepia-toned memories of Seth that filled me with sadness, yes, but also fondness. Rage takes their place, boiling fury that propels me toward my mattress, which I push with as much force as I can muster until it slides down to the floor several inches on the left side.

There they are. The bills. The envelopes. My nightmares laid bare.

It's a decent-size stack. I pick up a pile of them but manage to scatter the rest to the hardwood floor, then bend down to try to clasp them all in my arms. I fail, and several flutter to the ground. I lean down to pick those up, too, and finally manage to carry them all to my breakfast table, where I drop them in a heap.

"What were you doing in my room?"

I turn, startled and on edge, to find Sofie standing by the couch, quietly watching me.

I let out a breath. Sofie, I can deal with. Her mom, not so much.

"I had to get these. They're bills. Boring grown-up stuff."

"But you went in our room without asking my mom?" Sofie lets her backpack slip down from her shoulder, onto the couch, and with the toes of her right foot, she pops off the heel of her left sneaker. Then she repeats the movement on the other side. "She might be mad, just FYI."

Nope. Not falling for it. Not apologizing. It's my home. My room.

I straighten up. "This is my house, Sofie. I said it was okay for you to borrow the bedroom so you'd be more comfortable, but it's still my room."

"What are all those?" She's eyeing the bills.

"Bills. The ones we have to figure out how to pay before they turn off the water, the internet, the heat. You know—all the stuff that allows us to live here."

Sofie pops up and grabs one. I almost snatch it out of her hand. It feels like my private business, and I've waited so long to open these . . . I'm truly anxious about actually doing it. Almost . . . afraid.

Then I stop myself. Let her open it. Let her see what I'm dealing with. Maybe sharing this shameful secret with someone . . . even *her* . . . will help me tackle it. Maybe she'll report back to her mom that we need funds. Yesterday.

Sofie scans the paper, her eyes widening. "You owe four hundred dollars to the utility company?"

"Yep." It almost feels like a relief to admit it.

"Can I open the rest?"

I stare at her. She's for real? "Sure. You know what? Why not. Not sure why you want to, but . . ." I shrug. "Go ahead."

"I'm good at math." Sofie shrugs. "I won this big math award at school, and now everyone's saying I should enter this national math-competition thing. I could add them all up for you. Get a total."

I hand Sofie a letter opener and my phone calculator, and she gets to work, slitting open the envelopes one by one. She peeks at the first one, then unfolds a second. She starts typing numbers into the calculator. I turn away from her, unable to watch. I go to the fridge, open it, and grab something—anything—I just need to use my hands. I take an apple, then slide a chef's knife from the cabinet. Thwack. The knife hits the counter as I cut. Thwack. Another one. I pick up each individual apple slice and deposit it in a bowl, then move on to the next. I bring the bowl to the table where Sofie is furiously working, punching numbers into the phone. Ping, ping, ping.

The pile of opened bills is growing, the discarded envelopes lying in a small heap. Sofie's not done—there are at least five more bills for her to reconcile—so I return to my bedroom to push the mattress back onto the bed frame. I straighten my duvet too. Then I remember the closet, and with an energy and fervor that surprises me, I begin tearing my clothes from the hangers. My soft-from-too-many-washes T-shirts. The wide-legged jeans, several pairs, I got from some epic thrifting adventures with Aunt Viv in the Mission. My cardigans, my floral grandma dresses. I toss them all into a giant heap on the bed.

My bed.

It feels good, taking charge, taking control, acting out. I will never again let these two own me, no matter what I have to do.

"Emily?"

I wrench myself away from the room and head back to the breakfast table. "Yeah?"

"I don't know if I did this math right. The total . . . Is this a lot?"

Emotionless, I stare at Sofie. She really is an adorable girl. Her face is so eager, so innocent. She even wears her hair in a long braid. It's a childish hairstyle for a near teen, but it makes me like her all the more.

"I don't know, Sofie. You have to give me a sum before I can answer that."

Sofie looks down at the phone as if to check herself before speaking.

"Twenty-two thousand, five hundred, and forty dollars," she says breathlessly. "That's what you owe."

Chapter 17

Outside my building, I'm standing directly in front of the police tape that rings the area where Nathan's body was found. I can still see bloodstains on the sidewalk that no one has bothered to wash away. Or perhaps the police don't want that. Is this spot still official evidence? They already took a million pictures. Has the yellow tape been left here for any particular reason, or have they simply forgotten to come fetch it?

It's a nightmare, seems surreal: over twenty thousand dollars in debt. Nearly three months of the mortgage, plus all my other bills, including medical payments that went beyond my shitty insurance coverage. Those I can put aside; you can't be penalized in California for not paying your medical bills, not if you can't afford them. At least, that's what I've heard. Regardless, I'll worry about those last.

Staring down the bleak portion of sidewalk where Nathan lay last night, I feel physically sick. I may have problems, major ones, but Nathan is still dead.

"They're saying it was someone in the building."

Goose bumps prickle up my arms at the sound of it. Her voice. Serena, one of my neighbors.

I turn, feeling a mix of shame, embarrassment, and jealousy at the sight of her. She was Nathan's girlfriend before he slept with me.

And now he's dead, Emily.

What difference does it make that she's gorgeous and accomplished? Someone murdered Nathan. The two of us have more in common now than we ever did before.

Both of us were involved with the victim.

I shake off a chill in the air—or is it coming from her?—and wrap my yoga cardigan tight around me. Serena and I don't know each other well at all. Before Nathan's death, we were cordial, mostly trading quick hellos when we passed each other in the lobby. She's never been anything other than nice to me, so the coolness I'm sensing from her right now could be many things. Grief, shock. After all, she dated Nathan for months. No wonder she looks like she hasn't slept.

"You mean—whoever killed him? Whoever did it lives here?" I squeak out the words, almost stunned to be saying them. "And who? Who's saying that? The police?"

"That Detective Mason guy," Serena breathes. She's petite and slim, wearing sweats that are oversize, a big trendy jean jacket that's long and hits her at her knees, giving the effect of swallowing her up.

"But—" I answer, tripping on the words. "But there aren't that many of us. You, me, my roommate and her kid, and Wally from the top floor. I don't think he's even emerged in a decade. Surely he didn't do it?"

"There's also Jane from 4D. She's super chatty and doesn't exactly seem capable of . . . of killing anyone," Serena says, shrugging.

"Well, none of us do. And why couldn't it have been someone he invited over?" I roll this idea around in my head. It could have been anyone—someone who showed up to hang out with him. A colleague. A drug dealer. Yet another woman he was sleeping with. Hell, it could have been a delivery person or literally anyone, so what makes Mason think it was one of *us*?

"I don't know." Serena sighs. "All I know is I miss him, and I'm scared. If it was someone who lives here . . . that means we're literally living with a murderer."

I let that sink in. It doesn't seem plausible. I mean, who? Who would do this? And why?

"Listen," I say. "I wouldn't be so sure the cops know anything. Maybe they're floating this idea to deliberately make us nervous. Or force someone to cough up some info."

Serena stares at me. "Maybe."

"Do you, um, need anything?" I feel for this woman, knowing she genuinely cared about Nathan. She knew him intimately, more intimately than I did. They appeared to be a real thing, not like the casual hookup situation I was in with him. "I'm here if you do."

"We aren't friends," she says quickly. "We're neighbors. That's it."

I'm completely taken aback. Stunned, if I'm being honest. Is she angry at me? Why this hostility?

Seeing the look on my face, she sighs. "It's not your fault. I know you were with him—*with him* with him—after me, and frankly that freaks me out. It did before he died, and now . . . now." She studies her hands, I assume so she won't have to keep facing me. They are impeccably manicured. "Now you just trigger me."

"Oh," I manage to respond. "Okay. I get it."

"Thanks," she says. She starts back toward the door. "But look, I don't hate you or anything. Nathan and I were broken up, when . . . anyway, if you really do need anything, I'm here. We can still look out for each other. I'm not a monster who can't stand the sight of my ex's new flame. I don't, like, want you dead or anything."

Wow. Um, I would hope not. "Just so you know, I wasn't his flame, not really. And, well, this is awkward because I don't want to add to your, um, triggering. But he slept with my roommate too. After me."

Serena stops in her tracks. She looks crestfallen. "That Pip woman who's living with you?"

"Yes," I say, then bite back all the commentary on Pip I'd love to unleash but know I probably shouldn't. As long as we are tied to each other, in Mason's eyes . . . But are we? And even if we are . . . I can't trust her as far as I can throw her. Maybe I should stop worrying about what Pip thinks of me. What good is an alibi if your alibi would throw you under the 92 bus? "That Pip woman who's living with me."

"They slept together?"

"Yep. I mean, they both basically confirmed it."

Serena looks like I've run her over with a truck. "When?"

"I think it happened the day he died. Or maybe the night before." It's getting cold. I'll have to go back for a heavier jacket if I'm going to take a walk. My knee needs one. I need one.

"Did she *know* you two were a thing?"

"I don't think so. I think he flirted with her first." But as I'm saying the words . . . I start to doubt them. I never told Pip that Nathan and I had had a romantic relationship. But this is Pip we're talking about. If anyone could, and *would*, find out something like that—it's her. I don't know how, but I wouldn't put it past her.

"So you're taking your friend's word for it that she had no idea you were dating him." Serena wraps her denim jacket around her, her hands trembling.

"You know how you just said *we* aren't friends? Pip's not my friend either." And Serena's right. I shouldn't take Pip's word for a single damn thing.

"She's not your friend? I assumed since you took her and her kid in, you must be like, old college besties or something."

"Pip's a fucking stranger from Craigslist," I explode. "I'd never met her before a week or so ago."

Saying it out loud, now, unburdening myself like that, feels like exhaling. I've been living with this person—these people, this secret— feeling like a prisoner in my own space for days. Now, someone else knows. Not the full extent of it, or even the half of it. But it's something. Human connection, with someone who isn't trying to sabotage my life.

"Wow," she finally answers. "I did not expect you to say that."

I shrug. "Money problems. I needed someone to share the rent."

"But," she sputters, looking like something's marinating in her head. "But you know nothing about her . . . Do you?"

She's right, of course. I don't know anything about Pip Stone, except that she's a lying, manipulative bitch.

But hearing a third party say this now, it's like a blow to my already-frayed nervous system.

"Not really," I admit. "No."

I don't know where she's going with this, and maybe she doesn't either. But there's only one *obvious* way to interpret her comment. She thinks Pip could have done this.

She's implying that Pip could have murdered Nathan.

"She's a mother," I remind her. It's not that I'm defending her. Pip's insane, but a murderer? She's too invested in her daughter. Wouldn't risk going to prison and leaving Sofie an orphan.

At least, I don't think she would.

"Also, she was with me the entire night. We're each other's alibis," I add, though those words sound laughable now.

"Lucky you," Serena says, the sarcasm dripping from her voice. "I don't have one."

She turns to go, then pauses for a second like she has something to say to me. But she doesn't. She keeps walking, back inside the condo building. I watch her go. Then I do the only thing I can right now that will make my head stop spinning, my heart stop feeling like someone's sucker punched it.

I run. Forget the coat. I will go so fast that I'll heat up from the inside out. Down the street I fly, bolting through the crosswalk. My knee throbs as I put pressure on it, forcing more and more weight on it, faster and faster. I'm challenging myself, but it feels good, and real. Standing still right now isn't the answer. I will combust if I do. I have too much to sweat off and work through. My knee screams as I go, pumping, pounding the pavement, but I don't stop. All I can think about is Nathan . . . and Pip.

I can't stop replaying the conversation with Serena over and over in my head. One thing, and one thing alone, stands out to me. The words she spoke that I wish she hadn't. They are all too true. I wish to God they weren't.

"You know nothing about her."

Chapter 18

I have no idea who I'm living with.

Sure, Pip's a grifter and Sofie's a kid; that much is obvious. But when I stop to think about what I know to be quantifiably true about the people who share my small apartment, it's next to nothing. My talk with Serena was unsettling on so many levels. But it's stirred something in me. A determination. A fire.

I realize, now, I've been letting this woman play her games, play *me* like a fiddle.

But I don't have to. She may hold a bunch of rights as a tenant, and she may be far more skilled than I am at conning—and winning. But I have the truth on my side.

And I won't let her do this to me. Not anymore.

Serena was right. I don't know her, don't know her at all.

But I can change that. I can find out. I can turn over every rock until I've learned who Penelope Stone really is. Information is power. And then I will use it to do whatever I have to do take her down.

I return from my run, red-faced, winded, but feeling a release like I haven't in days. My knee is angry with me, I can tell, but having the tension melt away as I traversed my beloved neighborhood is worth whatever damage to my body I might have inflicted. I approach my building, willing the yellow police tape to be gone as I round the street corner, but naturally, it isn't. It confronts me like unfinished business, stopping me in my tracks.

I push past it, starting up the steps, feeling the high from my run dissipating as I get nearer and nearer to my apartment. The irony is not lost on me. My home, my precious oasis, is the last place I want to be right now.

I stick my key in the lock of my front door and open it, expecting to find Sofie doing her homework. I brace myself for Pip's cheery, affected greeting, which will have the same effect on me as fingernails on a blackboard.

Instead, Pip and Sofie are sitting on the area rug in the living room. Laid out in front of them is all Aunt Viv's jewelry. "Take it," Viv told me before she left for assisted living. "I'll have no use for it in lockup." It was our little joke, that her new "home" would be a jail. We both knew it had to happen; she needed dedicated memory-care professionals. I couldn't possibly look out for her alone, with a job, a life. What if she wandered out into the street? It had happened twice already, and once she'd nearly been hit by an Uber as she crossed the road, confused.

I can't close the front door behind me. I cannot *move*. My stomach clenches; I feel that same panic rising up through me that sent me straight to the medicine cabinet for Pip's Xanax.

Aunt Viv's rings, gem studded and chunky, are tossed in a heap on the rug. The charm necklaces procured at estate sales—ladybugs and elephants, and my all-time favorite piece, an oversize circular pendant boasting the moon on one side and stars on the other—lie tangled on a footstool. There are chains—gold, silver, some thin, some with double or triple strands intertwined like DNA—strewn on the ground. The jewelry box itself, a vintage metal piece decorated in tiny roses, with little feet like an old wood-burning stove, lies on the floor, tipped over, empty.

My heart beats at an increasingly rapid pace. I have to stop myself from hurling. Don't panic again, Emily. Don't panic.

"What the fuck are you doing?" I hiss. My fingers curl around my phone. I have half a mind to call the police. Heck, I'll call Detective Mason if I have to. Aunt Viv's jewelry box lived at the top of the bedroom closet, tucked away. They are sifting through it without my permission. They might as well be stealing it.

"Emily!" Pip looks up from the carpet, where she sits cross-legged, and grins up at me. "Look what we found!"

"It's mine," I nearly growl at her.

"Really?" Pip knits her eyebrows together. "You collected all these? Bought all these beautiful pieces yourself, on a yoga teacher's wage?"

Inhale, exhale, Emily, so you don't fucking murder her.

"They're my aunt's," I say, squeezing my hands into fists so I don't scream. "And most of it's costume jewelry. Not valuable, except to her. And me." Put it down, is all I can think. Stop touching it, defiling it. I've never felt my privacy invaded more in my entire life. And that's saying a lot, given that they took my actual bedroom.

"My mom says some of these would sell for a few hundred bucks," Sofie says, then looks up from sorting through some chains—my chains—and stares at me, wide eyed. "But she said this one we found might be super valuable . . . Where is it, Mommy?"

Pip gingerly holds up a gold chain with several charms attached: a tennis racket, a kite, and a snake. The snake's eyes are diamonds, and the tennis charm is ringed with sapphires. I'll never forget when Aunt Viv acquired it. It was at the estate sale of this old Hollywood star who died in her nineties. We'd been in LA, visiting Aunt Viv's best college friend, when we saw the ad for the sale. Viv's friend thought we were nuts, but we took the afternoon to drive to the address on the posting, which turned out to be this massive compound in the Hollywood Hills, gated and sprawling. There were more jewels and expensive vases than I'd ever seen in my life, all in one room. Most of it was way beyond our budget, even for a splurge, but when Viv found the charm bracelet hidden away behind some other, splashier gems, she held it up, and we instantly knew it was "the one." It had cost Viv nearly two thousand dollars and was the most expensive piece she ever purchased, she told me. But it was special. And even more special was the day we spent together—after purchasing the charm bracelet, we wandered the grounds of the estate, pretending to be fabulous rich ladies as we sneaked past the enormous swimming pool and imagined we lived there, throwing themed parties and dancing all night.

The sight of Pip holding Viv's most treasured bracelet in her soulless, lying, manipulative hands almost does me in.

"Give it to me," I say, teeth clenched. "Now."

Pip raises an eyebrow. "Are you okay, Emily? Because you seem . . . on edge."

Don't lunge at her. Don't lunge at her. I've never felt like this in my life—almost wild, like a feral animal. My hatred of Pip is literally making me see red.

"Give me the bracelet. It's my aunt's, and yes. That is the only piece of the lot that has value."

It's now I notice that Sofie has her laptop open next to her on the rug, and she's typing something into it. "This website called ThingsWeBuy.com says we could get fifteen hundred dollars for it! Fifteen hundred, Mom!"

I cannot believe what I'm hearing and seeing. Pip has told her daughter that these items are theirs to sell? And Sofie's going along with it? I get that she's still a kid, but she's precocious, very smart. Surely she knows this isn't right. I'm this close to grabbing it all out of her hands. Or screaming at her.

"Sofie," I say, turning to address her. "We can't sell that one. Or any of these. But especially that one. It's my aunt's, and it's really meaningful to her. So please close the laptop and put all this back where you found it."

Sofie looks up from her laptop. "Oh. But my mom said . . ."

"Your mom misunderstood."

I'm going to do this the generous, diplomatic way if it kills me. I want to strangle them both, but Sofie is a child. She's learning all this despicable behavior from her mother. She's old enough to know better, but then again, look who her role model is.

"But . . ." Sofie crinkles her forehead. "But I told my mom about all your debt. All those bills we tallied up. All twenty-two thousand dollars of it. I know you want me to quit ballet, but don't you think you should be willing to make some sacrifices too?"

This one hits me, hard. A left hook to my gut. But I'm not taking her bait.

"Pip," I say, teeth clenched. "Put all this away. It's mine."

"You said it belongs to your aunt."

"It's mine, by way of my aunt. She left me here in charge of it. We can't sell it, and that's nonnegotiable."

"But you're so hard up for cash," Pip shrugs. "I was trying to help. What's more important to you? Keeping your home? Or a couple of necklaces? They aren't even that in style anymore, just saying."

Inhale, Emily. In-fucking-hale.

"This jewelry won't solve my debt problems. What would is you paying me what you owe me." I don't want to have this conversation in front of Sofie, not like this. Pip has left me no choice.

"But you could take a huge chunk out of the mortgage with this one silly bracelet, Emily! It's a no-brainer. I can take it to a shop tomorrow and get you the cash pronto. It would be so easy . . ."

"No," I practically bark. I feel my hand shaking as I reach out and grab hold of the bracelet, ripping it from her tightly held grip. The feeling of the cold metal under my fingertips is a relief. I won't let Pip steal one more thing from me, not as long as I'm alive.

I let out a breath, clutching the bracelet.

"I think it's pretty, Emily." Sofie's trying to extend an olive branch, but it's too little, too late. She already treated all Viv's jewelry like it was a grab bag of items she could take and keep on taking. She may only be twelve, but she's entitled as shit. "I don't think it's out of style. Old stuff is coming back. It's OG."

I don't answer her. I'm afraid of what I'll say.

"Fine, fine. We'll put it away." Pip shrugs, as though I'm the inflexible one. "Sofie, hand me those . . ."

I stand there, watching, while Pip and Sofie pack all the jewelry back up and place it carefully in Viv's jewelry box. Her rings, her bracelets, her art deco sunburst pin, its little rays crusted in tiny diamonds. That one's worth $500, maybe more. It's not all junk. I'm also not letting them bully me into selling it.

Everything back in the box now, Pip stands up and hands it over to me. "Here ya go," she says with a shrug. "Think about it, Em. It's only jewelry. Maybe not worth digging in on this one, ya know?"

I slip Viv's charm bracelet into the box and carry it over to my futon, clutching onto it for dear life. I set it on the windowsill, where Pip would physically have to get through me first, if I were sleeping and she tried to take it.

Would she actually try? It seems so preposterous.

Who am I kidding? Of course she would.

Chapter 19

I sleep fitfully, yet also like the dead.

I wake in the morning to the sounds of Sofie eating breakfast. Turning on my phone notifications, I find a brief text from Alli. Did someone in your building die??!

News of Nathan's death has gotten out.

I can't stop myself from googling, and what's the point, anyway? I'm going to know sooner or later what's been said online.

Possible homicide says the first article I find, this from a local news source. It's short, lays out what I mostly already know. That he fell. That foul play is suspected.

I close the tab, then pull up Pip's LinkedIn page. I ignore the clinking and clanging Pip's making as she sets a frying pan down heavily on the burner. I don't say good morning, pretending I'm invisible behind my beaded curtain.

It's a new day. The day I'm going to start to take Pip down.

"Penelope Stone," I type in. Before sending Pip the lease, I googled her, of course. Cursorily scanned over her résumé, registered that she seemed like a capable, gainfully employed person, and in my haste to seal the deal, closed my browser, satisfied.

Now, I will look more closely, with an eagle eye. Up pops her profile. There is her smiling face. Dirty-blond hair frames her, and she appears professional and capable in her photo, wearing a crisp white button-down shirt. It's as expected: she looks like someone you'd hire.

I scan down her list of résumé items. I remember seeing all these, before: a host of different gigs, some part-time or consulting work, which jibes with what she told me. Her current position is at PL Consulting, the years listed the last three. That lines up with what she said when she handed me the bad check.

Her more solid, full-time work appears to have been in the years when Sofie was younger. There's a four-year stint listed at the Gap headquarters, which is entirely plausible since Gap is based here, in San Francisco . . . and I wouldn't doubt that Pip could work in a retail capacity. She's stylish and seems to know what's on trend. A slick bullshitter. And her degree, from CUNY in New York, says she majored in fashion merchandising, so that aligns as well.

What I'm seeing on her profile page appears reasonable and robust, but I know better—especially now—than to take any of this at face value.

I could run a background check. I quickly google "background checks California," and a host of sites pops up. I have no experience in this and no way of knowing which of these are legit. But I will figure it out. Feeling the fire under me, I shut my laptop and get dressed, quickly—Pip has laid all the clothes that I put on the bed yesterday over a chair near my futon. Another passive-aggressive move; any normal person would have asked me what I wanted to do with them, or simply have hung them back in the closet where they belong. *My* closet. I can't dwell on that now, can't think small anymore, need to focus on the big picture. Getting Pip and Sofie out of my life. Keeping my home, no matter what it takes.

I pass through my curtain to the bathroom, where I get ready as fast as I can. I won't spend the day here with Pip, waiting for her to harass me, push my buttons, provoke the shit out of me, raise my blood pressure. I grab my laptop, slip it into my purse along with a granola bar and Aunt Viv's jewelry box. No way I'm leaving that behind with this viper. I slip out without saying a word to either Sofie or Pip. I'm still vexed with Sofie, too, for sifting carelessly through Viv's jewelry like trinkets at a flea market. For speaking to me that way.

I head to my favorite coffee shop. I can't afford store-bought lattes, clearly, but I need a place where I can think, and Beans is that place. It's a neighborhood hole where you can sit outside with your dog or in one of the tiny booths inside.

"I'll have a coffee, black," I tell Fi, the barista with a sleeve of tats and a perky smile.

"Sure thing, Emily," she answers. "How's your aunt?" Her face grows more serious.

"Fine," I reassure her. No point in telling her the whole truth. What good would it do? "She likes it there. They play a lot of board games in prison. Direct quote from Viv." Fi laughs at the joke—I've made this one before—but I know she can see right through my fib, her face falling a fraction before she lifts it again.

"Great!" she answers. We both know that Viv's life summed up in board games is a sobering thought. She was so much more than that, *is* so much more than that. Getting old sucks.

I pay, and Fi hands me my coffee. I settle into a booth and google the background-check sites again. I spend an hour clicking through them and finally settle on one that seems promising, GetVerifiedNow, which costs thirty-two dollars a month to use. It's thirty-two dollars I don't have, but a drop in the bucket of my debt, and besides, finding out Pip's dirty secrets is well worth it. I go through the steps, inputting as much info as I have about her, then get an email telling me I'll get a result in one to three business days. Crap, I was hoping it would be instant.

I sigh, then resume looking at Pip's LinkedIn profile. I won't rest while I wait for the background-check results. There is more I can do, more I can find . . . I'm sure of it. The background check can tell me about her criminal history, if she has one. Her driver history, like if she's gotten tickets or has any DUIs. And, of course, her credit score. But it's only the beginning. I can dig into her work history myself.

I spend the next three hours going down a rabbit hole to locate the managers Pip worked for and reach out to them. I contact Melanie Hopper from Gap, sending her an email asking her to confirm Pip's employment details and attaching the link to Pip's profile page. I tell her I'm a new potential employer doing my due diligence. Another lie but at this point, a harmless one.

I reach out to the folks who offered up the shiny blurbs at the bottom of Pip's profile page, one who called her "a reliable and insightful team member" and another who praised her work ethic at Kaplan, the tutoring company where she lists a yearlong stint prepping kids for the SAT and ACT.

Then I reach out to CUNY. I google the alumni office and call but get a recorded message. I pretend to be an alum myself, and I ask them to call me back.

Then I take a pause, sipping my last drop of the coffee and settling in to finally respond to Alli, who has continued to barrage me with texts asking about the dead guy in your building. I wince. She has no idea I slept with Nathan, no idea there even *was* a Nathan. It's not her fault that her texts are insensitive. I would probably take the same tone if our roles were reversed.

Don't know any details. Guy from downstairs. Super tragic

I add a crying emoji and set down my phone. I have work today, thank God. My single shift at the yoga studio is scheduled at 1 p.m. But I have several hours more until then. Hours I can use to my advantage.

I reopen my laptop, noticing a new, bold email at the top of my inbox. A response to my Gap inquiry. I click on it greedily, my heart pounding.

Hi, Emily.

I wanted to write back quickly, so excuse any typos.
This is in response to your inquiry about a Penelope
Stone. I have never had anyone by that name working on my team. I checked with a few colleagues,
as well, who have been here at Gap longer than I
have, and they said the same thing. I'm sorry for any
confusion, but I can't help you—I checked out her
LinkedIn profile and her photo doesn't look familiar
to any of us, either. None of us have ever seen her
before. Just so you know, I plan to report her profile
to LinkedIn, since she's falsely listing me as her former boss.

Best of luck, Melanie

I stare at the email, read it a second time. Then a third.

Falsely listing me as her former boss.

Pip described her role as directly reporting to Melanie. I click back
to her LinkedIn profile to confirm that I'm not going mad. It's right
there. She mentions Melanie explicitly.

Sitting up straighter in my chair, I head to Melanie's own LinkedIn
page. She is still at the Gap, still in charge of customer relations, though
she's moved up, been promoted a few times since Pip was supposedly
there.

If she was there. Which this woman is saying never happened.

And I'd bet my life it didn't. Pip's a master, an expert liar. This
would fit right in, squarely, with all her bullshit. This is simply proof of
yet another one of her transgressions.

Feeling energized . . . feeling, for the first time in *days*, like I might
be on to something . . . something big . . . I shut the laptop and start
to leave Beans, waving goodbye distractedly to Fi.

131

———

I sling my bag over my shoulder, checking first that Aunt Viv's jewelry box is safely tucked inside. I am hours too early for my yoga shift, but I don't feel right about staying here unless I order another drink, and I can't justify throwing away another few dollars on coffee.

Mind churning, I step outside into the crisp fall air, then hear my phone ring. I grab it from my bag, nearly dropping it, then manage to answer just in time. It's a New York number I don't recognize, could be a job offer. Could be a telemarketer. Could be anyone.

"Hello?" I answer.

"Is this . . . Emily Hawthorne?"

"Yes. This is she."

"Great, this is the CUNY alumni office returning your call." The woman on the other end sounds polite but slightly bored. She has no idea how important this call is to me. I straighten, pausing my steps to make sure I don't miss a word.

"Oh, wonderful. Thank you for calling me back so quickly."

"Sure," she answers. "Look, I don't have record of a Penelope Stone in our graduate database."

I let that sink in. Another no Pip.

I don't answer right away, so the woman continues. "Maybe she's listed under another name? A maiden name, perhaps?"

I consider that. "Stone" could be a married name. Sofie's last name is Stone, or at least, I think it is . . . Maybe Pip *was* married and is now divorced? Or she separated from the guy?

"I do, however, have a Penelope Stone who registered under our night classes a few years back. It's not the same as having a degree, but she took a few business courses under our adult continuing education program."

A bus whizzes past me. A cyclist who should really be wearing a helmet nearly collides with a pedestrian. They share angry looks, then keep moving.

"Is there anything else I can help you with?" the woman prods. I haven't said a word in probably a full thirty seconds.

"No," I answer her. "That's extremely helpful. Thanks for your time."

I hang up the phone. No Penelope Stone alums. Only a Penelope Stone who registered in the continuing education course. Sure, there's some chance Penelope did graduate, and her maiden name is something else . . . But what are the odds a Penelope Stone recently signed up for CUNY continuing ed? And wouldn't it track that if Pip never got a degree from there, she'd list CUNY as her lie because it was just close *enough* to the truth to keep anyone from digging further? Because let's face it—who actually calls alumni offices to verify college degrees?

I step out into the crosswalk, and a horn honks loudly. I startle and look to my left. A blue Tesla has stopped mere feet from me, and the driver looks pissed. My eyes flit to the walking-man signal. It's not a walking man, as I thought—it's an orange hand. It wasn't my turn to cross.

Embarrassed, I mouth an apology to the driver and hurry across, my whole body on high alert.

I am going to take that woman down.

Chapter 20

PIP

Pip wanted the other mothers to like her.

Well, no, it was not a matter of wanting. It was a matter of needing.

Pip was a good mom. It was one thing she knew about herself, the only thing, if she was being honest, that she knew to be 100 percent true. But knowing she was a good mom didn't make her one in the eyes of the others. And that's what Pip required, if she was to set her child up for success.

She would die trying.

At her core, she didn't give a rat's ass about what the other mothers at the school thought of her. How could she possibly care what a bunch of superficial, arrogant, and downright bitchy women thought of *her*? She was above all of them. But they were the gatekeepers, and that made them important. Critical, really. Fundamental to Pip getting the life she wanted for Sofie. And that meant playing their silly, artificial game.

Sofie had not come into this world with any advantages. It had been quite the opposite, if anything. Still, Pip had known the minute she'd given birth, and they'd handed her daughter to her swaddled in that pink-and-blue, rough newborn blanket, that even though she and Sofie had next to nothing, in the material sense, they had each other. That was enough. It would have to be.

Pip spent the next few years of her life attempting to prove it true: That she was not, in fact, wrong to trust her instincts. That she could live up to the ideal she had in her head of what a "good mother" said and did. A good mother provided for her child: adequate food, medicine, clothing; those were givens. Even she'd had those as a kid. She had never starved or gone without clothes and shoes that fit, though sometimes they were hand-me-downs that bordered on unacceptable and humiliating. Despite the crushing sense of shame, she'd known how to make them work from a young age, rolling up the cuffs of outdated clothing or scouring Goodwill for items that had been tossed by wealthy kids with no idea that their fifty-dollar sneaker castoffs would qualify as her treasure.

She wanted much more than that for Sofie. Anyone could give their daughter the most basic childhood possible, hitting a low bar for parenting. But Sofie deserved everything—all of it. Pip wanted her to shine, to feel worthy. Sofie was all she had in the world, and as clichéd as that sounded, it was true. Sofie's father wasn't in the picture. It stung. Good mothers provided their children with two loving parents, didn't they? And Pip knew from day one that wouldn't be in the cards for her and Sofie. She wasn't 100 percent sure who Sofie's father even was. The two possible candidates were equally undesirable. One was an alcoholic druggie; the other was the druggie's dealer friend who'd roofied and assaulted her while the druggie pretended not to notice. Either way, it was humiliating. Neither of those men was even remotely dad material, so she'd gotten the hell out of that situation as soon as the cheap-ass pregnancy test had turned blue. Pip had never told Sofie anything about who her possible dad might be. They avoided the subject entirely, for which Pip was grateful. If Sofie ever did think to ask when she was older, Pip planned to tell her he was a one-night stand.

She'd never once regretted that decision, though she did wonder, at times, if it was right to bring a child into the world with only one parent who literally had nothing.

She vowed to be such a good mom to Sofie that it would make up for everything she lacked.

It was pickup time at the school, which meant it was a scene. Pip had never considered herself "carpool mom" material. Even when she'd shuttled Sofie to the playground as a toddler, she'd felt "other" from the perky moms with their snack pouches and had assumed she'd do things her own way. She'd been broke but fancied herself unconventional. She'd imagined taking Sofie and traveling to far-flung places together, skipping out on chunks of school to see the world and live like bohemians, learning about the world in a hands-on manner that would ultimately prove far more educational than what every other boring, by-the-book parent was doing.

Then Pip noticed how well adjusted and downright happy the other kids were with their stupid snack pouches, and her old way of thinking went out the window. She realized, in time, what she'd really wanted her whole life, and it was what she became determined to give her daughter: normalcy.

Standing outside the school, Pip resisted the urge to pull out a cigarette. She'd quit months ago but still kept a pack buried at the bottom of her hobo bag, just in case. In case what, she wasn't sure, but it always seemed like a good idea to have them there as a sort of insurance policy. Against boredom, or the utter meaninglessness of life.

Pip knew that good moms don't smoke, that popular moms don't indulge or wouldn't be caught dead doing so publicly, that they condemn the practice. Which is why she'd never light up there, outside Franklin Elementary.

No, Pip needed to fit in. It was what was best for Sofie, what would benefit her, and what benefited Sofie benefited Pip. To that end, she played the part, wearing the requisite mom costume: jeans in the most current mom style, though slightly behind what was on the cutting edge of fashion. She wouldn't want to show anyone up, and besides, she couldn't yet afford anything that wasn't thrifted, so she was always choosing from the wares that wealthy parents had deemed stylish six months prior and now cast off. She was a master thrifter. She could scan a display—a whole store, even—in five minutes flat, then pull the best pieces off their hangers before other shoppers had managed to get their footing inside. Dressing the part was step one of keeping up the illusion of good mom.

Step two was the script. More specifically, saying all the right things. She waved to a mom who approached her. This was key. Pip knew how to be friendly, how to engage, how to seem breezy but just interested enough in the other women and their petty concerns. She asked about their kids' gymnastic class, the uniforms for soccer. She knew which moms were upset about the nonorganic apples in the cafeteria and which ones wanted to gossip about Scott the librarian and whether he was, indeed, single.

This mom approaching her now was one of the worst, the most mundane, the most generic. The most critical to impress.

Pip turned on the charm.

"Carrie," she said warmly, smiling at this thirty-something PTA fanatic who had a degree in psychology but seemed to only apply it toward analyzing the motivations of spoiled kids at birthday parties. "How's Izzy? Is she adjusted to the move?"

Carrie had recently moved her family from a spacious condo to an even more spacious house, right in the heart of Noe Valley. It was one of those super-desirable developer flips that was overpriced but move-in ready. According to Carrie, they hadn't even had to paint before they arrived. Pip didn't give one shit about Carrie's move, but it was exactly the right question to ask. She could see Carrie practically drip with appreciation for being "seen."

Carrie sighed. "Kids are so funny. Who ever thought my daughter would be mad about no longer sharing a room with her little brother? Can you believe she's been sneaking over to his room at night to sleep next to him? In a *twin*, for God's sake!"

Pip made the most empathetic face she could muster. "That's terrible. All that work you did to move to a house where she'd have her own room, and she doesn't even appreciate it!"

Carrie sighed again. "I know I should be grateful she loves her brother that much. I am, of course. I see how other siblings treat each other . . . ripping each other's throats out. God, you're lucky Sofie is an only child, so you don't have to deal with that bullshit!"

Pip nodded in agreement. "Only children are truly the best." She smiled pleasantly, even though she did not share the same feelings. She felt like a failure for denying Sofie the lifelong bond of a sibling. She beat herself up for it daily. But a second child wasn't in the cards for Pip, and anyway, it didn't make sense, financially. Giving Sofie the moon was a reasonable goal. Giving two Sofies two moons seemed impossible.

Speaking of Sofie, she now came marching toward her mother, and Pip felt a rush of relief. Pip was good at these vacuous small-talk conversations. Good at being in the right place, at the right time, to absorb all the relevant gossip and ensure she was an essential part of the fabric of Sofie's class. Parents thought of her when they hosted get-togethers, and being thought of was another step in ensuring she was giving Sofie that normality, that stability, that she craved. Still, she hated talking to the Carries of the world. Give her a cigarette-smoking, wisecracking girlfriend any day of the week. The Carries were so aggravatingly oblivious. So simple. So ungrateful. They had no idea that every step Pip took, every move she made . . . it was calculated, out of necessity. Pip had found a few friends over the years who really "got" her, and sometimes they texted, or got together for happy hour. But those friends were few and far between. And they weren't the people Pip needed in her life if she was going to give Sofie the childhood she deserved.

Pip was always happy to take Sofie's hand and walk off toward home. But this time, something stopped her. Carrie's own daughter, Izzy, was skipping two paces behind Sofie. Having caught up to her, she got close and whispered something in Sofie's ear. Pip watched the exchange intently, working hard not to let her inner thoughts appear on her face. This was something she was practiced at: always appearing calm and collected, in spite of whatever mental gymnastics were going on in her mind, which was always churning, marinating, strategizing. She couldn't help it. Years of having to scrape and self-advocate had made it so her brain was never calm.

Sofie didn't look happy about whatever Izzy had said to her. She said nothing and moved imperceptibly away from Izzy. Pip was probably the only one who'd noticed that tiny stealth move. She was a mother. She noticed everything her child did.

"Can we go now, Mommy?" Sofie asked, not looking toward Izzy or acknowledging her.

"Of course, sweetie," Pip said, scanning Carrie's face, and then Izzy's, for some sign that something was wrong. They looked as pleasant and bland as always.

Pip felt her stomach flip as she and Sofie traversed the crosswalk.

Being considered normal was a valiant goal, but it was harder to achieve than Pip had ever imagined.

Chapter 21

I arrive home fighting tears. Wren has canceled the one shift I had left.

Only two students showed up today. This time slot has never been popular. People prefer early-morning yoga classes on a Saturday, or late afternoon. Most people are eating brunch or running errands or hanging in the park at 1 p.m. That other instructor got all my best shifts. This one yoga shift wasn't keeping me afloat, not even close. Whether or not I make that seventy-five dollars per week isn't even the point. It's that I'm off her payroll.

Maybe it's because I feel like I literally have nothing left to lose now. No job, not even one shift. No Seth. No certainty about my future, if I have one, or if I'm staring down an eventual cancer diagnosis. And no home. Maybe that's what makes these embers start to rumble in my gut and fill me, one atom at a time. Starting to catch fire.

Pip's standing outside the building when I arrive. She's not alone. Next to her is Serena, and they're talking animatedly with a woman I don't recognize. She's wearing a blazer and looks professional, put together.

I walk up, cautious, feeling my chest start to tighten at the sight of Pip. My muscles tense like they're preparing to fight off a predator.

"Call us if you need anything else," Pip is saying to the woman. "You have my number?"

"Yes, I do. This is enormously helpful," the woman says before turning around and walking off.

It's now that I notice Pip and Serena are standing close to each other. Talking quietly. Seeming . . . friendly.

"Pip?" Be calm, Emily. Be Zen. "Serena? Who was that?"

They stare at me like I'm the outsider—which is so infuriating I want to scream—then finally Serena speaks. "She was a reporter. She's writing a piece on Nathan's, um, death, and she asked if we had any info she could use in the story."

Is she for real? They spoke to a reporter? Gave her details about Nathan's fall?

"It's an ongoing murder case!" I sputter. "Are you sure that's even allowed?"

"Mason never told us we had anything to hide, did he?" Pip asks. "Unless he told you something different?"

Of course he didn't. But leave it to Pip to try to destabilize me. My head is spinning, my chest tightening, a screw turning inside my torso, by the second. Why do these two seem like they're in cahoots? Have Serena and Pip even crossed paths before today?

"Emily?" Pip moves up to put a hand on my arm. I flinch instinctively. "Are you okay? You look . . . kinda off."

Inhale, exhale, inhale, exhale . . . "I'm not sure talking to that journalist was a good idea. What if she misconstrues what you told her?"

"We simply told her the facts, Emily," Serena pipes up. "I don't think it's a big deal. She seemed to know most of it, anyway . . ."

"Text if you need *anything*, okay?" Pip's addressing Serena. Serena nods, looking small and pitiful in her oversize sweater. And then Pip is hugging her, scooping her in her arms like she did with me the night that Seth visited.

Serena doesn't seem to mind.

I'm beyond disgusted by Pip's insidious pattern of ingratiating herself to *everyone*: Mason. Serena. The PTA moms. Everyone but me.

Post-hug, Serena picks up her bag from the sidewalk and slings it over her shoulder. "Thanks, Pip. It's been really healing talking to you. Bye, Emily."

Serena leaves, opening the front door to the condo and disappearing inside. The door shuts behind her with a thud.

"Poor girl . . ." Pip fishes in her bag, presumably for the keys I never should have freaking given her. "She's really beat up about Nathan's death. I think she might have actually loved him."

I'm having none of this. My wheels are spinning, faster and faster. What does Pip have to gain from befriending Serena? Isolating me? Making me feel like there's one less person in the building I can count on, because the two of them have formed an alliance?

We take the stairs briskly. I go first, and I let her follow. When we reach the condo, I take my key out, but I stop in front of the door without unlocking it, spin to face her, feeling those embers flying up to my chest and propelling me, galvanizing me. "Is Stone your married name?"

Pip's jaunty smile drops. For one minuscule second, she looks put out. Or is it something more than that. Does she look . . . caught?

"Oh! Huh. Why are you asking?"

"No reason. Well, actually, that's a lie, there is totally a reason." My plan here is two pronged. I'll keep digging, keep investigating her lies, and letting her know I'm onto her, until I scare her into packing up her and Sofie's stuff and moving out. After all, she clearly doesn't want anyone knowing the truth about her. Why? Because she's likely hiding things. Things she doesn't want anyone to know. That leads me to the second prong. Maybe, just maybe I'll uncover enough about her, some crimes or lies or fraud, to alert the authorities. And *that* will force her to leave on her own, before getting formally evicted.

"Did you ever work at Gap?" I press. "Did you really get your BA from CUNY? Because Gap's never heard of a Penelope Stone, and CUNY has you on record as having taken a few continuing ed courses. No degree."

Pip seems to compose herself, and she's as in command as ever, now—that fleeting look of vulnerability I sensed on her face, and in her stance, has vanished. She pushes past me to the door, takes her own key out, and opens it.

"It's not a married name, no. But it's not the name I was born with. I changed it a few years back."

We step inside the condo, where I spot Sofie sitting on the couch next to a girl her age. A schoolmate, I assume.

"Mom! This is Roxy." Sofie and Roxy are chowing down on chips, and they've got their schoolwork spread around them on the sofa, and on the rug.

"Hi, Roxy! It's wonderful to meet you!" Pip has turned on the charm, big time, and is bustling around, neatening the condo and heading to the kitchen, presumably to bring more snacks. Sofie hasn't had a friend over since they moved in, and Pip seems primed to impress, like she did with the PTA moms.

"It's Roxanne! I'm phasing out my nickname. New year, new me, you know? And thanks, happy to be here."

Wow, this Roxy, I mean Roxanne, is confident. Maybe it's her name. Her parents did her a favor. I move to the kitchen to corner Pip. What she just told me is wholly unhelpful. I need an explanation, not more vagaries.

"What do you mean you changed it?" I ask under my breath.

"I mean, I changed it. Can we talk about this later?" She indicates Sofie and the friend. "I don't want Sofie overhearing, and I certainly don't want her classmate to get the wrong idea about our family. My ex was an abuser, okay? I changed our last names for safety concerns."

Another excuse. Possibly true, but more likely fabricated.

"So you *did* work at Gap? If I reached back out to Melanie Hopper, she'd remember you under a different name?"

Pip sets down the milk carton she's holding. "What do you mean, reached back out? You contacted my former employer?"

"Of course I reached out to her." I am not apologizing. Not backing down.

"That feels pretty invasive, Emily." She has a look of outrage on her face. One I'm sure is as practiced as everything else about her. "If you'd asked me, I could have explained."

"Just like you asked me before you started ransacking my aunt's jewelry? And it wasn't just your name. Melanie didn't recognize your photo either. I find it a little hard to believe she wouldn't remember your face, if you worked there for a few years like it says on your LinkedIn profile."

Pip lets out a breath. "Look, I didn't want to make a thing of this, but . . ." She lowers her voice so I can barely make out what she's saying. "Roxanne's one of the bullies at Sofie's school. I encouraged Sofie to invite her over here to extend an olive branch. So I'd prefer we not discuss my personal history right now, okay?"

It's all the confirmation I need—she's deflecting, using her daughter to avoid answering me because she *can't*, and we both know it.

"Guess what, Emily!" Sofie shoots me her hundred-watt smile from the couch. "My mom had this great idea the other day, and I wanted to keep it a secret until the right time to tell you!"

There's that on-fire feeling again. Whatever this "great idea" is, I'm not going to like it. And it might just push me over the edge. I brace myself for the onslaught.

Sofie's standing up now, bouncing from foot to foot. Roxy looks mildly engaged but is mostly focused on the chips she's devouring.

I glance over at Pip. She's pouring herself a coffee and looks checked out. What a surprise.

"What's this big secret, Sofie?" I clasp my hands together, channeling my energy inward. Don't yell. Don't freak out—not yet.

"We started a GoFundMe! It's already gotten four hundred dollars, can you believe it? Roxy helped, right, Rox?" She looks over at her friend, who shrugs.

"Sure, yeah. I told some people about it. My cousin threw in five bucks."

"My mom asked me to do it since I set up one last year for the class hamster, and I know how the site works," Sofie continues. "She thought, hmm, if we're strapped for cash, why not try it? Everyone else does! And now we have the money for ballet!"

I take that in. The money for ballet. But not the rent.

This has to end. Before I do something I'll really regret.

Chapter 22

I ate dinner in my nook last night. I spent the rest of the evening googling other people's terrible squatter experiences and searching for tidbits. I opened up a fresh Google Doc on my laptop and titled it PIP, documenting anything and everything that could possibly prove helpful to me. I read about the Flower Lady in Bernal Heights who managed to stay put without paying rent for *years*. She'd gotten the media on her side.

I'm positive that's what Pip's planning. To make sure, if I fight her too fiercely, that she comes out smelling like roses while I look like an evil, money-grubbing landlord.

I will protect myself. I must.

I spent this morning running errands, including a trip to Walgreens, where I picked up a few items that are now safely tucked under the blankets of my futon.

It's 9 a.m. when I hear Sofie grabbing her things, telling her mom she's going to take the bus to Roxy's house to work on their joint science project. They'll have to work all day since they've got to filter their own water and have barely started.

Great. Sofie's gone. I will wait for Pip to leave the house, and then I will begin.

It's nearing ten o'clock, and Pip's only just exited the bathroom. She is snappily dressed, her hair blown out nicely. A wolf in sheep's clothing. Attractive, with a way about her that screams ease and confidence. It's what Serena latched on to, I'm sure of it. The way Pip speaks to you, when she really wants to get you on her side . . . it's a skill, a talent.

Almost like a calling.

She did it with me, I recall with a lurch in the pit of my stomach. That day we spoke on FaceTime, before I invited her into my life. She snake-charmed me. Made me believe I'd be gaining not only a room-mate but a friend. I fell for it.

It's an agonizing wait for Pip to leave. My heart rams into my rib cage while I pretend to check my Instagram account, doomscroll and search for any and every distraction. There's a new hair straightener by Dyson that claims to be magic in a stick. It's $600, which would cover a whole month of utilities, phone, and groceries. I scroll past.

Twenty minutes pass, and she leaves the condo—finally. As soon as I hear the front door latch shut, I spring up in my futon, the hair standing up on the backs of my arms. It is imperative that I move quickly.

It's go time.

I grab the Walgreens bag from under my covers and a random tote, then slip out one minute behind her, careful to follow as quietly as I can. The last thing I want is for her to accost me in the hallway. As long as I remain a few steps behind her, this will work. It has to.

Down in the lobby, Pip pauses to reach for something in her purse. I stand back, several paces away, waiting, heart in my throat.

She pulls the object out. It's only her phone.

She scrolls on it, seeming to have no idea I'm nearby, watching her from behind. Good.

After checking her phone—for a text? Directions?—she starts for-ward again, toward the front doors of the building, and pushes the right side open. She walks through it, and it shuts with a click. I remain a few paces back.

She's heading down the street toward the bus stop.

Perfect.

I pray she will stop and wait there, and it feels like a small gift from the universe when she does. She transfers weight from one foot to the other, checking the bus times, I assume, on her phone.

This is good. This is *working*. I can watch her from across the sidewalk, and she'll be none the wiser.

I rip open the Walgreens bag and pull out the Halloween costume I procured at the drugstore. Lucky it's September. Any other time of year, this wouldn't have been in stock. The set includes a wig—long black witch hair, which I throw on—along with some cheap five-dollar sunglasses from the revolving rack. The final touch—the cheapest workwear boot I could find, not real Timberlands but knockoffs I spotted at a consignment shop several blocks from my house. It wasn't even open yet for the day, but I'm friendly with the owner. We've both lived in Noe Valley for years. She opened the shop for me and sold me these for ten dollars. I'm pretty sure she was doing me a favor. She said she remembered my parents and was fond of them. The boots don't look anything like shoes I would ever wear, which is the entire point, and I hope—no, I pray—that in this disguise, I won't be recognizable. I slam my feet into them, toss my cheap flip-flops into the tote I'm carrying, along with the Walgreens bag.

It's a good ten minutes before the bus arrives. I wait until Pip has boarded before running up and hopping on at the back entrance. I pull my Muni card from my bag and scan it. I slip into an open seat, avoid looking in Pip's direction. The last thing I need is for her to have some kind of sixth sense about what I'm doing and get suspicious. She could easily recognize me if she were really trying, or had reason to, but I'm hoping right now I blend in as the quirky lady at the back of the bus. At least I don't stand out as strange, not here in my home city. You could walk around naked, or in a mummy costume, and no one would blink.

We head down Market Street. I stare at my lap, careful to look up briefly every time we stop, to make sure Pip hasn't gotten off. Two stops, three, four . . . it's six later, near Civic Center, that she stands up from her seat, and I tense. So far, so good. I will follow Pip today until I find out something, anything, I can add to my Google Doc and use against her. If I can catch her in a lie, or better yet, uncover some criminal behavior on her part, learning just enough about her past to panic her, she might just leave my condo and get out of my life. Evicting her may prove too difficult, but scaring her a little won't cost me anything. I will follow her as long as I have to.

We pull to a stop at Larkin Street, as Pip makes her way to the front doors. I do the same, toward the ones in the back.

She steps off; I step off. The bus pulls away, and I follow behind her. It's crowded now, a bustling city morning, which makes it a lot easier for me to go unnoticed. I breathe out a sigh as a man in a suit nearly mows me down, not looking where he's going. He shoots me an angry look—go figure—and I compose myself, relieved Pip hasn't gotten much farther ahead.

I see now where she is headed.

The public library. Interesting choice, but she clearly does read. She exudes sophistication, and that must come from somewhere.

I speed up, not wanting her to get too far away. The main branch of the library is enormous, and once she heads inside, she'll be swallowed up. She walks toward the sprawling building that takes up an entire city block, and I quicken my pace.

She reaches the front double doors and heads inside. I follow just steps behind, making sure a few other patrons pad us in between. Then I pull open the hefty door and slide in after her.

The foyer is enormous. I haven't been here in ages, probably not since I was a high schooler. There are school groups here, kids who aren't nearly as quiet as they probably should be, and the sound echoes off the monstrously tall ceilings. It's an open atrium. You can see the floors above you, like one of those fancy hotels where the elevator climbs up the side, leaving open floors that are visible from the lobby.

Pip heads to the information desk, and I follow, maintaining a short distance.

She approaches the counter, then reaches in her bag and pulls out books. A whole stack of them. Some look like textbooks, others like novels. Hers, Sofie's, or both?

She sets them on the desk, and the librarian behind the counter says something to her—I can't hear what—before Pip walks off, over to a bank of elevators, and presses the button.

Dammit. I can't follow her into the elevator—surely I'd give myself away in such close quarters—and this place is vast. Who knows what else is on Pip's agenda here, but likely I won't be able to investigate her, up close, without risking her finding me out.

I watch out of the corner of my eye as the elevator doors open, and Pip steps inside.

There is only one thing left to do. I walk up to a different librarian from the one Pip talked to. Pip's books sit right there, in a stack. They haven't been tossed into a bin to be sorted, not yet.

I study the titles. A psychology textbook . . . twisted, considering Pip's probably reading this to gain strategies to con me. But it's not particularly alarming on face value. There's also a text on education philosophies—fair; it's on brand with her supposed tutoring gig, I guess—and I was right, there are a few middle-grade titles I assume are Sofie's picks. The Front Desk series. A couple of Judy Blumes.

"Excuse me," I say, feeling emboldened. I never would have done something like this. Never would have considered it. Guess there's a first time for everything.

The librarian looks up. She's straight out of Central Casting, curly silver hair and chunky tortoiseshell glasses connected to a beaded cord. "Can I help you?"

"Yes," I say, pulling my sunglasses down and flashing my biggest smile. "What phone number do you have on file for me? I just dropped off these books. They're under my name."

The librarian sighs, picks up one of the books, and scans the barcode.

"I have 415-555-2231." She doesn't look amused. She probably thinks I'm a dolt for not knowing my own phone number.

"Great, that's the one." I smile at her, again. No return smile from her. Nothing. It's probably this witch wig she finds off-putting. I feel the need to explain it away. "I'm headed to an event at my kid's school." I indicate the middle-grade books. "I have a twelve-year-old. It's share day in sixth grade. All the parents are dressing up. I'm a Harry Potter character. It's a shitty costume, but it's all I could throw together . . . my kid informed me this morning it was happening and claims she 'forgot.'"

The lady stares at me, still not responding. Who can blame her? Since when do sixth graders have costume days where their parents show up? They'd probably rather die.

"Anyway, thanks," I add, doing my best to sound as perky as possible. "Quick question—I just got divorced, and yeah, big bummer. So I'm wondering what name is listed on my library card. I lost it," I add, "but if it's got my husband, I mean ex-husband's, last name on it, I'm gonna need to rectify that. He's a big douche."

The librarian sighs, types something into her keyboard.

"You're listed as Penelope Baker. Will that be all?"

"No, that's . . . that's good. Thank you," I mutter, no longer feeling the need to impress as I stumble away, across the foyer.

Penelope Baker. Baker? That's the name Pip uses at the library? And probably other places, too?

Mason, I think. Does Mason know?

Because if Pip lied to the police about who she really is . . .

She could be *anyone*.

She could even be a killer.

Chapter 23

A text comes in from Alli.

Are you mad at me?

No, I write back, emphatically. I add a heart emoji so she doesn't get suspicious. She gives it a thumbs-up.

I stuff my phone in my bag. It's tempting. If I went to Alli's right now and spilled everything to her . . . . if I really told her the truth . . . about Pip. About Sofie. About my debt.

About Seth.

She'd take me in. She'd probably go so far as to hire me a lawyer. Both to advise me on evicting Pip, and to make sure that if the police come knocking again, with more questions about Nathan, I'm protected.

But I won't. I can't do that to her. She's already told me how much debt she's in over the IVF. Good lawyers cost tens or even hundreds of thousands of dollars. It's one thing to rely on friends for support. It's quite another to burden them. And anyway—I already know what I need to do. Handle this myself. If it kills me.

I pull off the wig and stuff it in my tote, shedding the disguise and acknowledging that what I did was justified, and not only that: it was valuable.

Penelope Baker, either a fake name or a pseudonym. Or maybe it's her real name, and Stone is the fake . . .

My phone rings. If it's Alli, I'm going to send it to voicemail. But it's not Alli. It's Viv's nursing home.

Heart in my throat, I answer.

"Hello?"

"Is this Emily Hawthorne?"

"Yes." My nerves jangle. The assisted living doesn't call unless something's wrong. "Is everything okay? Is Vivian okay?"

"All is fine," says the woman on the other end. "I didn't mean to alarm you. It's your aunt. She wants to speak to you."

I let out a breath. Thank goodness. "Oh, put her on. Please," I add.

There's some jostling on the other end, then I hear loud breathing.

"Emily, honey? Is that you?"

There it is. Aunt Viv's voice, silky like honey but so wise, so fierce. God, I miss her. "It's me, Viv. Sorry I haven't visited. I've been . . . busy."

"Oh, don't you worry. I know you have more important things to worry about than me!"

She doesn't mean it pointedly. She's serious. She has always wanted the best for me, has never wanted to be a burden. She told me once that I could make her the happiest by living my life, by continuing to do all the fun and life-giving things we used to do together.

"I don't, Viv, truly. I miss you." My voice trembles. I do miss her, more than she knows. The trouble is, the Viv I miss is only half-there, now. She'll never be the Viv who stayed up late watching old black-and-white films with me. Who taught me how to navigate breakups, and tricky friendships, who helped me write a personal statement for college about our joint journey to become "Zen." That Viv is gone, and maybe that Emily is gone too.

"How's Seth?"

The question stops me in my tracks. She doesn't remember. Months ago, I told her we broke up—canceled our engagement. I didn't tell her the reason. I couldn't, because she might have tried to talk me out of it.

But now she's forgotten, and I have to do it—I have to break the news all over again.

"We broke up, Aunt Viv."

"Oh, no! Why? When?"

I sigh. "A while ago, Viv. It's okay. You must have forgotten. It was for the best. I'm okay—okay?"

"Okay, honey. I have to go, they're saying it's lunch time. I hope it's not that soggy brisket again. Soggy and tough as nails. Worst combination. At least I don't overeat!"

I smile. There's Aunt Viv. "I'll visit soon, okay?"

And I hang up.

As I toss my phone back in my tote, my aunt's bracelet jangles on my arm, the charms reflecting the morning light. My heart feels like it's leaping up in my throat as I study them.

I'm walking briskly now, but not toward home.

I arrive at the pawnshop twenty minutes later. This isn't a pretty stretch of Market Street. In fact, it's quite grimy, and as I push open the filthy glass door, I feel a quickening in my chest that I recognize: dread. I ignore it, walking up to the counter past the cases of jewels, trinkets, and junk. Viv's bracelet doesn't belong in a place like this. Some of these items might be worth something, but most are knockoffs, cheap imitations. I feel guilty even bringing her precious heirloom in here.

She won't ever know, I think. She can't even remember that Seth and I called off our engagement. It sucks to acknowledge it. But the truth is, she won't ever know the bracelet's gone. And I need this now. I have no choice.

A clerk walks into the store from the back room.

"Hi," I say, fighting tears. Be strong, Emily. You have to.

"Can I help you?" He isn't unfriendly, just blunt. That's good. I don't feel like making polite conversation. I need to get this done. That's all.

"I'd like to sell this." I hold up my wrist, showing off Viv's bracelet. I almost can't look straight at it. Such a beautiful relic, one that meant so much to me and Viv, should not be parted with.

But it's painfully obvious, too, that doing this is necessary.

"I'll need to see it up close," the man says.

I let out a breath. I don't know how I imagined this going. It's obvious I have to let this man examine it.

I unhook the clasp, then lay the chunky gold chain down on the counter. He picks up a magnifying glass.

"Real diamonds," I tell him, as though I need to sell him on its finer points.

He doesn't respond, simply looks it over, squinting a bit through the glass of the magnifier, then sets the magnifying device down.

"One thousand dollars cash, right now. Take it or leave it."

My heart sinks. Only a thousand? I know Viv bought it for more—a lot more. But the truth is, I have no idea what its value is. She may have overpaid. It's beautiful, and sentimental—to me—but could I get more than that elsewhere?

I steel myself.

"Cash," I answer him. "I'll take it."

He nods, then heads to a locked box, which he rifles through for the bills.

"You'll resell it, right?" I ask, suddenly feeling my heart start to race.

The clerk looks up at me. "Or melt it down. Why?"

Oh no. That thought hadn't occurred to me when I walked in. I can't bear the idea of it being destroyed.

"But won't someone want it? It's really special."

"Maybe." He shrugs. "But times are tough. If it doesn't sell in sixty days, I can't keep it on the shelf."

I could change my mind, snatch it up from the counter and run out of here. We've only made a verbal agreement. He can't hold me to it.

"It was my aunt's, and I hate to sell it."

He gathers up the cash and starts over to me. "Says everyone who ever walked in here. You want the cash or not, lady?"

I think of Pip. Taking over my house. It's enough ammunition to sell every single one of Viv's pieces.

I reach out and grab the stack of bills. I feel the heft of them—hundreds and fifty-dollar bills.

"Thanks," I say, not wanting to stay in this stuffy, musty store, this place where dreams go to die, for one second longer.

I turn to the door and walk out.

On the sidewalk, I count them, the bills. Eight one hundreds, four fifties.

I know what I should do. Go directly to the Chase ATM and deposit this, and direct the funds toward the mortgage. But I can't. I have other, pressing plans for this cash. I pocket the bills, am heading home when I receive another text from Alli.

Emily—is this YOU?

There's a link, and I click on it, feeling a sense of something unknowable start to crawl up my spine.

I open the link to a GoFundMe. It's called "Help us combat evil landlord."

It's so obviously the GoFundMe Sofie was referring to, and it's raised a lot more than $400. It's up to $1,800.

Right smack in the middle of the web page is a photo. Of me.

Chapter 24

It only takes a quick scan of the GoFundMe page to get the gist. Two anonymous residents of Noe Valley who claim to fear for their safety are asking for support for legal fees to fight the landlord who is trying to evict them.

That landlord, naturally, is me.

I don't know what to be angrier about. The fact that Pip's played me *again*, and in public this time, or the fact that some foolish idiots have donated to this shameless "cause." What do Sofie and Pip plan to use these funds for? Because it's clearly not going to be their rent. Cello lessons? A high-end luncheon, perhaps, for the PTA moms?

I head straight home, to *my* home, my brain whirling. I'll get this taken down. I will contact the site. Explain that my face is being used, exploited, that no one had permission to post my photograph like that. I'll get myself unassociated from this ridiculous smear campaign. I'm not going to let Pip get away with this.

Alli. What do I tell her? I need to say something. She's worried. She'll keep worrying unless I can persuade her not to.

> Saw this. Someone's using my photo in an internet scam, gonna report it. It's harmless. Love ya

There. That should do it. It's perfectly reasonable that someone could have gotten my photo from the yoga-studio website and repurposed it for this. I hope Alli buys my explanation.

I sprint toward home, trying not to spiral about who could see this GoFundMe, what they might think . . . Will I ever work again if I'm thought of as some money-thirsty slumlord who's mistreating her tenant? It's so outlandish, but I know how people are. It's likely why some random strangers donated to it. They want a place to direct their anger, their outrage.

This time, it's coming for *me*.

Well, fuck that.

I run. So hard, so fast, I know what a cliché I am, trying to outrun my anger. Without Viv's bracelet on my wrist, I feel freer. I can move quickly, and my knee seems to be holding up as I make my way over a crosswalk, then down Sanchez Street. But I miss the bracelet. I feel its absence like a hole in my chest. I know I did what I had to. It felt like the adult course of action, much as it pained me to let it go. It felt like letting a part of *Viv* go, and maybe my old life with it.

I pump my legs, pushing myself until my calf muscles burn. This is only the second time I've run like this since my recovery, and I'm going harder and faster than last time. I'm pushing through my anger, my shame, my fear—all of it.

It's not just Viv I miss, and our life together. It's Seth.

My stomach flips with the panicked realization that someone might send him the link to this website.

I can't imagine anything more humiliating than either having to confess the truth to him, or trying to convince him, like I hopefully convinced Alli, that someone stole and used my photo.

I care what Seth thinks of me. A lot. More than I'd admit to anyone else. We used to run like this, together, on weekends, those lazy Saturdays when we had nothing to do but stop for brunch at Le Marais on Eighteenth Street. We'd talk about the future, or I guess I should say, Seth did. I was always quiet, reticent, hesitant to make plans.

When he proposed to me, in Dolores Park, we were picnicking with all the other folks who'd come out to laze around on that clear, sunny day in October. It was eighty degrees, unseasonably warm anywhere else, but not in this city, where summer weather often surfaces in the fall. We'd carved out our own tiny patch of grass, in between the twenty-somethings tossing Frisbees to their dogs and the parents who were attempting to shield their young kids from the weed stench that was wafting across the grass. I remember being surprised when Seth unearthed a bottle of champagne from his bag of Bi-Rite goodies. It was chilled, and he'd somehow procured two champagne flutes.

"Wow, I thought today was just regular," I joked. It didn't even occur to me, in that moment, what he was about to do.

It's why I was totally blindsided, completely unprepared.

It's not that I hadn't imagined this day would come. That he'd propose, that he'd want to take our relationship to the next, permanent level. It's what I wanted too. Of course it was.

I loved him—love him, still—but I don't regret what I did. At least, I don't regret *why* I did it.

I reach my street, turn into my condo lobby, putting Seth and the abhorrent GoFundMe from my mind. Screw that and Pip. I will work this from every angle. I will fight her where she doesn't even see me. Starting with the info gleaned from my library trip.

Penelope Baker.

It's so obvious what I need to do.

I race into the lobby and up the stairs, taking them two at a time. When I reach my door, I pull out my key and charge inside—my house—with efficiency. I'm a woman on a mission.

Sofie is there, in the living room, sprawled on the couch with her headphones on. Pip's futzing around in the kitchen, or maybe she's actually cooking. I don't take the time to find out or let her distract me. There is no time left. I must act.

I reach my futon in mere moments and slip my laptop from under my pillow, where I last left it, then open my purse in search of a pen and the miniature notebook I carry around with me.

After yanking my beaded curtain closed, I shove my earbuds into my ears and then flip open my laptop. The first thing I do is head to GetVerifiedNow and run a second background check—this time, for Penelope Baker. Once I've done that, I begin my Google search. I don't think about it too hard. In fact, I don't think at all. I type the first combination of words that pops into my head.

"Penelope Baker San Francisco mom Sofie grifter"

I wait with bated breath for the results to appear, knowing full well this could be a bust. There might be a million Penelope Bakers on the World Wide Web. Realistically, there have to be at least a thousand or more. What if all I get is a string of other Penelopes and nothing concrete to use against *my* Pip? What then?

A list of entries appears.

The first result: a Penelope Baker who works at Stanford as a grad student in their biology lab. Definitely not my Pip. I move to the next one.

An obituary for an eighty-year-old woman. Also not Pip.

Next, a bunch of Google images, one an old-school painted portrait for a Penelope *Barker* who was an activist in the eighteenth century.

The next few entries are equally irrelevant.

Dang. This is not what I was expecting. But I refuse to give up. I've barely begun.

I'll have to change things up. I begin again, this time typing in the same search terms but starting with Penelope Pip *Stone*, instead. I've looked at Pip's LinkedIn, of course, but I've never typed "mom" along with her name, and I've definitely never typed "grifter." Before hitting return, I add one more word. "Baker."

I wait, my midsection clenching with nerves. I can't fail. I won't. There is too much at stake here, too much on the line. I don't know when I last ate a stitch of food, but the idea of consuming anything right now makes my insides twist even further. I wouldn't be able to keep anything down if I tried.

The results appear. First is Pip's LinkedIn. No surprise there, but I've already seen it.

Next is another Penelope Stone, unrelated—this woman's a lawyer in Rhode Island—but after that, there's an Instagram post from 2021 that looks promising. I sit up a little straighter as I click on it, and up pops a photo of a bunch of women smiling from their chairs at a pizza restaurant, wineglasses in hand. The location is tagged as Delfina in the Mission. They all look to be in their thirties, and the caption to the Instagram post, which is displayed on the profile of a lady named Abigail, reads "Third grade moms night."

Bingo.

I spot Pip among the moms right away, looking the same as she always does. Messy blond hair arranged in a topknot. Trendy but casual T-shirt and jeans, a couple of gold necklaces slung around her neck. She's sitting on the end, glass of red wine in hand, and she's smiling. The mere sight of her makes my blood boil and my face heat up, but I remind myself to focus.

This could be the key, or *a* key, at least, to cracking Pip's identity wide open.

I scan the comments on the post. "Such a fun night" says @daisywilson1230. "When are we doing the next one?"—a question from @totallystressed_mom52. No comment from Pip, but I see now why the post came up in my search: the last commenter has tagged @pip-baker_tutor. Thank you so very much, @MotherhoodisCrap.

I click on Pip's handle, but dammit—I'm directed to "page not found." Clearly, if that ever *was* Pip's Instagram page, it's not now.

I don't know how to proceed. This is Pip, clearly—I'd recognize that aggravatingly inscrutable face anywhere—and she's here under the name Baker, just like they told me at the library. This tracks, sort of. Pip told me she changed her name from Baker to Stone because of an abusive ex. So I can assume she made that change, if it's even true, in the last few years, and that this particular post is from three years back, when Sofie was in third grade. This tells me very little but that these ladies knew her as Baker, not Stone . . .

The ladies. The *moms*. They knew her. They know her! I click on the profile of the poster, Abigail Jennings. Her feed pops up. From a quick glance, I can tell she's a regular thirty-something mom, with two cute kids, a nice-looking husband, and a dog that appears to be a variety of doodle.

She only has 234 followers and a smattering of posts. But I skip over all that. It's her connection to Pip I care about. I'm logged in to my own Instagram account, which I've mostly populated with yoga poses and some selfies of my thrift-store finds. I have about two thousand followers, mostly folks in the yoga world, and I don't spend too much time on here, but these days a social media page is a calling card of sorts. I keep it so people can find me. Or offer me a job.

And now I'll use it to send a DM to Abigail.

I click on the message button, am about to start typing, and abruptly stop. What do I say?

I've been bulldozing through this like a bat out of hell, determined to find something, anything, that can help me take down Pip. But now I force myself to take a minute to pause and reflect. A random DM from a stranger might not get this woman's attention, or worse, it could garner the wrong kind of attention. She might think I'm a nutjob and delete without even reading. Well, I can't help that, but I *can* compose a message that she'll be more likely to respond to, if she reads it at all.

> Hi Abigail! Sorry to bother you—we don't know each other, but my name's Emily, and I'm vetting a potential new roommate. I know it's weird to reach out like this out of the blue. SORRY!! Are you still in touch with Pip Baker? She goes by Stone now, I guess. She seems like she'd be an amazing person to live with, and her daughter's adorable! But I guess you can never be too careful! Thought I'd track down some of

her old friends and double check before making her
a copy of the key. Thank you so much in advance!

I've composed this message strategically. No point in admitting I already live with this nightmare person. If Abigail knew the entirety of my situation, she might think I'm too far gone and not even bother responding. But telling her I could be about to embark on a potentially life-altering journey with this old friend of hers, that I haven't taken the plunge yet . . . if she has any qualms about Pip, she may feel compelled to speak now.

Of course, there's every chance she has nothing negative at all to say about Pip, that she only knew her tangentially. Or even likes her.

That thought is sobering. What if this is all a wild-goose chase, and I go to bed tonight no closer to finding out who Pip really is?

I don't think I'll be able to sleep if that happens. Not here. Not with them. This has gone on too long, too far. My head pounds, likely from hunger and lack of sleep. Maybe it's a caffeine headache. Or stress; could it be the stress? My mouth is dry, too, like I've been sucking in breaths. Feels like every inhale is pressing up against an intractable rib cage.

The thought of my yogic breathing, now, is laughable. It won't save me. Nothing will, except getting some information, something concrete I can use to change my circumstances.

I stare at the message box, willing a response to appear. But a watched pot never boils, does it? So I leave my laptop open but lie down on my futon. I'm so tired—logically, I recognize that—but at the same time, I'm so wired it feels like torture to try to still my body.

How far I have fallen from my peaceful days filled with yogic breaths and mindful meditation . . .

If Seth were to see me now, really see me . . . I squeeze my eyes tight, a desperate attempt to wipe out my shame.

It takes every effort I can muster to still my body, force myself to rely on my wellness skills—if there ever were a time to fall back on my self-healing practices, it's now . . . Isn't it?

I breathe in, feeling my chest expand painfully. It's the anxiety, the overbearing sense of uncertainty. That's what's making my torso feel like an overstuffed aluminum can.

I conjure up a ball of light—bright, shining, unburdened by Pip and my reality—and the imaginary ball starts to glow in my fingertips. It moves up my arms, as I force myself not to think of Pip. Of Seth. Of the bracelet I sold so I could fight an evil predator in my own home.

Ugh. The first rule of meditation is to quiet your mind, release your brain from all your day-to-day worries. I've already failed.

I start over, determined to let that glowing ball travel from my lower arms to my elbows, my shoulders, my chest . . .

DING!

An alert.

My eyes slam open. I sit up, abandoning my meditation as I flip over and grab my laptop.

It's a message. From Abigail.

> I'm going out on a limb here to assume you're a real person and not a bot or a scammer but my conscience just won't let me ignore you.

I let out a breath. My DM worked. Thank God.

I'm real, I write, my fingers tap-dancing over the keyboard as my pulse speeds up to a breakneck pace. I promise. Thank you for writing me back.

I watch and wait, never filled with more anticipation than I am right now, as three dots appear.

Look, she types. I can't go on record saying anything that could get back to me and frankly I'm freaked you even found me . . .

My chest tightens. Crap. I do feel bad about that. But I had no choice. No choice at all.

But Penelope stayed with me for three months, she writes. When Sofie was nine.

I hear myself gasp. Holy shit. I feel my pulse race, my heartbeat speeding up as the three dots reappear.

I don't want this to get back to her, she types, and I haven't spoken to her since and never want to again, believe me. But let's just say it went really, really badly.

I race to type a response to her.

OMG. I answer. I chew on my lip, so hard I think I've drawn blood. What else to say? What else to *say*? That's . . . that's terrible.

My words feel wholly inadequate. But she thumbs-ups that last part, then continues typing. Does it matter what I say, now? She seems determined to tell me this. To inform me. To *stop* me.

Is that what she's doing? Stopping me? She has no idea Pip already lives here. That her "Penelope" has made my life a living hell.

Go on the local Nextdoor for Noe Valley, Abigail writes. I feel my erratic heartbeat morph from an adrenaline-fueled response into dread.

Search Pip Baker, she continues. Do that before you do anything else. Please. And if I were you . . . Well, you'll see for yourself.

See what? I type. See what. See WHAT.

I have to go. I'm sorry. Just do it, that's all I can say.
And Emily . . .

Yes?

Her last two words feel like the nail in my coffin—but also the ammunition I will use to get Pip out of my life once and for all.

Good luck.

Chapter 25

It only takes me thirty seconds to locate Nextdoor in the App Store on my phone. Downloading it takes a minute and a half, and creating a profile another three.

I type in Noe Valley as my neighborhood "area," fill out the required information, including uploading a profile pic—I choose one where I'm only partly visible, a hat covering the upper half of my face—and come up with a password.

I'm in.

Hunting down the thread about Penelope Baker–slash–Penelope Stone takes a mere fifty seconds. It was posted two years ago by a woman named Laura Jenkins. From the looks of her profile pic, she's petite, in her twenties or thirties, blond hair, and straight white teeth. It's hard to tell much else about her, but the truth is, I don't stop to look. My heart is nearly frozen in my chest as I scan her post.

SQUATTER! it reads. Major warning—do NOT let this woman into your home. Penelope Stone who goes by a bunch of other aliases is a total criminal. BEWARE, she is the roommate from hell!

I think I feel nauseous, but I can't even tell, so transfixed am I by what I'm reading.

Frannie Wilson says: "Pip" Stone or Baker or whatever the f*E)))@K her name is is a NIGHTMARE. Do not trust this woman for a second. She lived with me for seven months and paid rent for zero of it. I had to hire a lawyer to get her out of my home, and that cost me seven grand. I can't believe this happened to me. She is one of the shittiest POSes on the planet and the worst part is she's never had to pay for any of her crimes.

Alexa Marietta says: hard agree, I had the same experience and the crazy part (of many crazy parts) is that she gets you by using her daughter, it's the sickest thing. The daughter is cute but Pip is a freaking liar

Claudia Zhong says: I was about to let this woman live with me but thank GOD I read these posts first and OP stopped me! Her pattern is disgusting and sick. I'm so grateful this community saved me from her b/c I totally would have let her move in. I really needed the cash. Thank God I didn't! The fact that she's still doing this is so messed up. I wish someone could stop her but she's just so freaking sneaky and unless she's breaking an actual law and we can catch her, it's impossible! UGH!! I feel for the person who gets taken in by her next!

My hand drops the phone onto the bed. I let my covers bury it.

The person taken in by her next. The person taken in by her next is *me*.

But that's not what I'm focused on. I know I've been taken in by her. That's not news. The only thing I care about now is that I've found it, finally. The mother lode. Confirmation. Validation. This is me feeling suddenly very much like I have found the smoking gun that will allow me to get Pip out of my house forever.

I can't believe it. This was here, all along. If only I'd known to search for it—to search "Baker," to keep looking, combing the internet. But I didn't know, and how could I have? Most of these people didn't do a Google search, either, or at least not one specific enough to find all *this*. Claudia Zhong did, but she's the lucky one. The rest . . .

Pip screwed them over exactly the way she's been screwing me.

When I stop to think about it, really think about it . . . we were all, except Claudia, taken in by a master manipulator. An expert. A bona fide con artist. This didn't happen to me because I was too hasty to look her up. It wasn't because I was naive.

It's because Pip is a *professional*. And it's not my fault. They called her a criminal, didn't they? A piece of shit. What she's done to me *has* been the worst kind of shitty. She's heartless, ruthless. She's completely devoid of empathy, and worse than that, she knows how to *project* empathy when she clearly lacks it, on a fundamental level.

Is she a sociopath? A psychopath?

I have no idea how she'd be characterized, not officially, but I don't need to in order to understand what I already do, deep down in my bones.

She is either so insane that she has no idea how cruelly she is conning people.

Or she does know, and she's so calculating and cunning as to truly be evil.

Pip has shown me nothing since she moved in except that she's conniving, a first-class liar. But Nathan . . . *Nathan*.

With this new information in hand, it's becoming harder for me to believe his death was a coincidence.

The man died less than a week after she moved in.

No one *else* in this building is the subject of a Nextdoor post warning the general public about her sociopathic tendencies. No one else could possibly lack Pip's moral clarity. People like Pip, who con and lie and cheat so relentlessly, over and over—they are rare.

And sneaky. And secretive.

And that's what makes them so deadly.

Still, does that mean . . . Is she capable of murder?

I pull out the thousand dollars from my pocket and bring up my "PIP" Google Doc, dropping all these Nextdoor posts in it.

Then I change the name of the file. From "PIP" to "Evidence."

Chapter 26

I'm googling like a madwoman. The idea started taking shape earlier in the day, but now it's crystallized in my mind.

I know exactly what I'll be spending the bracelet money on. It only takes me a couple of searches to find who I need. Two service providers I reach out to right away. Can they do a job for me, tomorrow? Both are responsive, and within minutes we're texting. I'd need them here tomorrow around 10 a.m. Am willing to pay extra for speedy service.

The next morning, I set my plan in motion. I've asked Jack to do me one more favor. Could he text this number—I gave him Pip's—and ask to meet her for a tutoring job? Pretend he has a middle schooler. Say it's an emergency, the kid is this close to failing out. He can say he got her number from Desi's mom, who called Pip's services "a lifesaver."

Jack texts me at 7 a.m. that it's done, and Pip's already agreed to meet him and his fictional kid, Clara, at 9:30 a.m. on the dot in Hayward. It's far enough away that without a car, she's going to have to take Caltrain, which means getting up early and getting moving. For a brief moment I panic that she won't take his bait—what if she's even less hungry for work than she pretends? But my racing heartbeat settles again when I see her rushing to get ready, scooting Sofie out the door for school, and following her out with a travel coffee mug in her hand.

Obviously, there will be no Clara when she arrives, but Jack's prepared for that, with a long story and some other stall tactics that will keep her out of my hair for the necessary couple of hours.

Joe from Bay Movers pulls up in his truck twenty minutes after Pip's gone. I let him in, explain how urgently this must get done. A twenty-something dude with some dramatic tats on his arms who's honestly pretty attractive shoots me a smile and promises he's the fastest there is. He's agreeable, easy. I direct him around the condo while his coworker brings up boxes and has Pip and Sofie's books, clothes, and other items neatly packed up within the hour. I could have called 1-800-Junk, could have tossed all their things into a landfill, but I'm too nice. Besides, I hate waste. I don't have a problem with them going to get their things later. As long as I never see them again.

I decide to leave their coffee maker. Whoops.

A text rolls in from Jack.

All is well.

I don't know what he's told her or how he's kept her occupied, but I thank my lucky stars for a friend like Jack. True blue. Not many people would drop everything to help me out with a tenuous and morally gray scheme like this. But he knows it's important. I told him as much, without going into too many details.

While Joe hauls all Pip's things away, I peel off the right number of bills to pay them for their work, and to store the stuff for a couple of days. I'm not sure what I'll do with it after that—maybe I'll tell Pip she can text them if she wants it back. Like with a towed car, she'll have to pay any balance on the account—but for now, I don't care.

Next to arrive is Saul the locksmith. He's more than happy to change the lock on the front door and hand me two shiny new keys to it, which I slip on my key ring.

"There was a death in this building," I whisper. "A murder. I just don't feel safe."

Saul doesn't seem fazed—maybe he's heard it all before? Says I'll feel like a new person once the locks are changed.

If only he knew.

Saul's work only takes about an hour, and when he finishes, I bolt the front door and collapse on my living room couch.

I've spent most of the thousand dollars, but I have no regrets.

My condo is mine again. Pip and Sofie's things are gone. They won't be able to get back in.

The lawyer mentioned all this to me that day on the phone. Said if I could get them out, and keep them out long enough, it would become harder and harder for them to establish residency. It's why I needed to make sure I didn't let *them* run *me* out of my home. If I stayed away for too long, camped out at Alli's or Jack's or went to a hotel, I'd be risking them gaining ground, racking up an argument as to why this was officially their home.

I look around the room, finally scrubbed of Pip and Sofie's paraphernalia, and feel like, for the first time since Pip stepped in that door, I can breathe again. The fire that had been rising up this past week, the embers igniting with every new injustice, every new egregious manipulation on Pip's part, have suddenly, effortlessly, dissipated.

It's divine.

My house, my space. I still have to find a way to pay back what I owe so I can keep it, so I don't let Aunt Viv down. But for a moment—one small, peaceful moment—I feel like myself again. I'm not naive enough to think Pip won't try to get back in here, that she won't pound on the door and demand I open it. I have an eviction notice at the ready. It wouldn't hold up in court, but Jack's helped me make it look *quite* convincing. Over text last night, he even helped me get the fonts, city letterhead, and paper weight just so. If and when she shows up here, I will slide it under the door, if I have to, and threaten to call the police.

I walk over to Pip's Breville, sitting there on the counter. There are crumbs left there from Pip's hasty breakfast making this morning. Did she bother to sweep them up? Of course not.

I tamp my dark roast coffee and make sure it's compact in the filter. I didn't keep this Breville monstrosity as some sort of victory spoil. I'll sell it and use the money for the mortgage—after I drink this one last cup.

I'm sitting down on my threadbare couch, surrounded by my memories of Viv, and the days Seth and I spent here, at our happiest, when my phone rings.

I don't recognize the number, and for a moment I worry it's Pip, somehow.

I answer, wary. "Hello?"

"Is this Emily Hawthorne?"

I tense. "Yes?"

"Emily. It's Detective Mason. How've you been?"

My chest feels like it's on fire again. So much for the momentary infusion of Zen I was experiencing. "I'm fine. Did you need something?"

"Actually, yes. Can you come down to the police station, as soon as possible? We have a few follow-up questions. Nothing serious. If you have the time."

Those last words are a courtesy, I know. They aren't asking me if I have time, they are telling me I'm being summoned. Now.

"Is thirty minutes from now good?" I ask, trying to control the trembling in my voice.

"Perfect. We'll see you then. And Emily . . ."

"Yes?"

"Don't worry." Detective Mason hangs up, and I'm left staring at my phone screen.

Don't worry? I bet he says that to everyone. Well, guess what, Detective Mason. I'm worried.

I flop on my couch, feeling the empty, light space that had freed up in my chest begin to fill with dread.

I cannot believe I have to speak to the police again. At the station this time, no less. Do I need a lawyer? I can't even begin to afford one. Do they appoint you one, if you can't pay for one yourself? No, I think that's only if they charge you with a crime . . . Didn't I hear on a podcast recently that Amanda Knox got screwed because they let her speak without one, and they manipulated her into saying all that stuff that never happened? That was in Italy, but still, you're never supposed to talk to the police without a lawyer, not about a murder, anyway . . .

Alli's voice rings in my ears. She hasn't said it, doesn't even know she needs to, but God, if she were here. She'd be lawyering me up faster than I could get off the phone with Mason.

But I can't ask her for help. She doesn't have the funds either. No one in my life has the kind of funds you'd need for that. And besides, I'm *not* a suspect. Am I?

Would they even tell me if I was? What about Pip? Has she gotten this same call? I find myself wishing I could ask her. Then remind myself: I can't trust her, not even a little. We're alibis, but that word is meaningless.

I'm so focused on gathering what I need to head to the station—wallet, ID, laptop, bag—that I don't register Jack's text.

Pip's on her way back

Chapter 27

PIP

The next step in Pip's Project Normality was the security of a stable household, at least for a while, and that included a father figure for Sofie.

She tried to look at this as a glass-half-full sort of situation. Given that Sofie's actual father was one of two dirtbags, and that she had the opportunity to start fresh, she might as well choose from all the available men out there and find the ideal candidate.

Pip had no illusions that this man she found—whoever he was— would ever share half the parenting responsibilities or hold the same level of importance in her daughter's life that she did. He would be a "sometimes" presence in Sofie's life, which was how she wanted it. Sofie was *hers*. She had given birth to her and had raised her thus far, and she'd be damned if she was going to give up her control. She'd never trusted men, period, and she wasn't about to start now. But there were certainly holes a stepfather could fill. He could provide financial security and accompany Sofie to father-daughter dances, and if he stuck around for the long haul, they might one day send out a joint holiday card, the type of family portrait that showed the world you had made it. Pip hated those cards with the passion of a thousand suns. She also very badly wanted to send one.

Ultimately, what she wanted was for her child to never feel she was lacking. Sofie lacked so much: Siblings, a real dad, a mom with a steady, lucrative job. A big house in the suburbs with a lawn and a swing set and disposable income and regular trips to Disneyland. If there was any one part that Pip could rectify by interviewing, dating, and ultimately winning the love of a respectable, kind man, she was willing to do the heavy lifting.

Even if the guy sucked.

Pip's actual affection for this man, whoever he turned out to be, was irrelevant. What mattered was that he was stable. That he had a steady, well-paying job, and stellar health benefits, in a field that had long-term viability. He had to be cultured, nice enough, and, at his core, a good person who wouldn't screw her or her daughter over.

It was a pretty short list of qualities. Pip was sure she could find this man. It would just take time.

It did take time—several years, if she was counting. She always met these guys for coffee when Sofie was at school, never taking time away from her child. Sofie and Pip were rarely apart, if at all. The few times when she took things to the next level with any of these men, agreeing to go on an evening date or up to their apartment for a drink and sex, she made sure she wrapped things up efficiently, by 10 p.m., retrieved Sofie from her friend's house before it got too late, or relieved the babysitter in a prompt manner.

Pip took the concept of speed dating to the next level. She could have dinner with a guy, sizing him up with a list of strategic questions she'd honed carefully, questions that, much like in a job interview, elicited the targeted information that she was looking for. Once in the man's apartment, she could assess his domain with a quick glance around the living room. Was it furnished with IKEA fare, indicating he was a tried-and-true bachelor, or was this a real home? Was the TV massive, taking up an entire wall—signaling a sports fanatic—or was it modest? Was the house clean? She looked for just enough dust to ensure he wasn't an excessive neat freak, but conversely, she wouldn't dream of cleaning up after a pig. If she found the apartment unacceptable, she'd make up an excuse to leave, immediately. If it met her standards, she'd stay for sex. Quick, dirty, less than ten minutes, and she'd be out the door, back to Sofie, and her life.

The irony of all this is that Pip didn't find Mike on a dating app. It was an organic meeting, one she hadn't banked on. The truth is, she sort of didn't hate him. He wasn't hot in any traditional sense. His teeth were crooked, and he had a bit of a goofy smile. He also had a quiet confidence, in spite of his shortcomings. He was older; this was good. Closer to forty than thirty, divorced. He liked kids but hadn't desired his own, which was what had driven him and his previous wife apart. Mike admitted he was afraid of messing a kid up. His own childhood had been rocky, and he was sure it was his parents' fault.

Sofie, however . . . he loved the idea of Sofie. He practically lit up when Pip showed him her photo. He thought babies sounded insufferable and didn't want to be tied down to a child with no "out." But a kid who was at least partially formed already . . . *that* he could get on board with.

Bingo, Pip thought. This guy doesn't want more children, and neither do I. He can't commit to them, which means he'll only be peripherally involved in Sofie's life. Available for the holiday card and the dance. He won't dream of getting in the way of Pip's parenting.

It was a gamble. She had no way of knowing if this Mike would turn out to be the father figure she constructed on paper, but she was willing to give it a try.

She even let him meet Sofie.

That had gone exceptionally well, Pip thought. Mike had come over and played board games with them. He'd brought wine for Pip and a shiny new pack of playing cards for Sofie, which she loved. Four months later, Pip could not stop pinching herself. Mike had stuck around, and he was *good.*

She felt bad for him, at least a bit. He had no idea what she was capable of.

But this was the way it would be. The way it had to be.

If this worked out the way she hoped, it would be the only time in her life, besides Sofie's birth, when she felt the universe was looking out for her.

Chapter 28

I leave the police station feeling clammy. Mason grilled me for what felt like hours.

I check my watch. It's almost 1 p.m. I was there a mere forty-five minutes, but every second I sat in that interrogation room, across from Detective Mason, with his inscrutable facial expressions, was torture.

Not least because every question, every comment, reminded me how cruel and tragic Nathan's death, his murder, truly was. I thought of telling Mason all about Pip, what I was learning about her . . . but I wasn't ready yet to present the ammunition I'd gathered. Not until I'd had time to analyze it, figure out what it all meant.

I answered Mason's questions to the best of my ability. Was I sure I hadn't left the house between the hours of 5 and 10 p.m.? Had I seen anyone suspicious coming or going from Nathan's apartment? Did I hear anything? Spy anything unusual?

My answer to all these was no. But bile rose up in my throat with every interrogation. I could hear Alli's, Jack's, and Seth's voices in my head, outraged that I hadn't called a lawyer. But I don't know any lawyers, besides Seth's dad. And after what I did to him . . . dumping him less than a week before our wedding . . . there's no way I could ask that favor.

I'd have to take my chances. And I did. Mason assured me this was all standard, that they always had follow-ups after questioning those in the immediate vicinity of the murder.

"How do you . . . know?" I asked.

"Know what?" he asked, crossing his arms over his chest and staring back at me. The room was so sterile, just like on a police procedural. Sterile, and surreal. If I weren't a suspect, or a potential suspect, why couldn't he have asked me these questions over the phone?

"How do you know he was murdered? Couldn't he have simply . . . fallen?"

"We can tell by his positioning. His injuries. That sort of thing," Mason answered lightly, as though I'd asked him what he'd eaten for breakfast.

Now, as I make my way home in a daze, I hope I didn't mess up, didn't say something that contradicted what Pip had already told them. Who *knows* what she told them?

I race home. I have to get my head on straight, not let Mason's questioning derail me. I check my phone: Jack texted me again, telling me to watch out for Pip, and that she'd likely be back at the condo by 1 p.m. It's 1:30 now.

I pull my keys from my purse, feeling the weight of the shiny new silver keys to my condo, reminding myself that I've done it, Pip won't have a way in.

She and Sofie will simply have to find someone else to con, someone else to drop in on, someone else to bail them out.

I run toward my condo, picking up the pace with every footfall, even as my knee begins to throb. I've pushed it too hard these past few days, but I can't stop to worry about it. I need to get back, to hold down the fort, to lay my claim on my house—in case Pip tries something.

My head is starting to pound, as I realize I haven't eaten a single thing today. I've been too busy trying to get my home, my life back.

I reach my condo by two o'clock, stopping in my tracks, panting, out of breath, every atom in my being pulsing from how hard I've pushed myself.

I notice that the police tape is gone, the chalk perimeter washed away. I'm relieved, but then I feel the wind being knocked out of me. Standing in the spot where Nathan died are an older couple and a man who looks to be in his twenties, and I know, in an instant, who they are. Nathan's family. I recognize the younger man, vaguely, as Nathan's little brother from the Grand Canyon photo that lived on his desk. The parents flank the brother on either side, the dad with his arm around his son. He's attractive, with salt-and-pepper hair and thick glasses, and his wife is slim, although frankly, she's gaunt. Her outfit is put together, a soft cardigan over loose black pants. They both look wrecked, and how could they not?

Facing them right now feels wrong. I didn't know him, not like they did. What could I possibly have to offer them in the way of comfort? And yet, I know I must. I start toward them, but before I can cross the last few feet to reach them, someone else advances and cuts me off, gunning straight toward them.

She's reached them, now, has her arms around the mom. The dad wipes a tear from his eye, and the brother, who looks stricken, says something to my roommate that I can't hear.

What. The. Actual. Fuck.

I shouldn't be surprised. This is Pip's pattern. Her game, the one she plays with the skill and ingenuity of a card counter at blackjack.

When did she ingratiate herself to Nathan's family? The thought of her doing that, in her cool, calculated way, makes me sick.

"Emily!" she calls out, having spotted me.

Has she tried her key yet? Does she know yet what I've done? If she does, she's not letting on.

"Come meet Nathan's family. I told them we're all here, all of us from the building, to offer as much moral support as they need."

"It's so shocking," the mom says as Pip squeezes her hand. "We don't understand. How? Who? Nathan wasn't mixed up in anything illegal or sketchy. He was good. My good, good boy . . ." She breaks down in sobs, and Pip folds her arms around her.

My God. How can this woman live with herself? She's so two faced I honestly can't look at her. The way she paints herself as some paragon of virtue when she's literally a vile manipulator.

"I'm so sorry," I say, feeling numb but knowing I must speak before it seems odd, or I come off as insensitive. Here is Pip, putting on this whole fake song and dance freak show for this devastated family, and I can barely string two words together. "Nathan was a wonderful guy. Honestly, his loss, I know it's incalculable."

"Thank you," the father speaks up. "We appreciate that."

"We'll find whoever did it," Nathan's younger brother says. I stiffen. The brother has seemed to come out of his trance long enough to say the words that shake me to my core. Not because I have anything to worry about. But because it's a reminder to me of how real all this is. How unresolved. And how tied I am to the woman who's pretending to comfort them in their hour of need.

A prickling sense of dread starts to crawl up my spine. There's something about Pip, here, now, that makes me suspicious of her in a whole new way.

Did she do it? Murder Nathan?

"Do the police, I mean Mason . . . Does he have any leads?" I ask, feeling shameful for asking this of Nathan's family. It's not their job to have to educate me on the case of who murdered their son, their brother. But there's no one else to pose this question to. I can't possibly ask Mason. I don't want the police engaging with me any more than is absolutely necessary.

"I don't think we should discuss the case with strangers," the brother says, looking me straight in the eye.

"These aren't strangers, honey," says the mom, who puts a hand on her son's shoulder. "You're Nathan's neighbors . . . Right?" Through her heartbroken expression, she is forcing lightness. I get it. She's still in that phase of grief where she's hanging on to every last tidbit about her loved one. She's hoping I can give her some memories of her son that she didn't already know about, that she can file away for a rainy day in the not-too-distant future, when she will be past the denial phase of his death and living through the dark days of her worst nightmare.

I know because I've been there. Twice.

For years, I told myself that my parents dying in such proximity to each other, rather than one of them leaving the other to live for another forty years, alone, was oddly a gift, because I imagined them in on some secret pact where they'd agreed to leave this earth at exactly the same time. That was all bullshit, of course, a yarn I spun, an interior monologue I fabricated so that I wouldn't crawl into a hole and never return. There was certainly no gift, only highway robbery. I'll never forget the moment my dad told me about his diagnosis. It was on the day of Mom's memorial. We were home afterward, in our cozy house in the Inner Richmond, where I'd grown up, and it cracked him in half having to reveal to me that he, too, had cancer. That his, too, was incurable.

Those odds were cruel. Outrageous. How the dice had been rolled this way, leaving me parentless at sixteen, is not something I'll ever reconcile.

But here I am, sixteen years later, having lived as much of my life without them as with them. I'm a member of that club I never wanted to join, that no one ever does, and now Nathan's family has joined it too. Only, their son has been murdered. It's too heinous, too unfair. Mother Nature took my parents, but this—if Nathan were truly killed, then it was a pointless waste of a life. Preventable. The worst type of death possible.

"Let us know if we can help," I offer. "We are so sorry for your loss. So very sorry."

"Can we make you dinner?" Pip has clasped Nathan's mom's hands in her own. It's like watching a train wreck.

"Thank you, dear. We have a dinner reservation nearby. But that's very kind of you."

"Please. It's the least I can do. I was fond of your son. I'd like to say we had a special connection." Pip is hugging the mom now, and it's all I can do not to scream. How long does Nathan's mother even think Pip's lived here? The whole thing is an insane rewriting of history, playing out before my very eyes.

Nathan's family walks off, and Pip turns to me, slinging her bag over her arm like she hasn't got a care in the world. She smiles. "How'd it go with Mason?"

Chapter 29

My heart pounds as Pip follows me up the stairs.

I haven't said a word. I'm rolling *her* words around in my head. Mason? How the hell did she know I met with Mason?

He must have met with her too. It's the only explanation.

Two minutes ago, I thought about walking away. I considered it. Turning around and sprinting down to Beans, letting Pip discover the locked door on her own. I didn't need, or want, to see it live. Her face as she realized her key no longer worked. Her confusion, which would morph into realization, and ultimately anger. I don't want that anger directed at me, not in person, anyway.

But walking away would have made it seem like I was giving up. Surrendering. I want to stay and fight for my home, my freedom, my sanity. Not slink away like a coward.

Maybe seeing her reaction will buoy me. Maybe it is actually what I need, and deserve.

We reach our landing, and I press open the door to the hallway. Pip is right on my heels, and I fear my own nerves are showing in my body language. It's about to be the moment of truth. I will say I don't have my key, and can she open the door?

Then she will discover what I've done.

Pulse racing, we approach the door. I root around in my bag, act surprised.

"I don't have my keys. Must have left them inside. Can you . . . ?" It's my best acting. I should win an Academy Award.

"Sure." Pip shrugs. She roots for her keys in her bag. I stare, watching, waiting, feeling my heartbeat in my eardrums.

Then she pulls out a key, sticks it in the lock, turns it . . .

And it opens.

She strides inside, where Sofie's sitting in a straddle position on the ground, leaning forward flexibly on her elbows, her homework laid out in front of her.

I don't move. I can't. It's like I'm experiencing this moment through the wrong end of a telescope. What is happening? How can this be?

Pip tosses her keys on the console, slings her bag on the ground.

I feel my reality starting to slip, and slide, like I can't get a foothold, or a handhold, or any sort of hold on what's happening.

"Sofie called a locksmith. You know—to fix whatever issue was going on with the front door."

"She called . . . a locksmith."

Pip turns to meet my eyes. "She was confused when she came home early from school again—the bullies, those girls suck—and her key didn't work. Did you know there are emergency locksmiths who can come get you in within the hour? They charge twice as much—here's the bill, it's $526 when you get a chance . . . but they work *fast*. And when Sofie explained this is her house, well, who wouldn't believe a twelve-year-old? By the time I got back from that wild-goose chase you sent me on, the locksmith was already here. Easy-peasy!"

I'd sink down on the floor and completely melt into a puddle if I weren't so enraged.

A locksmith changed the locks again for them. Just like that.

Sofie was so cute. And Pip, I'm sure, was so *charming*.

You can convince people to do almost anything for a quick buck. Or 526 of them.

Oh, my God. All that money I spent. Viv's bracelet. All that effort . . . no, no, no. I won't berate myself. It was necessary. She threw a punch, proved herself once again a formidable foe. I will get back up, and punch back.

"We don't really need our things, by the way. It's just stuff. We'll be lighter this way! Breezier. Glad you kept the Breville, though. Good call." And she walks over to brew herself a cup.

———

I'm at Beans, my laptop in front of me, my eyes glazing over as I stare at my search engine. She's a lunatic. A *lunatic*. I can't believe she bested me. She outsmarted me, again. And my plan . . . it had been so foolproof. Hadn't it?

Pip must have seen through Jack right away. It's the only explanation. She must have gotten in touch with Sofie, texted her on her Apple Watch and told her to come home. Then Sofie waited for me to leave the house—to see Mason—and that's when she pounced. Called the locksmith. Made up a sob story, said I was her mom . . . Who the hell knows? Do they have copies of my ID? My bills? It's not like I've tried to keep any of my things private from them. She could have used any amount of documentation to convince a locksmith to let her in. Maybe she told him there was a dying pet inside. Whatever she said, it had the desired effect.

Is this what they did to all those other people on Nextdoor? I haven't tried reaching out to them, but I'm desperate enough now to do it, should have done it already. I log in to the app on my phone. Those posters might be some of the only people who can help me, now. If I can get even more proof of Pip's lies, her grifting, her conning, I can present it all to Mason with my "Evidence" doc. Put the pressure on him to investigate *her* for Nathan's murder, not me.

Especially because I highly suspect she did it.

I go to the OP Squatter post, and as I scroll down to the bottom, desperate for something, anything I might have missed the first time around—I see it.

A comment that wasn't there before. Or else, I missed it. That's entirely possible.

It's by a woman named Tabitha. She has no photo, only the provided Nextdoor purple "T" for the first letter of her first name.

> Penelope Baker/Stone and her daughter caused me more distress than I'd ever imagined possible. I can't emphasize enough what a terrible person she is. She literally ruined my life.

I don't know what it is about this particular comment that makes my heart lurch. Maybe it's because I relate to it in a way that makes it feel visceral, like I could have written it. I can almost feel this Tabitha's desperation seeping out through her words. And not just her words, but those she *hasn't* said. Pip ruined her life? How? When? This doesn't sound like a cut-and-dried example of a grifter who refused to pay rent. This sounds so much worse. More distress than she ever imagined possible?

That's me. That could *be* me.

I click on Tabitha's profile, eager to find out more about her.

There's nothing. She hasn't filled in much of her personal information at all, only stating the bare minimum, that she lives in the neighborhood, which you have to do when you sign on to Nextdoor. It's the whole point of the app, to connect to others in your immediate vicinity.

I could DM her. It's what I do now, my MO—isn't it? Sliding into the DMs of people I barely know? Hoping they'll write back and not block me?

I hit the message button on her profile page—noting this is the only post she's commented on in the past couple of years—and stare at the blank message box.

I don't have time to waste, not a second to spare. I'm just going to have to wing it.

Hi, I write. I'm Emily and I saw what you commented on Laura's post about Penelope Stone, Penelope Baker, whatever you want to call her. Can we meet? I don't know if I can even bring myself to tell you this—you're one of the only people I've admitted this to—but I'm Penelope's latest con. And worse than that. She might be a killer.

I hit send, but I don't stop there. I wonder how I must look to the patrons waiting at the counter for their coffees: my clothes falling off me, unshowered, hair in a ratty bun, cowering at this table, shivering. If they think I'm a disaster of a person who needs major help, they won't be far off base. But I don't care. I begin DMing all the others who commented. I give them a similar version of what I wrote to Tabitha. Can we speak? Can they get in touch with me? We'll only take her down if we band together.

And anyway, I add. I may be living with a murderer.

———

I get a ping on my phone. It's from Nextdoor. Heart in my throat, I click on it.

You're in Noe Valley? Can you meet now?

I feel my chest tighten. Tabitha's written me. She wants to *meet*.
Absolutely, I type back so fast I jumble all the letters and have to start over. Where?

We can't meet at my house, but how about the wine bar on the corner of 24th and Sanchez? Ten minutes?

Yes, I type. I'll be there.

Good. Because I need you to understand something: you are not safe in your home.

Chapter 30

Tabitha's words haunt me, ring in my ears as I head toward Toast, my brain spinning, my body feeling like it's running purely on adrenaline, now. My home isn't safe. If Pip did this, really did this, killed a man in cold blood—how can I go back there?

I run my meeting with Mason over and over in my mind, grasping for specific words I can't remember now. If only I had a recording, could remember exactly what we both said.

Does he really think I did it? It feels so implausible—I'm a yoga teacher. A law-abiding daughter and niece who wouldn't hurt a fly, hardly even eats meat. But Mason doesn't know that. There's no explanation for why he could possibly think I'd do it . . .

Unless.

Unless Pip has *given* Mason a reason. A reason why I hated Nathan enough to murder him.

Unless she's lied, strategically fabricated some story about me. A motive.

I feel my stomach drop like a stone to my feet.

I don't have to think too hard to know why she'd set me up. It's because she fears being the prime suspect herself.

Which can only mean one of two things. Either she's throwing suspicion off herself because she's a con artist who'd stop at nothing to make sure she doesn't go down for a murder she didn't commit.

Or it's because she *is* the murderer.

My chest is constricting like a vise is being squeezed around my rib cage. Am I living with a killer? Is that the truth that's been staring me in the face this entire time? Have I simply been too naive to see it, to recognize it?

But how? And when? Pip was with me that night, the entire time. Wasn't she?

The truth is, I don't know. Not really. My head aches from lack of food and caffeine, I'm cold, and I can barely see my phone six inches in front of me, the screen looking blurred and washed out as I walk, racking my brain. Think, Emily. Think.

She wasn't sitting next to me the *entire* time. We paused *White Lotus* to use the bathroom a couple of times, and once or twice she left the living room to check on Sofie, to bring her tray of dinner scraps back to the kitchen. At one point, Pip was gone for about ten minutes; isn't that what I told Mason the day Nathan died? She looked annoyed that time, muttering something about having to yank Sofie's earbuds from her ears and force her to focus on homework, not Roblox with her friends. I barely paid attention, was so angry at her for everything she'd already put me through.

What time did that happen? When did she leave the couch, then return?

There's no way I can recall, not in that kind of detail.

The thought terrifies me. Because if I can't remember, precisely, then I can't help myself. And if I can't defend myself, or prove Pip did this to Nathan . . . What does that mean for me?

People have gone to prison on a suspicion. It happens—wasn't the podcast *Serial* all about that? Innocent people spend decades, their lives even, behind bars, especially when the police are desperate for a suspect and eager to pin it on some obvious person so they can wrap up the case and give the public, and the victim's family, what they really want: someone to blame.

I can only imagine the lies Pip might have told Detective Mason about me. She's a master at this, isn't she? Always at the ready with a convenient story whenever the need strikes. As sneaky and cunning as they come. But I have ammunition. So much evidence I've amassed. The Nextdoor posts. Pip's lies on her résumé. I can show all this to Mason. And I will, when the time is right.

I've arrived at Toast, the wine bar five blocks from my house, a bell jingling as I walk through. It's a cozy, dimly lit spot with booths and a jukebox in the back, likely decorative at this point, but giving off a strong eighties vibe. I've lived in this neighborhood for sixteen years but have never set foot in this joint, not once. I'm not a wine bar person. I don't drink much, and when Seth and I did share a bottle of vino, it was usually at home, curled up on the couch, watching one of our favorite shows or playing a board game. Monopoly was our favorite. It took hours and gave us an excuse to put our phones down and just be together.

My chest aches at the memory, but I resist it. I can't let myself dissolve into a puddle, not now. If I don't find a way to prove to the police that I didn't do this . . . that I'm the last person who would have ever killed Nathan . . . I shudder to think of what could happen to me. Without a fancy lawyer . . . I could be toast. Just like this bar. The truth is, even my friends can't help me. Alli and Jack are well off, but not well off enough to pay half a million dollars in lawyer's fees. I know that's how much it costs to defend someone in a murder trial.

So I cannot let it get to that point.

I scan the room for Tabitha. I have no idea what she looks like, not even one clue, but the bar is pretty much empty. I spot two guys at one booth sharing a bottle of wine and some appetizers, the bartender with his back turned to me as he rattles a cocktail shaker, and a woman in the back, silver haired, wearing a fleece jacket, her face buried in her phone. It must be her.

Pulse in my throat, I walk toward her, feeling like I'm inching toward a future I can't imagine and almost don't want to. This woman may tell me exactly what I need—or she may have nothing. I brace myself for the latter but pray to the universe she will have something, anything, I can use to dig myself out of the hole I've sunken into.

"Tabitha?" I clear my throat, certain I sound as wrecked as I feel. She looks up at me.

"I'm Emily," I say quietly as I move closer to her booth. "May I?" She nods, and I sit down.

"Aren't you freezing?" She seems surprised by me, and I don't know why. Maybe it's because I look like I climbed out of a swamp.

"I'm a bit cold," I admit. I'm in a thin T-shirt, it's nearly 10 p.m., and it's fifty degrees out. "Thanks for meeting me," I say quickly. "Look, I know this is unusual, but—"

Tabitha waves me off as if to shush me, then takes a folded piece of paper out of her purse. It's wrinkled, and one corner is torn. She unfolds it, then lays it out in front of me.

I read silently.

Mom, we broke up. I'm gonna take off for a while. Need to clear my head. I love you and will see you when I get back, so don't worry.

I look up at her, not comprehending. If there are two halves of a whole to put together, I don't get what they are.

"My son," Tabitha explains. "He left me this note last year."

"Oh." I feel my cheeks flushing. I suddenly feel awkward, like I've walked into something unfamiliar and uncomfortable. Why is Tabitha showing me this? I'm a stranger. A complete nobody to her.

"It wasn't out of the ordinary for him," she goes on, unsmiling. I notice lines around her eyes and mouth, laugh lines, perhaps, though she looks weary, far from laughing, now. "My son isn't exactly a kid— he's practically middle aged. He rented a room from me, in the building I own. It's small, a couple of units, has been in our family for decades. It's not like I kept tabs on him all the time. But what *is* strange is that he never texted or called, not once after he left this letter on my kitchen counter . . . nothing. And he still hasn't come home. That was eight months ago. It's the longest I've ever gone without hearing from him."

A feeling I can't name starts to creep from my chest to my lungs, filling me, energizing me. I don't know if it's adrenaline or simply fear, but whatever it is, it causes me to grasp the table so hard my knuckles lose their color.

"Was Pip, I mean, Penelope . . ." I let out a massive breath, afraid to speak more, but knowing I have to. "Was she also your tenant?"

Tabitha nods. "She lived in my building for a year. And—here's the kicker. She dated my son."

I feel a tightness in my lungs that threatens to undo me.

"Fuck," I say, letting the word out in something akin to a long, low moan.

"Exactly," she says, picking up her glass of red wine and taking a careful sip. "He seemed happy, I suppose, but I wasn't. She never paid rent. Not once."

"Of course she didn't."

"He fell for her, my son. Even proposed, got down on one knee and everything. I got bad vibes from the day she and her daughter moved in, but he was lonely and vulnerable. Needy, and sensitive, too sensitive. He always said he never wanted kids, but I think he was taken in by them . . . by the idea of them. This sweet duo who had nothing, who needed saving. Like maybe they were the thing to bring him out of his funk, and it was fated or some baloney. His ex left him, you know, because he told her he wouldn't be a good dad. Thought his childhood had been lonely, which, of course, I blame myself for. We couldn't have more children . . ." She takes a sip of wine. Seems to steel herself. "Sorry—I can't help going over every inch of this, judging all my past actions when I know it's useless. What can I say, my son's always been hopeful, an optimist. Sees the good in people. Even some people who don't deserve it. I used to love that about him. Now . . ."

"I don't know what to say. Is he . . . Where is he?" I'm afraid to ask, but ask I must.

Tabitha takes a final swig of the wine left in her glass. I focus on the red liquid, watching it slide down the side of the wineglass and disappear into her mouth. Bloodred, leaving a stain. "I don't know where my son is. But I have my suspicions."

I feel my heart beating wildly, erratically. What is this woman trying to tell me? What are her suspicions—that her son might be *dead*?

"How did you . . . get Pip out?" I focus on questions with answers that don't scare the living daylights out of me.

"They left, finally, on their own. After my son took off . . . it was only a few days later, suspiciously enough. Pip and Sofie moved out, took all their stuff, didn't pay me a dime. I never heard from them again. Which I can't say I'm sad about."

My heart sinks. Pip left voluntarily? It's so out of character for her, it makes me think she *did* have something to do with this guy disappearing.

"Did you tell the police? Is anyone looking for him?" I sputter.

"He's not considered missing, not since he left this note. He's an adult, so it takes a lot for anyone to care. The police told me he's not required to call his mommy every day."

I wince; I can't imagine that felt good to hear, when she's obviously sick with worry about him.

"What are you going to do?"

Tabitha takes the empty wineglass in her hand and squeezes it. I hope it doesn't crack between her fingers.

"What *can* I do?" She meets my eyes. Hers are glossy, now, with tears. "I've hired a PI. So far, he hasn't come up with anything, but he's determined as hell."

"She lives with me," I say, breathless. "She and Sofie, they live with me. And our downstairs neighbor, he died and . . . the police suspect foul play."

Tabitha stares at me with such steel in her eyes, I have to look away.

"Get out of there, Emily. Do whatever you have to. Protect yourself. It's all I can tell you. That girl's a nightmare. You have to do what you have to do."

I nod, wishing like hell I had a coat as I pull my arms across my chest and try to make the thin fabric of my shirt warm me, which is a pointless exercise.

"Thank you," I say. "For meeting me like this. I hope you find your son."

I get up and walk out of the near-empty bar without a look back.

Chapter 31

PIP

Kids are mean.

It was a known fact. Pip had been a child once, herself, and though she was never on the receiving end of any kind of bullying—she made sure of that by being tough as nails and ready to pounce on anyone who even tried to mess with her—she saw how many were tortured, humiliated, and even eviscerated by stupid, insecure classmates who smelled weakness.

She vowed never to let that happen to Sofie.

That's why she insisted her child always dress impeccably. That they never allow anyone to visit their home unless the person had been vetted, and they could be sure no one would leave their apartment telling tales about Sofie being poor, or trash, or even worse than those things—uncultured. Any friend who came to visit for a playdate would receive the royal treatment. Snacks, soda, a fun movie to watch, and an even funner "fun mom" who let the girls do their nails instead of homework, or who took them to the day spa for massages. Pip couldn't afford day spas, but if it meant she had to skip lunch and dinner for an entire week to make up the cost, it was worth it.

This was what she signed on to when she decided to have Sofie, to leave behind the Neanderthal druggies—one who'd raped her, the other who'd let it happen—to start a new life with her daughter. From that night the pregnancy test revealed a faint positive line, Pip never looked back. She grabbed some cash from her boyfriend's drawer, hopped in the car, and sped off. She was only twenty, and more than broke. With no college education, barely a high school diploma. But she possessed something else that none of the other losers in her life did: grit, which manifested in a fierce determination to make sure none of the awful shit that had happened to her would ever befall her child.

Call it mother's intuition or a lucky guess, but she knew from the moment she saw the positive pregnancy test that she was having a girl. She was having a daughter for a reason. Sofie would live the life that Pip had been meant to. Sofie would never—*never*—be taken advantage of.

All this was clear as she drove out of town in the beat-up Chevy that barely ran, the one her alcoholic dad had left her before he dropped dead of liver failure. It was her one valuable possession, and even then it was fit for the junkyard. She had nowhere to go. No relatives, none who were doing any better than she was. Most of them were addicts, or she'd lost track of where they even lived. She'd miss her mother, but not the woman's enabling. So many times, her mother could have taken Pip and her brother far away from their abusive excuse for a dad. It wasn't her fault. Pip knew this. It still didn't make it okay.

Over the years, it got harder and harder to be the mom she knew Sofie needed, but she grew more fiercely determined with every one of her daughter's birthdays.

She made sure Project Normality was her top priority, taking precedence over everything else. And once she found Mike and checked "potential stepdad" off her list of to-do items, she was on her way to achieving her ultimate goal. All she needed, now, was for Sofie to thrive.

Which meant the other kids loving her. Thriving meant Sofie being popular, accepted, admired. Not just smart, but gifted. Academically and socially superior, or at the very least, not attracting the wrong kind of attention.

Thriving meant that Pip sought out the best schools for Sofie—public, of course, because she never would have sent her child to be a scholarship student at one of those elite K–12s, where everyone would have looked down on her. No, thank you. But she knew which public schools were the best, and she zeroed in on them. She was intimately familiar with San Francisco's GreatSchools ranking, and she and Sofie chose where to rent their apartments based on the city's lottery system and their proximity to the best schools—only the best.

When it came to the other children, Pip couldn't control those little shits, but she *could* control how Sofie appeared, how she acted, and how she presented herself. Every morning, they had a ritual that Pip took as seriously as a heart attack. They'd stand in front of the bathroom mirror together, adjust their outfits, hair, and accessories, and recite a little mantra. "No one else is better than me."

Pip told Sofie it was the absolute truth, and that she should never forget it. They weren't empty words. Pip believed it, too. When it came to Sofie, Pip had complete clarity. She believed, with every fiber of her being, that Sofie was the most beautiful, precious human who'd ever set foot on this godforsaken earth, and Pip had been chosen to be her mom. She didn't buy into any of that spiritual crap, not really, but she did believe that Sofie was here to save her from something—the horrible men who had conned and abused her and left her for dead. The mother who didn't think she was worth protecting.

And so, in spite of the crushing weight of poverty and single motherhood, Pip never lost sight of her goal. It was her North-fucking-Star. Sofie was the one thing, the *only* thing, that mattered, and Pip would go to her grave knowing she'd done everything possible for her kid.

Even if it meant breaking the law.

Pip didn't do it often. Only when it was absolutely necessary.

The day things started to unravel, the day that will live on in Pip's memory as a sort of line being drawn in the sand, was the day Sofie came home from school sobbing about the mean girls. The ones who had stolen her lunch and tossed it in the dumpster, uneaten.

It was Pip's worst nightmare. Why had these asshole children done this? More importantly, why had they done it to her precious, gifted daughter? As she stared at Sofie, curled up on the couch, weeping from her distress, she berated herself. Had she not done enough for this pure and innocent being? Sofie was dressed adorably, in an outfit of the most current fashion, her long locks brushed and coiffed. Even at that age she was lanky, and elegant, and moved with sophistication. On top of that, Sofie was funny and perceptive, knowing how to get along with others and avoid conflict. What had happened?

"I don't know, Mom," Sofie sobbed into the couch pillow. "I kept looking for my bag in my locker, and when I finally figured out what was going on, it was too late. They'd thrown it in the trash."

"But did they have a *reason*?" Pip asked, appalled.

"No. They're just mean," Sofie cried.

In that moment, Pip knew that what she had done had not been enough, that Project Normality was not living up to her expectations, that she would have to take matters into her own hands.

Chapter 32

I've never felt so cold, so alone. I jog back to my apartment, my mind whirring with such intensity I almost can't bear it.

Did Pip set me up for murder? Is she the murderer herself?

I realize there could be a perfectly good explanation for what happened to Tabitha's son. We don't even know that he's missing, that anything's wrong at all. Maybe he left town because he was heartbroken over their breakup and needed a fresh start. As Tabitha said herself, he's a grown man. He has no obligation to stay nearby or inform his mother of his whereabouts.

Still, people usually act in line with their past patterns. Tabitha's words come back to me in a feverish rush. "It's the longest I've ever gone without hearing from him."

I can't get that sentence out of my mind as I jog over a crosswalk, barely checking for cars, chilled to the bone, my sneakers quite literally pounding the pavement. I'm starving, truly so hungry now, but still, the thought of food makes me want to retch. I'll try to put something in my stomach when I get to my house. I'll shower and change into clean clothes. Then I'll be able to think. I hope.

I'm a block from my home now. It's nearly 10:30 p.m., so I'm either going home tonight, or I'm not.

I remind myself that Pip could be a killer. Am I really going to knowingly return to the hornet's nest?

I stop in front of my building, trying as hard as I can to make sense of things, to be smart, to not let my fatigue and panic and fear overtake my critical thinking.

Am I in immediate danger if I go back inside? What if this is Pip's sick pattern? Moving into condos where she cons and manipulates, lies and steals, strikes up a relationship with an unsuspecting guy in the building—like Tabitha's son, and Nathan—and then *murders* them?

Is that why she rented the room from me? Why she changed her name, never settles down, always sneaks around finding new places to live . . . to *hide*? Never using her real name so she can never be pinned down . . . ?

Did Pip decide to live with me because she's on the run? I'm surely her latest con, not only because she's so entitled she thinks she can get away with never paying rent, but because this is how she lives—how she *must* live—if she's going to commit murders and dodge the police indefinitely.

I'm nearly home when my phone rings in my pocket. I startle, jump out of my skin.

It's Mason.

Well, if I have to talk to him again, if I have to be interrogated by him again . . . this time I can at least show him my "Evidence" doc. I can build my case against Pip. I can convince him she's the one he should be investigating, not me.

It's risky, but right now, it's all I've got.

"Hello?" I try to sound breezy, unaffected, though my body and brain are screaming anything but. "Detective Mason? Hi! I've been wanting to reach you!"

"You have?" he asks. I get the feeling he's surprised. Probably his suspects don't usually sound happy to see him.

"Yep, I'd love to talk to you. Better in person, though. Can I come down to the station?"

I feel like an impostor, like a different person entirely. I don't think Emily of two weeks ago would have ever thought I'd become so bold—so gives-no-fucks.

There's a pause on the other end. I think I hear Mason cover up the phone, then return, his breath audible in my ear.

"Sure. How's right now?"

———

I stopped at PO Plus on my way to the station and printed out the Google Doc. Better to come prepared with a paper trail.

Now, I sit across from Mason in the interrogation room.

I have the papers laid out in front of us on the Formica tabletop. The evidence. The proof.

"Every single person on here was scammed by her. Her name's not even Stone, it's *Baker*. She's a serial con artist. Lives in places and never pays a dime. And look at this—"

I pull out the results from GetVerifiedNow.com. They finally came in earlier today. Just in time.

"This shows major inconsistencies in her work history, none of which matches her LinkedIn page . . ." I pull out a printout of that too. "To be honest, I'm not sure if Baker's her real name either. She's opened bank accounts under fake names, which I'm pretty sure is a crime in itself. I've talked to her supposed former employers. They've never heard of her. You can contact Melanie Hopper directly, she's reached out to LinkedIn to report the fraud . . . and there's Tabitha. From Nextdoor. Her son, he's missing."

I'm so caught up in what I'm saying, so driven and convinced I'm doing the right thing, I only just now notice he's recording me.

It gives me pause. Maybe I should have called a lawyer. Could I have put *that* on a credit card?

Mason shuffles through the papers. "This is all . . ."

I'm alert, on edge. I'm expecting him to say it's all very relevant, and shocking. I'm expecting him to say he'll open up an investigation into her person ASAP.

"This is interesting, but—"

"Interesting? Excuse me, Detective, and sorry if this is inappropriate, but *what*? I've just given you oodles of evidence that my roommate is a freaking squatter and liar. If anyone had the capability to murder someone—it's her."

"Perhaps. But what would her motive have been?"

I stop in my tracks. She slept with him. But beyond that—it's true. I don't have a motive for Pip.

"We'll take this all under advisement. But in the meantime . . ."

I stare at Mason. Holy shit. I haven't convinced him of anything. And now . . . "I'm a suspect. That's what you're about to say, isn't it? Am I going to be arrested?" The words come out before I can stop them. It hadn't occurred to me until saying them that I might not go home tonight.

Or ever.

"You aren't being arrested. Not tonight."

Oh, good. That's a relief, I think cynically. I'm glad I can still go home to the condo I can't afford that's been taken over by a criminal.

Mason pushes a glass of water toward me. It's aggravating. *I'm not thirsty!* I want to scream at him, but I know better than to let myself show my emotions on my sleeve. It'll only make me look guiltier.

"So why am I *still* here, then?"

Mason sighs. "I'm getting to that. Believe me, I want to get out of here as much as you do."

Um, no.

"We have come across . . . information that makes us unable to discount the role you may have played in Nathan's death."

"Information? What kind of information?" I place my hands on the table, trying to steady myself. "Did Pip give this to you? My roommate? Because we just proved she's certifiable . . ."

"No," he interrupts. "She had nothing to do with it. We found it routinely, through our standard investigation."

It's only now that I see he has a piece of paper in hand. He sets it in front of me on the table.

"What is this?" I feel my eyes blur from fatigue as I try to make sense of what I'm looking at. Words on a page . . . typed words . . . not densely spaced. Not many words at all.

"It's a text thread," he says gently. "Between you . . . and the victim."

I stare at it, forcing my brain to compute what's on the page.

Emily: I thought I meant more to you

Emily: I thought you cared

Nathan: we talked about this, hooking up was a mistake & I'm sorry

Emily: you think of it as a mistake? Of me as a mistake? it didn't feel like you thought I was a mistake when we were hooking up

Nathan: I shouldn't have gotten involved with someone in my building. Major mistake on my part and I really regret it but we aren't a thing.

Emily: so you made the same mistake twice? Slept with Pip? She lives in our building too you know

Emily: you hurt me, really hurt me

That's it. That's the last line of the thread. There's nothing more.

I set the paper down, my head spinning. These aren't my words. I never, *ever* would have written anything like this. It's humiliating and not representative of how I feel. It's not *me*. Sure, I was pissed to learn

Nathan slept with Pip, but it wasn't like we were an item. My God—this makes me look desperate and pathetic and . . . *guilty*.

"I didn't write this!" I stand up from my chair. So much for keeping my emotions in check. But I'm not just panicked, I'm *angry*. Angry as hell.

"It came from your phone," Mason says, still emotionless. "Time stamped Thursday afternoon—the day of the murder—at one p.m."

One p.m. That's after I saw Nathan in the hall and had that little run-in with him. When I was gone . . . this would track, if it were real, which it 100 percent isn't.

"Check." Mason shrugs. "Go ahead. I'll wait."

I reach for my phone in my pocket. "It won't be there. It won't *be* there because I didn't write it!"

I open my text app and scroll to find Nathan's name. Clicking on it feels wrong. I should be texting him something flirty and fun, not trying to disprove I killed him . . . I shake the feeling off. It won't help me, not now.

I audibly gasp when I see it. There it is. Plain as day. The last thing I wrote to him are those words that, of course, I never did write: you hurt me, really hurt me.

"This is impossible."

"But the texts are there?"

I scroll back and wince as I see all of them, laid out right in front of me like a nightmare.

"I didn't type these. Someone must have cloned my phone!" I fold my arms over my chest, feeling like a caged animal in this stuffy, windowless room. "Or took it, and wrote this."

"But that's assuming someone would have had a reason to have done that," Mason says carefully. I want to throttle him for being so aloof when my entire life and future are on the line here. "Who?"

I know exactly who.

I take in a breath so I don't yell. I will tell him calmly. I will be patient. He will get there, where I am, if I can just explain it. "It's Pip.

How many ways can I tell you that she's ruined my life and now wants to bury me in a shallow grave? She's a professional. A con artist. She cons people for a *living*, and this is one more of her tricks. I'm not even safe there, in my home. I'm not *safe*."

"If you don't feel safe at any time, you can call 911. Or my cell, directly."

I want to lash out at him not to placate me, baby me, give me lip service, but I know it would be a mistake. Of course he doesn't believe me. Because this is what Pip does. She's done it a thousand times, and if I don't prove to everyone that she's a lying manipulator, she will do it to more people after I'm . . . gone. In prison. Dead. Who the hell knows.

"That's it?" I wheel around to stare at him. "You show me this, I tell you it's fake, and then you just tell me to leave?"

"For now, yes," Mason says. "But expect to hear from us again soon."

I leave, incensed, but never more driven in my life. Pip set me up, I think as I walk home. There's no other explanation, except that she got her mitts on my phone and texted Nathan . . . she's always *there*. She could have grabbed it, shot off a couple of texts . . . put it back in my pocket or bag before I was even the wiser. While I was sleeping or taking a shower. Knowing Pip, she learned my passcode . . .

What am I going to do?

I'm off the hook, but only for tonight. For all I know, Mason's getting ready to arrest me in the morning. I have to think. I have to *act*.

Twenty minutes later, I'm in front of my condo again. I pull out my keys, head into the lobby, and start for the stairs. I'm clutching my key chain in my hand when I realize: the key I had made just this morning isn't going to work.

And I left the house without any reassurance I'd ever be able to get back in.

I'm locked out of my condo because I didn't think to *insist* Pip give me the new key.

I'm going to have to pound on my own front door and hope those two snakes let me in.

I reach Nathan's floor, gripping my key chain even tighter as I pass the stairwell door that leads to his hallway.

The damned keys. These useless keys! I stare down at them, loosening my death grip.

The keys.

I separate them to find a plain gold one that's been on here for years. It's been here so long, unused, unassuming, that I forgot I even had it.

A key to Nathan's apartment.

His isn't the only one in the building that I keep on this ring. Serena's is on here too. Aunt Viv was so well liked and respected here that several tenants entrusted an extra key to her, in case of emergency.

It's not like I have Nathan's key *because* we were sleeping together. We absolutely never reached that level of intimacy—not even close. I have it because he gave it to Viv, years ago . . .

I walk through the fire door into Nathan's hallway and approach his door.

There's no police tape here, and I'm surprised. Does that mean his actual apartment isn't a crime scene? Only the ground, below?

This is a terrible idea. I know that. It's reckless, foolish, insane—whether the apartment is technically a crime scene or not. No one knows I even have this key, and it's going to look mighty suspicious if someone finds out I came in here.

For several very compelling reasons, I have to do it.

Chapter 33

Hands shaking to a nearly nonfunctional degree, I stick the key into Nathan's lock. I fumble on the first try and almost drop the entire collection of them, then finally turn it.

I'm inside within seconds.

The first thing I do is inhale, attempting to ground myself. It's truly shocking being here. Intruding on Nathan's space feels wrong. I back up a little, smacked in the gut by the sheer absurdity of it—this bachelor pad that I associated with a fun, flirty romp now seems tinged with the cruelty of its owner's untimely death. Spying his sofa, the low midcentury coffee table with books still stacked on it, and the set of coasters he picked up in Rome, I'm brought back viscerally to the two nights we spent here, together. We were carefree and buzzed, and on the kind of high you only experience when you've got nothing to lose and everything to gain. We shed our clothes in this very room before heading to the bedroom. Flashes of our intimate moments together flicker before my mind's eye, once thrilling, now painful to recollect.

I dare to take a step forward and walk around the room, taking in all his things, untouched, like nothing happened here. His desk is still in the corner, set up for his workday. There's his cup full of chewed-up pens and that snapshot of him and his little brother at the Grand Canyon. No one's moved anything. Not a single item, as far as I can tell.

Someone will come to clear all this away. His parents, and brother. I bet they haven't been able to bring themselves to do it yet, or perhaps they've been ordered not to. His death is an open murder case, after all. It was different when my parents died. There was no investigation. Cancer doesn't necessitate one. I ended up with one single weekend to sort through, catalog, and ultimately dispose of—or keep—the objects that were all I had left of Mom and Dad. Then the house transferred to a new owner. I ended up taking only five boxes' worth of things, mostly books. I knew Aunt Viv didn't have extra space, and I made a point of not burdening her with a truckload of useless items. The ones I did keep are still some of my most treasured possessions, though when I think about them now, they seem unimportant. Vestiges of an old life.

I walk to the window. The fire escape is right outside. I push away the intrusive thoughts of Nathan hurtling from this very landing.

Nausea creeps up my throat as I look out the window, past the fire escape itself, to the street below. I can spot a yellow blink of police tape, still on the ground, and I can imagine Nathan's body lying there. Those high-top sneakers of his . . . and the blood. So much blood. I'm back in that moment, the night of the murder. I can feel the crowd of onlookers, the eerie silence as everyone stood, motionless, staring blankly at Nathan's form, bent at odd angles. The way a body should never bend.

I feel a panic attack coming, but I tell it to fucking back off.

I wrench open the window. It's not locked, thank God. Once I've opened it as far as it will go, I wedge my body through it, planting one foot, then the other, on the metal landing. The fire escape from where Nathan was pushed. Where he died, below, surprised, likely shocked, with mere seconds in the air to consider what was happening to him before he hit the ground at full velocity, and his life was terminated forever.

I look up, above me. The fire escape stairs lead directly from here to my bedroom window. I knew that, was counting on it. I will climb them, and open my window, which I know for a fact doesn't properly lock. It hasn't in years. Viv and I never felt the need to get it fixed. Who was going to rob us by going to all the trouble of climbing the fire escape?

Let's hope Pip didn't decide, on one of her whims, to fix it.

The stairs are more a glorified ladder, very thin and without a side handrail. It's easy enough for me to climb, going hand by hand, foot by foot, rung by rung. I'm at the top and slip up to the landing in less than a minute.

I peer in the window, thankful that it's dark, and late, and if Pip and Sofie are inside, they're already asleep. I can't tell, can only make out some dark lumps in the bed, which could be bodies, or might just be pillows . . . though I suspect Sofie's asleep. It's midnight, after all.

I reach for the window, beneath the sash, and pull up with all my strength.

It starts to open.

I let out a massive breath. This was never going to work if Pip had managed to secure this window. Thank God she didn't.

The window fully open now, I slip one leg through, then the other, until I'm inside. I reach to close it, pulse throbbing. They aren't going to love me climbing into the room they consider *theirs*, but too fucking bad. It was my only way in, besides begging, and I won't give them the satisfaction.

Heart pounding like a brass band, I close the window and tiptoe to the bed. As I approach, I realize it's empty. The forms are only bedding. The duvet and pillows. Where the hell are they?

I creep to the door, feeling like an intruder in my own house. I push it open slowly, not wanting to make any sudden, jarring movements.

I can't believe what I'm seeing.

Pip and Sofie are sitting in the brightly lit room playing checkers.

And not only that. Pip is wearing one of my sweaters and a pair of my dark-rinse jeans. Of course she is—because I sent all her clothes to storage.

She looks up at me, cheerily meeting my eyes. Calm, cool, collected—psychopathic—as always. "Oh, Emily! Hey!"

I stare at her, not registering what's going on here. Is she seriously saying hello after I've climbed into my own locked apartment via the fire escape?

"You should have knocked!" Pip adds peppily, before moving her red piece over Sofie's black one on the game board. "I have a key for you, by the way. You only had to ask." Pip searches the sofa until she locates it, grabs it and tosses it to me. "Here ya go!"

I manage to catch it, palming it like it's on fire, without taking my eyes off these snakes.

My phone rings, startling me out of my skin.

I don't want to look, but I have to.

It's Mason. *Crap*, it's *Mason*. I silence the call. He already questioned me not two hours ago . . . What more could he want, except to arrest me?

Pip sighs, is quick to comment. "You probably don't want to do that."

"Do what?" I can't believe I'm having this conversation with her.

Pip moves a checker. "Ignoring the police just isn't a good look."

I stare at her. "How'd you know it was the police?"

Pip shrugs. "Lucky guess."

"Well, I'm not ignoring him. It's the middle of the goddamned night. Am I not allowed to sleep?"

She raises an eyebrow. "Sure you are, but avoiding a detective will only make you look guiltier. I'm just saying." She tosses her checker down. "I gotta pee. Sofie—don't you dare cheat while I'm gone!"

"When do I ever cheat? You're the cheater, not me." Sofie rolls her eyes.

Pip walks over to the bathroom and shuts the door.

Guiltier? Guiltier than what? Than whom? What has Pip done to me? What has she told Detective Mason? Why is she acting like I'm already a dead man walking? If I ever thought she had any shred of decency left in that soulless form of hers, I know now that I was wrong.

She wants me arrested. She wants me to take the fall. She wants to take my bedroom, my home, my life. There is no other way to look at it.

I have never been surer of anything. She is capable of murder.

My phone rings *again*, causing phlegm to jump to my throat. I can't keep ignoring him, can I?

"Quick, we only have a second."

I nearly jump out of my skin. Sofie is standing right next to me, whispering in my ear. When did she get up from the table?

"Only a second . . . For what?"

Sofie looks toward the closed bathroom door, then back at me. "For me to tell you. My mom lies. About *everything*. The reason that detective keeps calling, it's because of her. She lied to the cops . . . about you."

Chapter 34

"What do you mean, 'she lied to the cops'?" My heart hammers, and I sneak my phone from my bag. Stealthily as I can, I click on to Photos, start a new video, and hit record. If Sofie sees what I'm doing, I'll be DOA.

"My mom lies," she answers, twisting her glossy hair around her finger. "About everything. You didn't . . . notice that?" Sofie creeps closer to me, and while it's clear that she wants to communicate this as quietly as possible, still, it sends prickles up my spine. "She knows you didn't kill Nathan." Her eyes widen. "You could never do something like that, obviously. But . . ."

"But what?" I say it nearly inaudibly. But Sofie hears me. I know she does.

"My mom loves this apartment so much. It's on such an amazing street and everything. My walk to school's only three blocks! I guess maybe she thought, if you went to prison . . . we could stay. Forever."

My heart thunders in my chest. If what Sofie's saying is true . . . I glance to the bathroom again. Pip could reenter the room at any moment. She *will*.

Sofie isn't safe here. *We* aren't safe here.

The truth is, I can't stand Sofie, not since she ransacked my jewelry . . . started talking to me like she owned the place. But she *is* just a child. And look at who her mother is. If I'm not safe here . . . neither is she.

"Sofie, if you know something, we have to go to the police," I whisper, never feeling greater urgency in my life. "Can you tell Detective Mason what you told me? About how your mom lies, makes things up?"

Sofie crumples her forehead. "I don't know . . . Maybe? That sounds . . . scary."

"No, forget it. I'll talk to Mason. I'll tell him what you just told me . . ."

But the text thread. It's on my phone. How can I disprove it? We should go straight to the station. I'll play this recording. Maybe I won't convince Mason right away, but with Sofie backing me up . . . it would be something. We'd be closer than we are now, at least marginally closer to the truth . . .

My eyes scan the condo. What should I grab in case I can't come back here, and have to stay at Jack's—or worse, though I don't want to think about it, in jail? My wallet and ID, keys, laptop, Viv's jewelry box . . . the small bit of cash I've stashed under my futon.

I'm getting ahead of myself. All I need are my wallet and phone. No one's taking my home from me unless it's the goddamned bank. And if I did go to prison, God forbid, it's not like they'd let me have a laptop in my cell.

"Sofie," I say slowly. "Grab your backpack. And a sweater. And any homework you need, because we might . . ." I don't know how to say "we might not come back." I settle on less alarming and loaded words. "We might be out for a bit."

Pip still hasn't returned from the bathroom, but I know if she does before we've left, she'll prevent Sofie from going with me.

Still, I can't urge Sofie on any faster. I'll run the risk of spooking her, and then she might not agree to go with me at all.

"Sofie," I whisper, as loudly as I can. "Your backpack . . ."

I check that my phone is safely inside my purse, as well as my wallet.

"Hang on, I'm just getting a snack first!"

I breathe in to try to subdue the pounding in my heart. It's going to be okay. I will take Sofie to Mason, and we'll explain. Together. If her own daughter can vouch for Pip's lies, that might be enough for him, along with all my evidence . . . this video recording . . . if he can start to see Pip for who she really is . . . it's all I need, to get him to believe me, then empathize. To see my side of things. He's a detective, sure, probably ruthless and hardened. But he's also a person. And he wants to pinpoint the truth, doesn't he?

I look up to see Sofie standing right in front of me. A snack wrapper has already been ripped open, and she's taking a second or third bite of a granola bar.

"Bring that with you," I say, holding out her backpack. "You can eat on the way."

"Wait," she says after a good, long chew. "We're going *now*? It's the middle of the night. I thought you meant we'd *call* Mason. Or talk to him in the morning. Is he even *at* the police station right now?"

She makes a good point—he probably isn't still there—but I can't lose momentum. This is my moment to get Mason to believe me. To believe *us*.

I'm about to explain this to Sofie, am slinging the strap of her backpack over my shoulder, when I see she's not moving her feet, is, instead, solely focused on taking another bite of that snack.

My stomach clenches, and I assume it's because we've made no progress to leave, and unless Pip's planning on camping out all night in the bathroom, she's bound to exit it at any moment . . . we'll lose our chance to go.

But, no, that's not it, or not entirely, anyway. There's something else . . . something else is making my stomach churn and my veins turn to ice.

I remember it so vividly, almost like a movie trailer played back at me on a massive screen, only the screen is in my subconscious: Sofie and Pip throwing away all that food on their first morning here. Sofie explaining about her very serious coconut allergy. It was why she had to toss nearly fifty dollars' worth of my pantry items.

Now, as I watch Sofie peel down the wrapper of the bar, the almost visceral memory of that morning—of how sucker punched I felt as I started to suspect, deep in my gut, that I'd made a huge strategic error—nearly bowls me over.

Because that's no ordinary granola bar. Not the chocolate chip kind, and not a PowerBar.

It's an Unreal bar. One of *my* Unreal bars, that Pip allegedly threw away that day.

Its core ingredient is coconut.

It's unmistakable, in its robin's-egg-blue wrapper, the photo right there on the front of it, featuring a chocolate bar cracked into two generously sized pieces, the raw edge of each half revealing the snow-white coconut inside.

Did Sofie nab one before tossing all my coconut items? Did she have a reason to keep it, or did she just miss one, thrown in the back of a drawer somewhere? Maybe, but that detail of the story is not what stops me in my tracks now.

Sofie's *allergic* to coconut. It's what they told me when they moved in. It's why they had to toss all my groceries that might have contained even one trace.

My mind whirls. Why lie about food, of all things? What kind of elaborate ruse *is* this?

I remind myself that everything about Pip and her daughter has been an elaborate ruse since the day they set foot in my life.

But this . . . this feels different from the other times.

As I watch Sofie chew and swallow another bite, I try to figure out why. This gaslighting, or trick, or whatever it is, just doesn't make any sense. It's illogical. Why lie to me, concoct a fake coconut allergy? What did that accomplish, besides throwing me off balance?

Was that Pip's game? Emotional manipulation, such that I'd start to feel, bit by bit, day by day, hour by hour, that my home wasn't mine, so that I'd lose my footing and crack?

Sofie just told me that her mom lies all the time. Was this just one more? That she forced her daughter to go along with?

Pip has literally lied about everything. Her name. Her résumé. Her liquidity. But those all had a specific endgame, part of a long con. One she's pulled on many others in the past.

Why does this one feel like something else entirely?

Something occurs to me.

Something far more unsettling than revisiting all the ways Pip has conned me—and that's saying a lot.

With a pounding heart, I take my phone from my pocket, forgetting all about my video recording, and, at breakneck speed, type out a message on Nextdoor—to Tabitha.

After I hit send, I hear the bathroom door creaking open, and Pip finally returns to the room, that Cheshire cat grin on her face. I know it all too well.

We've lost our window to leave. But maybe leaving isn't the smart move anymore. Maybe . . . I need to stay. And see this through.

"I hope you understand, Emily," Pip says, not missing a beat as she slips back into her chair and picks up a checker piece, contemplates where to place it on the board. "I had to tell Mason all the suspicious things I've learned about you since I've lived here. How you're collecting unemployment fraudulently. The fact that you don't actually even own this apartment. Not legally."

My back stiffens. I will not let her do this. Not to me. Not now. Not again.

"I paid the mortgage. It's more than you can claim."

Pip laughs, and the sound pierces me to my very bones. "Good for you, but you're still a criminal, Emily Hawthorne. You left your fiancé at the altar—"

"How does that make me a criminal?" I breathe.

She doesn't dignify my question with a response. She barrels over me in true Pip fashion. "Don't even get me started on what you were doing the day you killed Nathan."

Keep it together, Emily. Don't crumble now.

"I didn't kill Nathan, and we both know it."

Don't let her win. Don't let her ruin you.

"Are you sure, because I'm pretty certain you screamed at Nathan for getting together with me, then shoved him over the fire escape . . . taking it out on him when what you probably really wanted to do was kill Seth. Or maybe you just have it in for all men. I know you used your secret key, Emily, to sneak into his apartment."

How does she know . . .

"It's obvious, isn't it? You climbed in from his bedroom just now. You clearly have his spare key."

Shit.

I feel the ground shifting under me. Pip figures out everything. Knows everything.

Yes, I've done things I'm not proud of. Things Pip *drove* me to do. Things I never would have considered before I met her. But you know what? Past Emily would be fucking proud of me if she saw me now.

The apartment *is* mine. Viv entrusted it to me. It's the deal we made when she left for assisted living. I would pay the mortgage, so she could spend what funds she had left on her assisted living fees, which were steep. There was no way she could cover both, but she didn't want to have to sell the apartment, our *home*. She wanted me to hold on to it, so that after she died, I'd stay, indefinitely. It was her legacy, this apartment. Since she had no children, the condo and our special connection to it meant the world to her. She wasn't just doing me a favor by having me stay. She asked me to do it. For her. She felt that losing her mind and her memory was bad enough. She wanted something that would remind me, always, of the old Viv. The one who was vibrant and playful and brilliant and carefree. The condo symbolized that for her.

I couldn't bear to tell her I was failing to make the payments.

As for the unemployment checks . . . it's true, but also complicated. I received my first benefit the week after I tore my meniscus. I'd lost my job—every single shift I had—after the injury, requiring emergency surgery. I was ordered by my doctors to stay off my knee for at least six weeks. And that was until I recovered enough to walk again—not teach. My true road to total recovery was far longer. Without disability benefits or any kind of paid leave from Roll and Flow, the piddly $300 I got every week from the California unemployment office was hardly keeping me afloat, but it was something.

Then I got the one shift back. One singular, hour-long shift that netted me about forty dollars a week after taxes. Barely enough money to pay my utility bill.

I still needed that check, desperately. For all intents and purposes, I *was* still unemployed. I just refrained from reporting that weekly forty-dollar income, in case they cut off my benefits. Who was I hurting? I asked myself over and over. I came to the same conclusion every time: no one. I would only be hurting myself if I adhered to a level of honesty that I assumed most others wouldn't. I *was* unemployed, about as unemployed as you can get in San Francisco, but I knew what would happen if I were exceedingly transparent and declared those pathetic earnings. The bureaucracy and red tape could sink me. I promised myself, as soon as Wren gave me a few more shifts, I'd stop collecting. It hadn't happened yet.

My phone dings, sharp and jarring, and I bristle at the sound of it.

With a pounding heart, and acutely aware of Pip and Sofie continuing their checkers game like nothing's happening, nothing at all, I pull my phone out.

It's a Nextdoor notification. A DM from Tabitha.

I glance at Sofie. She's finished the Unreal bar and has left the wrapper carelessly on the table. I steady myself, then turn back to my phone—only partly sure I want to see what Tabitha has to say in response to my note.

I open the Nextdoor app, reread my message to her.

It's me, Emily. Sorry to bother you again, but I have a follow-up question. What did you mean, earlier, when you said "That girl is a nightmare"? Who were you referring to?

I take in a yogic breath, then steel myself.

I was talking about the daughter, obviously. Sofie. She's a complete psycho child.

Chapter 35

I have been going at this all wrong.

This entire situation, the past week and a half . . . I've been viewing it upside down. Through the lens of a fun house mirror. If what Tabitha is saying tracks . . . and I suspect, deep in my bones, that it does . . .

Then nothing about what's happened here, since Pip and Sofie first moved in, has been what it seemed.

I have been oblivious to what was unfolding in my own house, right under my nose, in front of my open eyes. And now I must pretend, compose myself. I must not let on to those two what I suspect.

Channeling calm I don't feel, I stash my phone back in my pocket, keeping it recording, then glance over at Sofie and Pip, still joking and making moves on the checkerboard. It's 1 a.m., or nearly, and Sofie exhibits no signs of winding down. Pip, for her part, doesn't seem the slightest bit concerned that her tween daughter's up in the middle of the night, seemingly uninterested in ever going to bed. Like it's a rainy Saturday afternoon, all good, all normal.

But it is *not* normal. Nothing *about* this is normal.

The snack wrapper is still there, crumpled on the table, and I look at it now with new eyes.

If Tabitha is right—and God, is she right?—the implications of that are almost unimaginable.

Sofie is twelve. A child, not even yet a teen. My brain doesn't want to believe it. Doesn't want it to be so.

But Tabitha confirmed it, plain as day. She said the nightmare was *Sofie*.

She's a complete psycho child.

But *how*? How could I have missed it? How could I have missed what's been staring me in the face all this time?

The person hiding in plain sight.

Nathan's killer.

Was it Sofie? Did she murder him? Push him from that fire escape to his death?

No. She couldn't have. She's only a child. So tiny. And he was a full-grown man. But aside from the implausibility of how she could have accomplished something like that . . . she isn't a murderer—is she?

I have to think. I have to *move*. The longer I stand here, watching them . . . the greater the risk that they will suspect what I suspect. They will know what I think I know.

I move to the kitchen, determined to finally eat something. If I'm going to keep my wits about me, I can't keep operating solely on fumes. Robotically, feeling like I'm being squeezed from the outside in, I walk to the fridge and open it. Inside, I spy bread and vegan cheese. I take out the ingredients and mechanically begin to assemble a sandwich. I find a plate, then stand at the counter and force myself to take a bite, even as I fear I might throw it right back up. My hands tremble as I lift the food to my mouth, but I manage to chew, then swallow, my mouth and brain cooperating, at least, on this simple task.

Sofie and Pip seem unbothered by me, as I stare at the girl, forcing my mind to make this all compute.

It's *Pip* who conned me from the moment she arrived on my doorstep, Sofie in tow.

Pip promised to pay me and then never ponied up. *Pip* lied about her finances, about her job security, about their last name. She fabricated her LinkedIn page, manipulated me into vacating my bedroom. She threw a party in my home without informing me and is wearing my clothes as we speak. She rummaged through Viv's jewelry like a pickpocket and lied to Mason about me. *Pip* did all that. And the posters on Nextdoor—they told the same story.

But what if?

I force myself to take another bite of the sandwich, feeling my stomach start to gnaw at the food, requiring more now that I've given my body a taste of sustenance.

What if it isn't Pip who is to blame for everything that's happened here?

What if it wasn't Pip who ordered that DoorDash meal? What if it wasn't Pip who changed the Wi-Fi password, or sent the suspicious text thread from my phone to Nathan? And what if it wasn't Pip who fabricated the lie about the coconut allergy? What if Sofie made it up, and her mother simply covered for her?

Is that what's been happening here, all this time? Has Pip done everything she's done, not because she's a sociopath trying to cover her own tracks, hide her despicable grifting . . . but because she's been protecting her uncontrollable psycho *daughter*? Because she knows what she's capable of? Because she knows exactly what her daughter has done—conning me, changing passwords and lying and hustling—and she suspects she might be capable of far worse? Like killing Nathan?

And what if . . . Could Sofie have handwritten that note Tabitha showed me?

Is it not *Pip* whom Tabitha suspects of foul play, of driving her son off, or even worse, killing him . . . but *Sofie*?

As I stare at the girl, using her kinged black checkers to do a triple jump on her mother's lone reds, relaxed and smug . . . it begins to track. To actually *make sense*.

Pip has been tossing me under the bus with Mason, lying to make me look guilty, not to protect herself but to throw the scent off her own child.

Sofie, who is at once so beautiful and innocent seeming, as all children are. She is especially so; a likable child who I imagine, at the outset, garners empathy from all the adults in her life. Who is clever, well spoken, and elegant, with her lithe movements and endearing smile. It is entirely possible that she is not what she appears to be, not at all the person she presents to the world. Are there two Sofies? The one I thought I knew—and the real one?

I set the sandwich crust down on the plate, done, then I shove the plate away.

Could Sofie really be capable of murder?

I think back to the comments on the original Nextdoor thread. People saying Pip was the roommate from hell. She is—that's not debatable—but is it less because she's evil and entitled, lacking any moral character, and more because she's had to constantly run . . . to protect and hide her depraved child?

It seems ludicrous. Children aren't born killers. Or born evil. But it's not outside the realm of possibility. Children do all sorts of horrible things if they're truly sociopathic, or psychopathic, or some chilling combination of the two . . .

Is that what Sofie is? Had any of the other posters realized it? Or were they, like me, hoodwinked by her adorable demeanor? By the fact that she's merely a child?

I could be wrong. How I hope I am. But as I pick up my plate to carry it to the sink, my hands shake so much that I drop it straight back on the counter. It shatters into several large triangle-shaped shards. I'm so startled by what's happened that I jump, nearly leaping out of my skin, and I give a little shriek.

I hadn't meant to do that.

Sofie's eyes jump to mine. I stare back at her, unnerved.

How had I never seen it before—the lack of empathy in her eyes? The icy soullessness.

Or am I concocting something that I think I see, that I'm perhaps looking for, because it fits the narrative I've painted in my head?

But the wrapper. The snack wrapper. It's the smoking gun, isn't it? Undeniable? My eyes flit involuntarily to it, and that is my fatal mistake. Because Sofie sees me do it. She follows my eyes directly to it.

And the next thing I know, something strikes me painfully in the head.

And then all I see is nothingness.

Chapter 36

Pip

Pip hadn't known her daughter would turn out to be a pathological liar.

She'd certainly never predicted that her daughter might become a killer.

The first sign of a problem was when Mike was asking too many pesky questions. Wanting to know why, exactly, Sofie had been expelled. Asking how Pip had managed to find her a spot in a nearby school, equally top notch, and why they were suddenly using a different last name. Stone, instead of Baker.

Pip was clever with her answers. She relied on her powers of persuasion, which had been highly effective since she was a teenager, when she first learned that it was smarter to convince people of things than to try to argue with them. She had been able to manipulate her father that way, from an even younger age, to get what she wanted. Money, a ride, his affection.

Mike had asked Pip to marry him. She was thrilled, initially. For one glorious moment, right after he'd gotten down on one knee, and she'd answered yes, Pip celebrated, and allowed herself to feel fleetingly happy, the way she imagined the Carries of the world felt every single day of their lives. Marrying Mike would have been the final step of Project Normality, and it would have meant her dreams for her and

Sofie were finally within reach. It would have—except for the small problem of Sofie's conduct disorder, and the fact that Pip had only barely managed to hide most of Sofie's lies, not to mention her indiscretions, from Mike.

But she knew that would only last so long. She could only continue to persuade, and dodge Mike's questions, and use her charm to keep him off Sofie's scent. It would not be a long-term solution.

Still, Pip was not willing to break things off, not yet. Mike lived next door to her, and he had given her a key to his condo along with the vintage diamond ring that had been in his family for decades. It wasn't super valuable, he said, but it was sentimental, and he hoped Pip would love it as much as his grandmother had. Pip didn't care for the ring; it was too old fashioned. But the key—that was her ticket to vacating the shitty studio she and Sofie were inhabiting and moving into his much more spacious abode. A two-bedroom with city views.

It wouldn't be forever. It inevitably couldn't be. But Pip had learned to live in the now.

A few weeks into their cohabitation, Pip began to make contingency plans. She came home one day to find Mike with a whiskey in hand, and he didn't even say hello before firing off a slew of questions. About her past. About her life story. He demanded answers but wasn't satisfied with the ones Pip provided. Her powers of persuasion only went so far.

Pip had to think, and act, fast. She had only one goal as a mother, and it was to protect her child. Which meant that if Mike was going to suspect they were not the pristine mother-daughter duo he thought they were, she would make sure Sofie did not take the fall.

The truth, which Pip would never tell Mike, was that she had been grifting all these years, scamming and cheating, not because she was a bad person, or because she felt the rules didn't apply to her. It was because of Sofie.

It was all to protect Sofie.

When your child is a pathological liar, deceitful about anything and everything under the sun, often for seemingly no reason at all, and unable to form friendships or connect with people, for years on end . . . you have no out. No options. No chance for a regular existence.

You have no choice but to compartmentalize.

She no longer heard the lies, not really. She simply knew not to trust a single word that came out of her child's mouth.

Sofie's gaslighting, her manipulations, the locking out of babysitters, the stealing money from landlords, the tricking children in her class and calling them bullies. The running home with sob stories about the terrible things her classmates had done to her, when in reality, she had been tormenting *them*.

Don't think Pip didn't want to help her daughter. Of course she did—so badly it burned in the deepest places of her heart. The problem was, she couldn't. At the first signs of Sofie's issues, she had sought highly specialized child therapists. Expensive therapy, behavior modification, out of pocket, not covered by her measly Covered California insurance. Therapies she simply could not afford. Therapies that did not *help*. Providers were reticent to call Sofie what she was—a pathological liar with a conduct disorder. They feared they'd stigmatize the girl for life, that she'd never get out from under a diagnosis like that. Worse, they told Pip that there truly was no therapy that could fix someone as "challenged" as Sofie. Diagnosing her would only make Pip's life harder. It would label her daughter, making it even more of an uphill battle for them to get close to anyone. To earn anyone's trust.

And they were right. No one has empathy for someone who appears to have no empathy herself.

Eventually, after Pip had pissed away her savings trying to track down that one treatment that might save her daughter, and herself, from a lifetime of lying and running . . . she stopped. She reminded herself of that day, driving off in the heat in her Chevy, the pregnancy test stick bouncing merrily on the cracked seat next to her. It was her and her daughter against the world. She'd never have a chance for another child, not when raising Sofie was like raising ten children. She couldn't turn her back, or leave her alone—unless she wanted to come home to a burned-down apartment. She couldn't entrust her to a babysitter while she got a normal nine-to-five job; that had failed one too many times, with nearly disastrous consequences. She could barely send her to school, which in itself was a struggle, as she never knew what her daughter might do. Every morning after dropping her off, Pip prepared herself to wait by the phone. Every day she didn't get "the call" from the principal, informing her that Sofie had done something awful, was a win.

Playdates had run dry years ago, at least the ones hosted by other families. Everyone thought Sofie was delightfully cute and sweet when they first met her, but then her personality and troublemaking would catch up to her. The day the dead squirrel was dragged into Angela Walker's house, where it was displayed prominently on the Walkers' kitchen table on a serving platter . . . Sofie shirked all responsibility for it and tried to pin it on Angela's little brother. That was when Pip realized that her life thereafter would never, ever be normal or happy. There would be no peace, no ability, ever, to exhale, to not panic, to stop strategizing.

Chapter 37

It takes me a minute to get my bearings, to realize where I am.

I'm lying on my bed, which feels surreal—it's the bed I'm used to, the one I occupied, with Seth, for years before Pip arrived on the scene and snatched it from me. Along with my home, my clothes, my sanity, my life. I've missed it, my bed, my bedroom, and in some strange way it feels like only a day or two since I've lain here, so familiar are these sheets, this view of my dresser on the opposite wall, the black-and-white art print that hangs over it. But logically, I know that it's been over a week since Pip and Sofie waltzed in and pushed me out of here, began dismantling me, piece by miserable piece.

My head hurts like a motherfucker. And when I sit up, the throbbing intensifies, and I have to lean over my knees, head in my hands, to wait out the agonizing wave of pain that overtakes me. I run my hands over my hair, feeling the knots and tangles, wincing when I find it: the spot where Pip whacked me. With what, I wonder—a shard from the plate I broke? A pot? I wasn't able to spot her weapon of choice before I went down like a sack of potatoes. Gingerly, I remove my hand from the bump and look at it. There is blood on my palm.

Normally I'd panic seeing my blood like that, sticky and viscous on my fingers.

Maybe it's everything I've been through recently. Maybe it's my utter fatigue, or maybe it's that I'm woozy from lack of food, water, and sleep. But I don't panic. I study the blood like it's not even mine, feeling detached from it all. Vaguely, I consider I might need stitches but decide not to focus on that.

I stand up, dizzy, my head pulsating, but manage to shuffle to the door. I reach for the knob, already sensing, deep in my gut, that getting out of here is not going to be the simple task it should be.

My fears are confirmed when I turn the doorknob and it doesn't budge.

They have locked me in here.

I saw it coming—I *knew* it—and yet the truth of it gobsmacks me.

Sofie and Pip have trapped me in here, in the bedroom they stole from me, and I am completely and utterly at their mercy.

I stumble back, woozy, to the bed. Thinking. Spinning. Churning.

The window. I scramble toward it, the one I came through not long before, after letting myself into Nathan's condo and climbing the fire escape. This window doesn't lock. It's *never* locked. That's how I got in here in the first place. Thank God.

But when I reach it and pull upward on the sash . . .

Nothing. It won't move. I strain at it, engaging every last muscle I have and feeling them burn with exhaustion. A searing pain in my knee that I worry, deep in the recesses of my brain, is my meniscus, tearing once again, or on the brink of it.

I sink back on the bed, spent. The window is sealed off. Probably glued shut. Fuck! How and when did Pip do it? While I was unconscious? I scan the window for some obvious sign of a lock but don't see one. Is it on the outside? Did Sofie somehow climb up the ladder and wedge something on it? Did she take my keys, go through Nathan's apartment, and access it that way? What will these two not do to get what they want? I'm too numb to feel chilled, but my brain tells me I should be.

It's dark out, which indicates to me that it's still night, though I spy a few headlights below and wonder how close to morning it actually is. Was I blacked out for thirty seconds? An hour? Two or twelve?

I begin to shake. It's terrifying, not knowing how long I was unconscious. Knowing Pip and Sofie locked me in here to make sure I won't talk. Because if I were to tell Mason what I suspect . . .

That it is not Pip he should be looking at, but Sofie . . . that Pip is framing me to protect her minor child . . .

They would kill me. They *will* kill me, won't they? If Sofie's killed before . . .

I would just be one more victim.

Is that it, then? This room will ultimately become my tomb? I'll be trapped here for God knows how long—without food, without a toilet, without water, without a prayer—until Sofie and Pip finish me off?

I lie back on the duvet and shut my eyes, tight, tight, tight.

Think, Emily. *Think. You must.*

What is their endgame? Is it truly just to shut me up? Is it to hammer a final nail in my coffin, so that they make sure Mason believes their story and not mine?

Are they going to find a way to guarantee I take the fall for pushing Nathan off that fire escape?

The fire escape.

My eyes pop open with the realization: it's how Sofie killed Nathan. It has to be.

I came up the ladder easily, didn't I? And Nathan's window, it wasn't locked when I opened it. Which means it probably hasn't ever been locked. Nathan wouldn't have had cause to regularly lock it, just like Viv and I hadn't.

The night Nathan died, Sofie was in here, in this room, the entire evening. Playing Roblox with friends. Doing homework. At least, we *thought* she was here the entire night. She never left through the front door.

Pip came in to check on her . . .

I clutch my aching head.

I'd bet all Aunt Viv's savings on the fact that when Pip came in to fetch Sofie's dinner tray . . . Sofie wasn't here.

That's how Pip would have found out, or suspected, anyway, that her daughter had something to do with Nathan's murder. I was in the living room the entire night. So was Pip, with the exception of those trips into Sofie's room. It's why I really couldn't square away how Pip could have committed the murder, though I still believed she must have done it, or had a hand in it, somehow . . .

But this. This explains it. This is the answer, and unless Mason is far cleverer than I've given him credit for . . .

He has no idea.

I have to get out of here. Not just for my own sake, but because he has to know. Sofie did this. It's clear as day to me, now, so obvious I can't believe I never landed here before. The recording. I'll show it to him! But it might not even help, and anyway, I don't have my phone. They've taken it. Likely erased it.

I stand up, determined to get my footing. My head screams at me as I make it to my feet. There must be a way out of here. There *has* to be.

The room will save me. *My* room. There has got to be something in here I can use to help myself.

I open the closet door, leaving a handprint of blood on the frame. Crap, I'm going to bloody up everything in here. There's a towel on the floor, left by Pip and Sofie. Slobs, I think as I reach for it and try to wipe the blood on it. Then, with my left hand, I press it to my head. If my wound's still bleeding, this should stanch it.

I flip through the clothes hanging in my closet, searching frantically for something, anything I might be able to use. There's my yoga mat, some tote bags, some hand weights, my favorite books piled on the shelf. My shoes are crammed in a corner.

Done with the closet, and stymied, I move to the dresser. Pip's underwear and bras—the ones I wasn't thorough enough to send off with the moving guy—are in the top drawer. Socks are squashed into the one under that. What I wouldn't give for my cell phone . . . they must have slipped it out of my pocket before depositing me here.

If only I had it right now. If only I had a landline. Or a laptop, or something . . .

Aargh. I toss all the clothes from the bottom drawer to the ground in frustration.

This room is full of a whole lot of clothes and junk, but not much of use. And the effort of these simple tasks has caused my head to full-on pound.

I'm going to have to face the fact that I'm not getting out of here until and unless Pip and Sofie want me to.

I close my eyes, attempting some calm Zen breaths, but all I can see, in my mind's eye, is him.

Seth.

Why didn't I tell him what was really going on? Why didn't I confess to Jack how dire my situation really was? Why didn't I tell *someone* in my life how truly fucked things had become? My world has become so small as of late. That's how Pip managed to do this to me . . . isolate me. Prey on me. Make sure I had no one in my corner. What if I become like Tabitha's son—and go "missing" indefinitely?

Would Seth even care?

He loved me. This I know. It's exactly why I did what I did. Because he would have loved me through all of it. Getting screened. Finding out the results. Helping me through treatments. Freezing eggs and embryos.

The irony of it all is that he would have been the best possible partner through all of it, and I let him go. It was the right thing to do. Of this I was sure, at the time. I felt he'd entered into a false arrangement. I'd never explained to him the risks inherent in being orphaned by cancer. He never thought about it much. Why would he? He wasn't a worrier, always viewed the world as a glass half-full. He hadn't lost anyone close to him, barely a grandparent, so he didn't know what it was like for me, living under this constant shadow.

And even if he did know . . . he would have stuck by me. Would have loved me, unconditionally.

But if I had tested positive, and had to face having all those surgeries? I couldn't freeze my eggs knowing they might be tainted. So what then? I knew how much Seth wanted kids. We could hire an egg donor, but that came with an astronomical cost attached. Or adopt, but who would let me adopt their precious newborn baby knowing I might not live to be fifty?

And even if someone did, what then? Would I even be around to raise a child?

Deep in my bones, I didn't think I would be.

It kept me up at night, every night since he proposed . . .

I came to the conclusion that I was—am—damaged goods. And I wanted Seth to have the very best. I couldn't sleep. Couldn't *deal*. I paced this apartment every night, unsure of how I could tell him the truth . . . that I was terrified. That ever since I lost my parents, I'd felt like cancer was my own personal ticking time bomb. I never imagined myself making it past age forty.

And if we were to get married . . .

I would leave him, one day. Not tomorrow, maybe not even three years from now, or ten. It wouldn't be my choice, but I knew it . . . I wouldn't get longevity. It wasn't in the cards, not for me.

I wanted Seth to find someone who *could* give him that. Seth would have *said* he was willing to take the risk, take the gamble, on me. But I didn't want him to have to. And I worried that one day he'd regret his decision. Resent me. And that, I could not bear.

Not when I knew that if I ended things, swiftly and permanently, he'd move on. Find someone else. Stop loving me. And settle down with a woman who could give him everything he wanted, and more.

It's why I broke his heart too. I didn't tell him the real reason I was leaving him. It wouldn't have worked. He would have begged me to reconsider. Would have professed his undying love and promised to stick by me, thick and thin, till death do us part.

I couldn't let that happen. So I called off our wedding, and it killed me.

The evening I ended things, I finally slept all night. Like a baby.

Chapter 38

I wake with a start, having dozed off on top of my covers.

It's daylight, and my mouth feels so parched. I scan the room for water. Something, anything I can drink. An old water bottle left over from yoga. A cup on the nightstand containing even a sip of a beverage. Anything to quell my thirst—but there's nothing. How long can a person go without? Is it two days? Three? I doubt I'm even close to that threshold yet . . . but if they don't come back for me, I'll eventually get to a point of no return. But I have even more pressing concerns. I have to pee like crazy.

I try the window again, panting and straining and screaming to the universe when it doesn't open.

I fall back onto the bed, spent. The only food I've eaten in days was that cheese sandwich. At least I ate that. I gingerly take stock of my body. The pee, I'll have to deal with in a second. I'll find some empty container and . . . ugh. I can't believe I've sunk that low—that they've *forced* me to sink that low—but my humiliation is the least of my worries now.

I reach for the gash on my head and detect crusty, dried blood. At least it's not actively bleeding anymore. My knee is throbbing, but on inspection, it's not swollen, so that's a good sign.

I scan the room for a bucket. There's nothing suitable, but when I investigate a pile of Pip and Sofie's things, stashed in a messy clump in the corner, I discover Pip's fancy water bottle—checking it first for even a drop of liquid but finding it dry as a bone, dammit—and screw open the top. Luckily, the canister opening is wide enough to be remotely workable, though it still takes a great deal of maneuvering to properly aim. Never have I felt so hideous as I do right now, using that bloody towel to clean up after I'm done. There's some slight satisfaction in knowing Pip will never want to use this water bottle again. Of course, if I'm dead, that satisfaction won't mean squat.

I try the door again. It's still locked, of course. *FUCK.* The four walls of this room, which always felt spacious for this city, are starting to feel a lot less forgiving. I don't want to think about what would happen if the smoke detector went off—I'd be trapped. I *am* trapped, and the realization hits me like a truck to the chest. I could die in here. I *will* die if Sofie and Pip don't come back.

But I could also die if they do.

What is their plan? To leave me here to starve, with no water, until my body eventually breaks down, and I die of natural causes? They'd never be able to explain that away, would have to come up with an incredibly imaginative story to justify how I got locked in here in the first place.

But Sofie killed Nathan, and probably Tabitha's son too. Which means she, at least, has killed without thinking . . . without considering a cover-up or the consequences. And Pip hasn't turned her daughter in. She's shown she's willing to do anything to protect her.

Including killing me.

I have to get out of here. I don't know how much time I have left. If I have the cancer genes, if I'm destined to live to one hundred or only age forty . . . I don't care anymore. Whatever my time left on this earth is, I won't let it be only a day or two more because that psycho and her mother have decided to kill me.

I want more time than *that.*

I spend the next few hours meticulously picking up every object in the room, opening every drawer, considering if any of the crap in here could possibly, in any way, shape, or form, be useful to me. Could I break the window? It's the best chance I have at getting out of here. But what can I use to do it?

I return to my closet and the ten-pound weight covered in purple neoprene material that I haven't used in years. It's definitely heavy enough, compact . . . I let out a breath and pick it up. Please work—for God's sake, please *work*.

I take a swing at the window. Nothing. I take another—and another with all my strength, which leaves me winded. The glass reverberates a little but doesn't crack.

I don't know what time it is. I barely know what day it is. There's no clock in here—I always relied on my phone for an alarm—and no watch that I can find in a jacket pocket or drawer. Which means the time is passing, without me, my fate getting dangerously close to the brink with every minute that goes by. I try not to think about what's happening to my insides, what will inevitably happen to my body if I don't get access to water soon.

I've ransacked the room, picked through every last object in here. I'm desperate to find the Swiss Army knife that was a gift from Viv before I went on a required high school camping trip to Pinnacles National Park. But it's not here, in the drawer where I last stashed it. At least, I think that's where I stashed it. Did Pip and Sofie take it? Hide it?

I sweep a pile of Pip and Sofie's things aside in anger, a kind of primal frustration at Pip, at Sofie . . .

I'm getting thirstier by the second, my stomach is howling in hunger and emptiness, and with a dread that's beginning to fill my entire body, from top down, I realize that no matter how loudly or for how long I screamed, it's unlikely anyone would hear it. Nathan's condo is empty, obviously, and Serena, downstairs, practically lives in her noise-canceling headphones. My old neighbor upstairs is in desperate need of hearing aids. I don't know about the other upstairs unit. If anyone heard screaming, would they think to act, or would they chalk it up to city living? I'd have to scream for a very extended amount of time for it to seem odd . . .

I try anyway.

———

Hours later, my voice is hoarse, and my vocal cords feel permanently damaged. I've banged on the window, on the door, until my palms are red and raw.

I'm spent, and I don't have the energy left to try anymore.

I curl up on the bed and drift in and out of sleep, feeling guilty for letting myself indulge in unconsciousness when I know I should be using every single minute I have left to strategize my way out of here.

But what if there isn't one? What if I'm completely, totally at the mercy of my captors—and I'll either die a slow, painful death in here, dehydrated, alone, or I'll see them again when *they* decide it's time?

I wake to a darkened room. The incoming light must have shifted dramatically while I was asleep, and now it's twilight. I do a quick calculation. If they locked me in here last night at 1 a.m., that means it's been about nineteen hours. Nineteen hours with no water, no food. Nineteen hours not knowing whether they are close to being my last.

How did I get here? *How* did I allow it? Why didn't I give Tabitha my last name? Tell her more about what was happening to me, so someone, anyone, might have thought to check up on me?

A knock on the door.

A knock! On the door!

I spring to a sitting position. Did I imagine it? Am I far gone enough that I'm hallucinating? Is that the next phase of dehydration, like people see mirages sometimes in the desert?

"Yes?" My voice sounds raspy on the way out, my throat feels raw. "I'm in here! Please! Help me, is that the police?"

"Not quite," says the voice on the other side. A familiar voice. Pip's voice.

"Are you going to let me out?" I growl. I sound like an animal. Isn't that what I am, now? An animal reduced to living in a cage?

"We're here with sustenance."

I take in a breath. So she's feeding me. Probably has water too. In the near term, I will eat. I will live.

My long-term fate is far less clear.

I stare at the door. It will open any minute. I could attack, jump them both when they walk in. But I'm unarmed, and weak, and not even remotely in my best shape, given my knee. Besides, attacking offensively might cost me my life. If Sofie's with her, that's two against one. Sofie may be small, but she's strong, and if she's as merciless as I think she is, who knows what she's capable of. Especially without the burden of a conscience.

I brace myself as I hear a dragging noise, like Pip's moving aside a piece of furniture and scraping it over my hardwood floors. So that's how they did this—fucking psychos. I'd bet my life it's one of my bookcases. Then she opens the door, slides in with Sofie in tow. They shut the door behind them and stand directly in front of it, blocking it.

Seeing them in here, with me, after all this time in solitary confinement, is surreal. My eyes jump hungrily to the paper bag Pip holds. Fast food, I think. She takes a measured step forward and drops it unceremoniously on the duvet, like it isn't the essential item it is. Food. The key to me not dying, at least, not yet.

I greedily open the bag, finding a cheap plastic bottle of spring water inside. I turn and snap the cap and take a long swig, not realizing how thirsty I was until the liquid is in my mouth, running down my throat, hydrating me almost instantly. There's a McDonald's burger inside, too, and I unwrap it without a second thought and take a monstrous bite, one that nearly makes me gag. I haven't eaten red meat in years, but the last thing I can be right now is picky.

I chew, slowly, trying not to go too fast and choke, as Pip and Sofie look on.

Animal at the zoo, is all I can think. The question is—are they going to put the animal out to pasture? Or keep her as a pet, locked up?

When I finally finish chewing the bite and chase it down with another sip of water, I set the burger and water bottle down.

"What the actual fuck, Pip? You knocked me out? Locked me up?" She's still wearing my clothes, which is so twisted I would walk over there and rip them off her body if my life weren't in her hands.

"I had to," she says, crossing her arms over her chest. "It was obvious when you saw that wrapper that . . . you knew."

"Knew what?" I'm going to make her say it. Make her admit it. Until then, I'll pretend not to understand.

"That I killed him, dum-dum." Sofie stares at me with that piercing look she gave me last night during her checkers game. It chilled me then, and it chills me even more now. She's confessed.

I wish she hadn't.

Pip moves over to me, sits down on the bed beside me. She grabs my hand, and I'm so stunned by her action I don't think to yank it away.

"Don't fight it, Emily. You can't. I'm sorry." She looks at me almost fondly, but what I notice the most is the resignation on her face. "You can't leave now, I'm afraid."

My heart drops. I knew this was coming. I'm no fool. It's not like I thought they'd let me walk out of here . . . especially now that Sofie's admitted what she's done. But still. *Still.*

"She's my daughter," Pip continues. "My child. The only person I have in the world. The only person I've *ever* had in the world. I love her, Emily, obviously, and I won't let her rot in juvie. You understand, don't you? I know you don't have kids. You're not a mother . . . but if you were, you'd see. You're a daughter. Try to imagine how your own mother would feel. What she would have done for you before she died, if it came to it. I'm sure she'd agree that it has to be this way."

I know what way. I know exactly what she means. But I'll make her say it. I'll make her say it to my face. "What way?"

Pip sighs, like I'm a child myself. Then she squeezes my hand. "The only way. You can't leave here. Not alive."

Chapter 39

PIP

Sofie *had* killed before. She would do it again. Of this, Pip was sure.

In the early years, she'd thought her daughter was a liar but only viewed that as a minor character defect. She would grow out of it. All kids lied. (The therapists had shrugged when she'd suggested that, like they had hope but weren't going to bet their therapy licenses on it. Pip secretly thought they were morons. Wasn't it their *job* to know? Imbeciles, the whole bunch.) She privately considered the fact that her daughter wouldn't grow out of it but resigned herself to the idea that she would simply live a limited, albeit interesting, life. Some pathological liars even ended up famous or doing great things. It wasn't the end of the world.

When Sofie started her first dumpster fire, in third grade, Pip started to worry.

Words were just words. Fibs were only fibs. But fires . . . pyromania . . . that was a whole other ball of wax. One Pip wasn't prepared for.

The problem was, there were no consequences she could use, none that worked. Sofie didn't seem to care what happened to her. If you told her she was in a prolonged time-out, she'd simply shrug, go in her room, and read for two days straight. Then she'd reemerge into the light with a fresh new deceit on her lips and a big ole happy smile.

Regular parenting techniques failed when it came to Sofie.

As did expulsion from school, as a deterrent. All that accomplished was punishing *Pip*—who had to go to great, then even greater, lengths to find her daughter a new school. In between, while she waited for Sofie to get accepted to someplace new, Pip tried homeschooling, and it would not be an exaggeration to say that it nearly killed her. Not to mention the fact that you can't make money when your lying, pyromaniac child is by your side all day. Pip'd had to give up on being a stable breadwinner years ago. She realized grifting would be her only hope, so she got good at it—out of sheer necessity.

On top of the burden to keep her head above water was the biggest burden of all: hiding Sofie in plain sight. The minute anyone suspected she had lied, or cheated, or manipulated—or worse—Pip found a way to make sure she took the fall for it, not her child. This was exhausting, not sustainable, as a way of life. And yet, it's what she had to do, day in and day out.

It began when Sofie was in preschool. She bit other children, scratched their faces. She was kicked out of several home day cares, and Pip never got the remainder of her tuition back, in spite of her persuasive pleas to the directors, who showed little sympathy for Pip's situation. At that point, she could no longer work as a receptionist at the ballet studio and had to start working from home. She breathed a sigh of relief when Sofie went off to kindergarten. Free school all day gave Pip a chance to finally get a real job again. But within months, Sofie had managed to lock their landlord out of her own apartment when she came to check that everything with Sofie was okay, stolen from three babysitters and lied about it, and bullied another child at school so badly his parents threatened to sue.

Pip began running. Moving from apartment to apartment, house to house, hustling and conning but making sure to do it with charm and ease, so that by the time anyone suspected how shady she really was, it was too late. People were quick to take her in. Pip could count on the kindness of strangers or, at the very least, their need for some quick cash, which she always promised to provide. Sofie was adorable, and as long as their reputation didn't precede them, she was considered a plus to the arrangement. People feel safe and happy and more agreeable when children are around, and Pip counted on that.

By the time it came to actually collect rent, Pip was ready with her excuses. She hated that her life had to be this way. She hated that she woke up every hour, on the hour, for years on end, to check on her daughter—not to make sure she was breathing, as some moms do, but to confirm she hadn't hurt anyone *else*. It's why, a few days after installing the slider bar, she got a real, locking knob for the bedroom door, with a key to open it that Pip kept in her bra. Not to keep Emily out, but rather so that Sofie wouldn't hurt Emily. Or do something entirely worse.

She hadn't considered that she needed to lock the window.

As for Mike, only a few short weeks after the engagement, after Pip and Sofie had moved into his place, the sheen of his proposal was already beginning to wear off. Pip figured he'd been blinded by love, and lust, up until that point. But living together meant a whole lot more visibility into their lives than Pip was fully prepared for, and she quickly realized her mistake. She should have delayed their cohabitation, put it off for as long as possible. Because Mike was starting to get wise to the fact that the mother and daughter were liars, that their history was riddled with inconsistencies and inaccuracies. Pip had to make damn sure he never thought Sofie was the one who was the real problem. So while Pip worked twenty-four seven to keep the truth from Mike—spinning her wheels, lying, covering up some of Sofie's worst behaviors—she also had to manage Sofie. It had always been her and Sofie against the world, and Sofie didn't feel threatened. She could tell others her tales of being abused or robbed, concoct fantasies that she spun like delicate yarns, horrifying or delighting those around her. But with Mike in the picture, and in such proximity, it was a different story. He questioned Sofie, looked too closely at her behavior. Then one day, he told her—he didn't believe her lies, and it was time to shape up.

Pip realized then that she had made a fatal, and irreversible, mistake. Project Normality had been so alluring. She was a fool to ever think she could have it.

Pip didn't have evidence that could point to exactly what her daughter had done, but she had her suspicions. The three of them had gone upstate for a weekend, to stay in Mike's buddy's cabin. The friend had been nice enough to loan it to them for a getaway, and Mike'd had all these grand ideas about the time they'd spend there, screen-free, though Pip suspected he was thinking of it as a chance to turn Sofie around, to try to get through to her. People seem to erroneously think that "time in nature" can cure people of deep psychological defects, which was laughable in Sofie's case. If a little nature could fix Sofie, Pip would have moved them to rural Northern California years ago.

They drove up to the cabin together, and Pip did what she always did—kept a watchful eye on Sofie. What she underestimated was just how much Sofie resented the trip, and the fact that Mike was questioning her relentlessly about her recent expulsion. Pip felt like she was dancing as fast as she could to brush all that under the rug, attempting to distract Mike by talking about wedding planning. (The fictional wedding that Pip knew would never actually take place would be simple, modest, and inexpensive. A courthouse ceremony followed by a light lunch.) Pip was exhausted. She barely slept that first night there, waking up to check on Sofie. This cabin didn't have locks on the doors, and Mike would have thought it suspicious if she hadn't allowed Sofie to sleep in the guest room down the hall from the room she and Mike were sharing. (In his condo, which they now all lived in, Sofie had her own room, but Pip had created a system of locking the door late at night after Sofie was asleep, and unlocking it early in the morning. So far, Mike had not noticed.)

The next morning, Pip made the mistake that would haunt her forever, except for the fact that she did not allow it to haunt her, because it was not her fault.

Pip slept in, and when she woke, Sofie was not in the guest room. Mike was nowhere to be found. Pip ran outside, calling for them. She found Sofie a few paces down by the lake on the property, dragging a small rowboat to shore. When Pip asked her where Mike had gone, Sofie shrugged.

"Don't know. Haven't seen him."

Pip's stomach dropped to her feet as she scanned the pristine water of the lake. She knew, even then, that Mike was likely down in its depths.

Had Sofie lured him out on the boat to "talk," then hit him over the head with something heavy, knocking him unconscious so she could tip him over and he would drown? Had she drugged him with something? Stabbed him? It didn't matter, did it? He was likely dead, and her daughter was likely responsible, but Pip reminded herself of her core responsibility, what she had been put on this earth to do: protect Sofie.

That meant packing up their things, wiping the place clean of any of their fingerprints, and climbing into the rental car and driving home.

When they got back to Mike's condo, Pip took the engagement ring off her finger and slipped it into the back of his nightstand drawer. She didn't feel right keeping it, much as she could have used the money from pawning it. She suspected it wasn't worth all that much, anyway— hadn't its value been mostly sentimental? And more practically, she could not do anything to cast any suspicion on their family. If asked, she'd claim she and Mike had called off the engagement, and she'd given him back his family heirloom.

Of course, Pip knew Sofie had written that letter from Mike to his mom, Tabitha. She'd seen Sofie copying Mike's handwriting from a to-do list. If she felt guilt about the fact that she could have stopped it, she pushed it down—deep down. It wasn't her fault her daughter was this way. All she could do was what a good mother should. Even if it meant someone else got hurt. Even if it meant . . . the worst thing possible. Besides, telling anyone what she suspected would not bring Mike back. It would only bring her and her daughter a world of hurt.

Chapter 40

Stall them. Humor them. Your life depends on it.

I must make this take a while, make sure they don't act—not yet. And maybe, just maybe, I can convince them that killing me, too, along with Nathan, isn't the answer. That it will only spell more trouble for them, for Sofie, in the long run. Pip doesn't care about herself. I see that now. Everything she's done has been to protect her demonic daughter. Probably has been for years. Which doesn't excuse the grifting, the manipulating, the gaslighting—it doesn't make up for it. But it does explain it. And in some small way, it makes me hate Pip less. Not because I would make the same choices, were I in her shoes. Those are despicable, no matter how you spin it. But the way she's tried to love her daughter unconditionally, that's admirable, in itself, in a twisted way.

She's still an evil bitch.

I've almost finished eating the cheeseburger. I've dragged this out as long as humanly possible because I've done the calculations, and I know every second, every minute I get, counts. They aren't going to slash my throat while I'm sitting here chewing. At least, I don't think they are. They have a plan. A strategy.

Well, two can play at this game.

I'm past yogic breathing, way past meditating. Adrenaline is my best friend now, and I barely register the pounding in my chest that must be my wildly beating heart.

I'm not confident in my abilities, not sure I can succeed. But I'll try, won't I? I won't lie down and die, I know that much.

Now, only one question remains—what exactly are they planning? And how can I use it against them? My brain whirls with the only paths available to me. Appealing to them. Outsmarting them. Begging them to spare me. Which has a chance in hell shot of working? Which route to take?

I chew the last bite of the burger, wash it down with another sip of water. I'm acutely aware of the door, and the fact that Sofie's standing sentry in front of it. It's not locked, and there's no way they moved the bookcase back in front of it after they came in, which means it's not barricaded. That's something, one small thing I have on my side.

"You know," I say casually, ordering every muscle in my body to stay calm, summoning every ounce of willpower I have, to work these two. They're snakes, monsters—one of them more than the other. But both are predators, determined to devour me like this burger, to swallow me whole. "Killing me is going to look suspicious. So I'm not sure what you've got up your sleeves, but Mason will be on to you. You can't just poison my food, or slit my neck, without leaving a trail of evidence. So what's your plan? Do you have a gun? Are you going to forge another letter, Sofie, like the one you forged in Tabitha's son's handwriting? This time, a suicide note? And are you going to place the gun in my hand and make me pull the trigger?"

"Of course not," Pip says, gently. "Those are shitty ideas. And we don't own a gun. Who do you think we are?" I'd laugh at that, were I not facing down my imminent demise at the hands of two psychos. "No, there's no gun, no poison. You're going to take the easy route. Jumping from the fire escape. Just like Nathan did. Only this time we'll push you the right way. Face forward."

Face forward. So everyone will believe I killed myself.

These fuckers aren't playing around.

"I tried to protect you, you know."

Pip slinks to where the dresser is, stands to face me. My body starts shaking. I'm doubtful it will stop. If this is the end . . . but no. I won't let it be.

"You tried to *protect* me?" My voice comes out flat, devoid of emotion. The only emotion I feel right now is a deep, dull fear, unlike anything I've ever experienced before. It fills me, top to bottom, threatening to prevent me from doing what must be done. I'm so tired, so very tired. But I shove that thought aside. There's no room for it, not now.

"It's why we moved into the bedroom." Pip shrugs, picking up a trinket from the top of the dresser—a little porcelain ballerina that Viv got on one of our flea market jaunts. "So I could lock the door at night. Obviously."

My eyes flit to the door, where I notice the knob has been replaced with one bearing a keyhole. How didn't I see this before? The slider bar is still there, up above, in the unlocked position, but I get it now. Sofie could simply wake up and unlock *that*. This new doorknob must have a hidden key somewhere . . . and Pip must lock it after Sofie passes out every night. Pip never cared about locking it from the outside. Only from within. I glance now at Sofie, who's twirling her hair around a finger in that childlike way she has. I can't reconcile it, can't square it. This beautiful young girl who's sugar on the outside, poison within. She's an enigma inside a riddle, inside a puzzle. A sick, depraved one. Pip locked the door so Sofie wouldn't hurt me. It's hard to make that compute.

"My mom's lying, of course," Sofie pipes up. "She's going to lie to you now about a *ton* of things, BTW. She's going to say that I've locked out babysitters and scared our past landlords. That I've killed animals—which I absolutely would never do, gross—and brought their carcasses inside. That one's particularly insulting because she's never let me get a pet, not even a goldfish, and she knows how much I want one. She also likes to blame me for her failed career, and says it's my fault I got expelled from a bunch of schools because I guess that makes her feel good about herself? She's so annoying. I *hate* her."

Pip doesn't respond, and it occurs to me, now—she's simply tuning her daughter out. I've read about pathological liars before, and I know it's nearly impossible to have a real relationship with them. What I'm witnessing here: this is Pip's entire reality. All the time.

Well, I can ignore Sofie too. She's severely troubled, and besides, she's just a child. It's *Pip* I must appeal to. As a mother. As a human. If Pip has any humanity left in her, I must appeal to it, to her, now.

"You wanted to make sure I was safe," I say quietly. "I appreciate that."

Pip meets my eyes again. She looks mildly surprised. I bet she expected me to yell. To scream, to fight her tooth and nail. All that's coming.

"I've been kind to you too," I continue, weighing each word carefully. So very carefully. "I let you bring your daughter here, even when that wasn't the deal. I gave you my bedroom. I stopped asking you for the rent."

"You gave our stuff away and changed the locks on us," Pip reminds me.

I don't take the bait. "I'm asking you now. Please." I take in a dramatic breath. This performance needs to be the stuff of Oscars, of legends. "Can I please go to the bathroom? I'm not going to run. I just really, really don't want to use the water bottle again." I point to the corner where her teal Stanley water bottle rests.

Pip glances at her water bottle, as if imagining what's inside, and I think I see her resolve waver . . . just a bit.

"Fine," she says. "We'll walk you there."

"Thanks," I say. "I really have to go."

I let Sofie and Pip frog-march me out of the room, each of them flanking my sides. As soon as I cross into the living room, I feel sweet relief. I'll do whatever it takes not to go back there, into the bedroom. Not if I can help it.

At the threshold to the bathroom, they push me inside.

"No closing the door," Pip says blandly.

"Don't worry," I assure her. "I don't want it closed either."

It's the truth. Getting locked in the bathroom would be far worse than the bedroom, with the exception of the access to running water. Regardless, I have no plans to let them do that to me again. I move directly to the toilet and pee, marveling at how congenial I sound. It's all an act; I'm still in stall mode, desperate to make this last long enough for them to give up, change their minds, chicken out. But what if the act becomes real, and I'm the one who eventually gives up? I can't let it. I won't.

I reach the sink, turn it on, position my mouth under the stream, and take a prolonged sip. Might as well take my time washing up. I need a minute to consider my next move.

I let the hot water scald my skin, vigorously rub in the soap. Once I've made that task take as long as is reasonable, I reach up to turn off the water, catching my reflection in the mirror.

Holy fuck. Is that *me*?

I gasp at the sight of my wan, malnourished face. My cheeks are practically hollow, my shirt bagging on my angular shoulders, once thin, now downright gaunt. And my hair—oh God, my hair. Dreadlocks are starting to form in the back, it's so knotted, and the top, where Pip hit me, it's a dried mass of bloody tangles. I reach up a hand, touching that rat's nest like I'm examining a foreign object, not connected to me. It's a bloody scab, the whole area so much larger than I thought. I feel something sticky there and realize, when I take my hand away, that it's started bleeding again. I must need stitches. Funny how that's my last concern, now.

"This fits," Sofie says, watching me. I nearly leap out of my skin at the sound of her voice. "You were so depressed, so guilt ridden about what you did to Nathan, that you couldn't stand being alive anymore, and you jumped."

Right. Sofie's finding reasons why my starved and ghostly appearance actually gel with her narrative. That means I'm running out of time.

"The cut on your head is easy enough to explain," she adds, as if reading my thoughts. "You hadn't been eating, fell from dizziness and hit your head on the bed frame. We got some of your blood last night and will wipe it on the bed so it all tracks. Don't worry."

Her words are unbelievable—insane, completely detached from reality—but I can't stop to dwell on them. Think, Emily, *think*. What in this room could I use as a weapon? I don't have to look; I know this place by heart. I have to do something, *now*. I run a mental inventory of my home. There's the lamp on the side table we picked up in Venice Beach. Is it heavy enough? Maybe not. There are steak knives, but they'd suspect those. And if I go for those and they've moved them, I'm completely screwed. I settle on an item they may not have taken stock of and considered. The letter opener I keep on the console by the front door. It's sharp, for sure, but could I reach it in time, and without them knowing?

I have to keep them guessing. I have to keep them *talking*.

"I'll confess," I say, spinning around to face them. "I'll go see Mason right now, tell him everything you said was true. I was angry at Seth, angry at Nathan. I pushed him. It was me. You'll back me up, say you lied when you gave me that alibi. I actually left for an extended time while we watched TV. You were protecting me, but now you aren't."

"Not going to happen." Pip shakes her head. "You know too much. The second you leave . . . How could I trust you? How could I be assured you wouldn't take it all back later? Sofie's a child, Emily. Children must be kept safe. Children must be protected. Isn't that a cardinal rule?"

I can't believe she's claiming some high-road bullshit.

"You confess, then," I offer blandly, making sure I don't lose my cool. "Wouldn't it be worth it, to go to prison to save your daughter?"

"Of course not," Pip answers. "I'd get at least eight years, at a minimum, and by then she'd be an adult. No offense, but I'm not making my child into an orphan."

The words sting—I know she's meant them to—but I have no time to take offense. My wheels spin. I pivot.

247

"I'll call him, then," I offer. "I'll call Detective Mason right now, and I'll tell him, on the record. Right here in front of you. You won't even have to let me go."

"Did you hear my mom? That would never work." I spin to find Sofie right beside me, a syringe in her hand. She's aiming it at my forearm, ready to jab.

I can't believe what I'm seeing. This is next level. This is *fucked*.

"Where the hell did you get *that*?"

"Nurse's office at school. You wouldn't believe what they keep in the cabinet in there. If only they weren't so stupid about forgetting to lock it up when they take their bathroom break." I don't even want to know what medication's in there. I won't let it come to that. Sofie makes a sudden movement, like she's about to stab my arm, but I manage to slam my hand back just in time, knocking her to the ground. She yelps, but I don't miss a beat. I turn to Pip, who's coming at me with a bookend, one of the marble alphabet set Viv and I found buried under a pile of junk at a thrift store on Union Street. She raises it up to hit me, and I think I spy blood on the sharp corner—this must be what she used to make the gash in my head and knock me unconscious—but I manage to duck, kicking her in the shins as hard as humanly possible, then sprint away from her and toward my beaded curtain. I slam through it to my futon, where I locate my phone lying on the sheets.

They've smashed the fucking screen.

I pocket it anyway, eyeing the object I really want and need: the letter opener by the door. The one with the space unicorn on top that was a gag gift I presented Viv once, for her birthday, but ended up using every day to open our mail—until I stopped opening it altogether, began shoving all the unpaid bills under my bed.

Pip is helping Sofie up, visibly limping from where I kicked her in the shins but clearly unfazed. If she expected a fight, well, she's going to get one.

I make a beeline for the letter opener, nab it from its perch, and start to feel for the doorknob, never taking my eyes off them as they launch themselves at me from across the room. Pip grabs my arm, the one holding the opener, and wrenches it back in a move so agonizing it sends sparks to my head. Sofie moves up, and in one swift motion stabs me in the arm with the syringe, and I shriek in surprise, and fear—what has she stabbed me with that they'd keep in a school nurse's office, a tranquilizer?—and I can't get a grasp on the doorknob. She throws her body at me, landing at my feet and sobbing in what I know, now, to be a carefully constructed act.

"She made me do it!" Sofie wails. "All of it, the entire thing! She killed Nathan herself because he dumped her, and then she made up this whole crazy story. She thought it was safe to make me look guilty, she promised me they'd never make a child go to prison. I only went along with it because I'm terrified of her. Please, Emily, help me . . . she's been lying about everything my entire life, and I'm stuck here with her. I'm trapped!"

Pip's squeezing the flesh of my arm, pulling it back at a distorted angle and bending it to my shoulder blades, so blisteringly tight I can hardly breathe, and Sofie's grabbing me by the knee, my compromised knee, digging her fingertips into the delicate spot where my tender scar is, and preventing me from reaching the door.

"I'm sorry, Sofie," I whisper as I kick with all my might, sending her flying across the room as I scrabble for the doorknob. I'm not sorry, not really, but I *am* sorry that any child should have to live with being so immoral, so depraved. Sofie's a menace, a murderer, but it feels wrong that she's been made that way. I throw Pip off me as Sofie manages to crawl back over and bite me in the calf, but I flip the dead bolt on the door, open it a crack.

Something stops me from wrenching it all the way. It's Pip, now on top of me, her hands on the door as I prize it open, pulling inward as she pushes it closed. She's stronger, slams it closed, turning so her back is to the door and using her body as a shield in front of the lock.

"I told you," Pip growls. "You aren't leaving here alive."

I grip the letter opener with steely determination as I look her square in the eye. "Oh, but the thing is, I am."

I plunge it into her side. She screams, her eyes focused on me in horror and shock—did she think I didn't have it in me?—before she drops to her knees, falling to the floor.

I don't react, don't watch, don't wait to see how hurt she is.

I reach for the doorknob, turn it, and I'm out the door in seconds, flying down the hall on my vulnerable knee with only one goal in mind: Getting out of this house of horrors. Getting free.

Chapter 41

Sofie

The day of the murder, Sofie left school early. She always wanted to, because school sucked. Kids were immature and dumb, and Sofie was perpetually bored. Most days, she didn't actually do it. She knew she could only get away with it sometimes, and she knew, too, that her story of *why* she had left had to be good. Really good, in case she was stopped by a teacher, or worse, the principal.

Her story was good that day, especially good, and so she walked to the front door of the school, opened it, and left. No one questioned her, again because people are generally dumb, and 99 percent of the time, they don't ask questions. Well, not the right ones, anyway. But if they had, she knew exactly what she would say. She was prepared, always.

When she got to Emily's apartment building, which she still didn't think of as "home" but hoped one day would be their home, and only *their* home. One day when Emily would be mysteriously gone . . . which Sofie was working on. She had all sorts of plans in mind to spook Emily so badly, she'd leave. Like hacking into her DoorDash account and changing her internet password. Sofie was good with technical things. Most kids her age were.

When she got home, her mom wasn't there. Emily was, fast asleep on her sad little futon, which Sofie thought was weird because it was almost 10 a.m., and Emily was a grown-up. Grown-ups are supposed to get up early.

Sofie went back out into the hall, wondering where her mom was, when she heard them coming up the stairwell.

Her mom's voice. And his. A man's. Nathan, the neighbor from downstairs. She recognized his voice, had heard it a lot of times in the hallway as he talked on the phone or said a quick hello. They were laughing, and when they came through the stairwell door, Sofie's mom looked . . . different. Her clothes were rumpled, and she was holding her shoes, which Sofie thought was odd until she saw Nathan put his arm around her mom and touch her in a way that let Sofie know exactly what was going on between these two.

She did not like what she was seeing.

Sofie had not liked it when her mom had dated Mike, the man next door in their old building, and she would definitely not like it if her mom started dating someone in *this* building. They'd had sex, obviously, which was gross, but that wasn't what Sofie was focused on. She was single-mindedly concerned with making sure this guy never came back here again.

"Mom?" Sofie asked, as innocently as she could, to get her mother's attention. It worked. Pip stopped short in the hallway at the sight of her daughter standing a few feet away, outside the condo door. Sofie could easily predict what would happen now: Her mom would put on a show, for Nathan's benefit. She would act appropriately concerned, as moms are supposed to do. Her mother never believed her, not anymore, but Nathan would believe her, and her mom was good at playing along.

"What are you doing home from school?" her mom asked, exactly as Sofie knew she would. "Are you sick? Did the school nurse send you home? Should I take your temp?"

"It was the mean girls again. They bullied me. So I left."

Pip moved to robotically hug her daughter, which Sofie let her do. It was all part of the performance. But Sofie was also planning act 2 of the performance, which would include her mother letting herself into the apartment, and Sofie making up a reason to linger in the hall with Nathan.

When her mother left Sofie and Nathan alone for that brief moment, Sofie screamed, and accused Nathan of touching her inappropriately, which was, of course, a lie, because Nathan was a decent man who would never do such a thing. And then she told him: "Don't you ever talk to us again. Even in the hall—or I'll call the police and tell them what you did to me."

Visibly shaken, Nathan fled. Then, later that morning, he came back to try to make things right and overheard a conversation through the door, slightly ajar, between Sofie and her mom, which troubled him greatly. A whispered conversation where Sofie and her mother seemed . . . odd. Not normal. Maybe even a little bit deranged. A conversation they didn't think he'd been privy to. And then, icked out, he threatened them, told them his plans to call Child Protective Services and report their unusual behavior.

That was all it took for Sofie to decide she had to take care of things, take care of *him*, permanently. Her mother had always warned Sofie about CPS. They were cruel. They would take Sofie away from Pip, and there would be no getting her back. Sofie knew this was because of how she behaved, but that wasn't something she could change about herself, so she heeded her mother's warning: avoid CPS at all costs. Sofie certainly did not want to be separated from her mother. She understood that the outside world did not like her, not the real her, anyway, and that there wasn't much chance that they ever would.

Sofie's plan was simple: She sneaked out of her bedroom window that evening, while her mom and Emily were watching TV. Climbed down the fire escape to Nathan's window. Rapped on it, luring him out there with a promise to smooth things over. Then started videoing him and accusing him of touching her again, of being a bad "#MeToo" person who belonged in prison. Backed him up to the edge of the fire escape, and when he was vulnerable and had his hands up in the air to prove he'd never touched her and never would, made sure he was unsteady on his feet, then pushed him over. Watched him fall. Made sure he was 100 percent dead. Then climbed back up and resumed playing Roblox.

Sofie didn't know why she was always the one who had to take care of things, but she could handle it. Someone had to.

Epilogue

The letter from Myriad Genetics lies on my kitchen countertop, unopened.

But unlike all the other unopened bills that I stuffed under my mattress, I'm not afraid to see what's inside.

I'm waiting for the right moment, because no matter what the result of my BRCA test, I want to celebrate it. Celebrate my *life*, which up until this moment has been pretty damn great. Celebrate my options, because I have them, no matter what the exact results are. Even if my cancer risk is high. Even if it means reshuffling my future: I am ready to know.

It was the hours spent in my bedroom, locked in by Pip and Sofie, when it all began to crystallize. I knew if I ever got out of there, I'd stop running from my problems—real or imagined—and face them, head on.

Aunt Viv passed away last month in her sleep. I got to tell her everything before she died: All about Pip and Sofie's conning and gaslighting. How I'd done everything I could think of to save the condo from them, and then, to save my life. My shame was gone, as was my feeling that it was all my fault. When Viv told me she was proud of me, I stopped her.

"Be proud of me once I get the cancer testing. Then I'll deserve it."

I could almost see Viv smiling through the phone. "You've always deserved it, honey. I just wish you could have seen that."

The memory of that last call with Viv, when she was lucid for much of it, is a balm to many of my old wounds. Apparently, Viv *always* thought I was worthy of, well, everything. I was the one who was stuck, who thought my brokenness was something innate I'd never fix.

When they called to tell me she'd died in her sleep, I was devastated—but I also felt at peace. Viv hadn't wanted to live that way, and unlike my parents, who would have given anything to stick around and raise me, she'd chosen to go. I was sure of it. She left me the condo in her will, along with enough money to pay off my debts and store up some funds for future mortgage payments. I've picked up a smattering of yoga shifts, not enough, but they will get me by until I find more. And I know I will.

Alli and Jack will be here soon. I lay out wine and cheese, grab Pellegrino for Alli from the fridge because she's on another round of IVF, and isn't drinking. They only know part of the story—Jack more than Alli, of course, since he played a role in it—but I've promised to give them every detail. They've been waiting long enough.

I pad through my kitchen to grab napkins and glassware, grateful for the silence I'll never again take for granted. No Pip with her incessant chatter, no Sofie with her wisecracks. After I ran out of here that night, bleeding, bruised, barely standing—and with what I later learned was diazepam coursing through my system—I only made it as far as the corner store when I collapsed, malnourished and drowsy beyond belief. Someone called an ambulance, and I found myself in the ER thirty minutes later on a stretcher, pleading with a nurse to let me call Detective Mason at the police station.

I was in and out of that drugged state for who knows how long until I woke to find Mason standing over my bed. Confused, I blinked at him. Once, twice . . . What the hell was he doing there? And where was I?

"You're lucky to be alive," Mason said with a small smile. "How are you feeling?"

"I'm feeling like a tween girl stabbed me in the arm with some kind of narcotic," I manage to say.

Mason's smile slips. "About that . . ."

My heart began to race with apprehension and, yes, probably whatever drugs were still in my system. "Did you finally look at all that evidence I compiled for you, against Pip?"

Mason sighed. "I did. And it's quite . . . concerning."

I let out a massive breath. He believed me. He finally believed me.

Mason explained that Tabitha's PI had found reason to believe that Mike had disappeared upstate. He'd urged the police force there to dredge the lake. And just yesterday—unbeknownst to me—they'd done it and found his body.

Poor Tabitha. Poor Mike. This was the worst possible news—except it was exactly what was needed to prove Sofie had done something awful. Something that established a pattern and could get her behind bars.

"You should rest," Mason told me. I was eager to keep talking, but he assured me we could continue this conversation when I was fully recovered, and back home. "Don't worry. I know where you live," Mason said before turning to leave.

"Ha," I managed to mutter.

"I hope you'll reach out if there's anything you need."

"That's it?" I asked, trying to sit up but realizing I couldn't; my head hurt too much. "What about getting those two behind bars?"

"Text me. We'll talk." Mason waved, then left the room.

I planned to.

As I lay in that hospital bed, I felt myself exhaling as I stared at my hands, so discombobulated and groggy. Sofie must have given me a massive dose. Was that really from the school nurse's office? Or had she stolen it from someplace else?

Mason and I did text in the following weeks, and I learned that my evidence helped him build his case against Sofie. And now, well, now she's been detained in a juvenile facility until her trial.

I hope they lock her up so she can't ever do this to anyone again. They say people can change, but I don't know if that applies to Sofie. As for Pip, she, too, is being investigated as Sofie's accomplice to Mike's murder, and Nathan's—and for kidnapping me, with intent to kill me.

The prosecutor's hoping to try her for attempted murder. I know she did what she did out of love, for her child. She's still a criminal.

I'll do what I have to, to make sure she goes to prison. Testify. Whatever Mason needs to make sure those two don't ever fuck with anyone else again. I hope no one else ever gets the chance to write another Nextdoor post about Pip, because she'll be behind bars.

I stretch my legs, change into jeans before my friends arrive. I know Alli will ask me about Seth. I've told him everything—not only what Pip did to me, but about the BRCA testing. The real reason I'd called off our wedding.

If Alli's still holding out hope we'll get back together, I need to set her straight. Seth said he understood why I did it, but he wasn't ready to forgive me.

Still, we did agree to get coffee sometime in the not-so-distant future. I wouldn't blame him if he never wanted to see my face again, but I'm grateful that he might. It would be asking too much for him to give me another chance. And maybe we're different people now. I'm not the same Emily who was too afraid to build a future with him. That girl is gone, forever—and good riddance. Besides, I don't need his forgiveness. I'm at peace with my decisions. Maybe I've finally found my Zen. Or maybe I just don't give a fuck anymore what anyone thinks.

I call Viv's cell phone, knowing she won't pick up. I feel her absence like a wound that won't heal, but calling her is therapeutic. This isn't the first message I've left her since she died. Once I stop the payments to AT&T, I won't be able to do this anymore, so I'm savoring the chance to hear her voice. "Viv, it's me, Emily. I miss you like crazy, but I know you already know that. This place isn't the same without you, but I think you'd like the little changes I've made. I bought a new sofa—don't worry, I didn't spend too much on it!—and I've managed to get one of those fancy Breville coffee makers at virtually no cost. Don't ask me how I did that, okay? All right, I've gotta go now. I love you, Aunt Viv. I'm gonna be just fine."

Acknowledgments

Recently, I had coffee with a friend I hadn't seen for a month or two. As I stepped inside her house, she said, "Rebecca, you aren't going to believe what's been happening in the neighborhood. I have your next book idea for you." All ears, I settled in to hear what had been going on. It turns out, a strange woman had been discovered scrubbing the counters at one house on the block, ordering Amazon packages to another and picking them up from the doorstep, pretending one especially lavish home was her Airbnb, and answering the door at yet another house with a Southern accent. Over the period of a week, she was spotted by the residents of the neighborhood in various locations, calling herself by a fake name when confronted, and managing to dodge the authorities and even a pretty expensive PI. Eventually, she was arrested, having nabbed the keys to a Lexus parked at the "Airbnb" and driven it to Union Street for a shopping spree . . . funded by the gift cards she found in the kitchen cabinet of her "host."

When my friend finished her story, I had to tell her that, regretfully, I couldn't write that book—I'd already written one with eerily similar themes: this one! But the rest of the day, as I meditated on what she'd told me, I noted with a pang of guilt that, while I recognized how much havoc this woman had wreaked on an entire neighborhood, I still felt a twinge of empathy for the *perpetrator*. I couldn't help it. On some gut level, I found myself caring about this woman and wondering what her motivations were. Of course, that's easy for me to say; I'm not the one whose belongings were stolen. I don't know what it says about me that I felt more for the con artist than for her victims, but I think it speaks to how long I spent in my characters' heads during the writing of this novel. And how your manuscript becomes a tangible piece of you by the time you're done.

Still. As much as I love and empathize with *all* my characters—even the mildly psychotic ones like Pip!—it's actually Emily I most related to during the writing of this book, because I felt like I was channeling her energy throughout the (sometimes grueling!) process. Completing this manuscript felt like a test I hadn't studied for, and as Emily's anxiety increased, and her panic and dread escalated, so did mine. *Unlike* Emily, I had a whole village of cheerleaders, friends, and teammates bolstering me through it—so that in the end, the book became one I love very dearly. While I could never choose any of my books to call my "favorite," I'll always hold a soft spot for this little toxic roommate story. And not only that—I'm deeply indebted to everyone who supported me. And so, a very heartfelt and earnest thank-you goes out to:

Danielle Marshall, for your patience, and for your wisdom early on to shape this story into what it was meant to be. I'm a lucky author. Jenna Free—you know how pivotal you were to the editing process, and I'll be eternally grateful to you for the depth you brought to these characters.

Victoria Sanders, Bernadette Baker-Baughman, Christine Kelder, and everyone at VSA, for being so consistently in my corner. Sylvie Rabineau at WME, for your continued unflagging support.

Benee Knauer—I think you know how much I appreciate you, but I will continue to shout it from every available rooftop, and possibly some low balconies as well. Thank you for being the truest friend and confidante.

Megan Beatie: I can't thank you enough for your support of my work. Olivia Haase, Stephanie Elliott—you are so kind, fun, and badass. Thank you for all you do.

The Lake Union and Amazon teams, for your tireless efforts on behalf of your authors. Karah Nichols, Nicole Burns-Ascue, Katherine Kirk, and Alicia Lea, for making each manuscript sing.

Matt, Leigh, and Stephen, for working so steadfastly behind the scenes on my behalf.

My friends: Sonia, Amanda, Cathleen, Victoria, Celeste, Michelle, Gabrielle, Sarah, Nidhi, Chloe, Sabrina, Rebecca, Kami, Stephany, Winnie, Billy, Alexa, Biren and Hiromi, Mike and Sophia, Josh and Amanda, Andy and Caitlin—and Meredith L., who is the most supportive writer friend (and friend-friend) I could ask for. Thank you for "getting" me.

Laura King, for playing Cambio and making slime and being a homework whisperer. Thank you more than I can say.

Sofia Bresciani, for being my right (and let's face it, left) arm this year. Insert grateful emoji here.

My family: Mom and Dad, stop interrupting my writing with texts! (Kidding, I'm the one who does that.) Jessica: good thing you taught me how to write my name forty-plus years ago (whew). You mostly continue to teach me things, but sometimes I teach you things, too, so we might finally be even. Ray, Sonya, Nicholas, and Jacob, for listening to my outlandish ideas and not laughing. Amy, for being the ultimate writing confidante.

Ethan: when I told you that writing this first draft gave me chest pains, you were unfazed, and also certain I was not having a heart attack, which was helpful to hear when my own brain was not so convinced. Thank you for always being such a successful convincer. I love you.

Leo, Quincy, and Naomi: you can squat with me as long as you want, though if you're still here when you're thirty, I'll start charging rent (and a security deposit). I love you more than anything. Thank you for making me laugh, and for filling every day with more fun than I could have ever imagined.

About the Author

Photo © 2021 Kathleen Sheffer

Rebecca Hanover is the *New York Times* bestselling author of the young adult series the Similars. After graduating from Stanford University with a BA in English and drama, Rebecca joined the writing team of the CBS daytime drama *Guiding Light*, where she earned an Emmy Award. She now writes novels full time from her home in San Francisco, where she enjoys matcha lattes and a complete lack of seasons. *Seems Perfect* is Hanover's second novel for adults, following *The Last Applicant* (2023). When she isn't writing, the author can be found in a yoga class or reading anything by Dav Pilkey with her husband and three kiddos.